Copyright © 2024 by Steve Ryhn

All rights reserved.

No part of this publication may be reproduced, distributed, or transmitted in any form or by any means, including photocopying, recording, or other electronic or mechanical methods, without the prior written permission of the publisher, except as permitted by U.S. copyright law. For permission requests, contact RyhntopiaWritings@gmail.com.

The story, all names, characters, and incidents portrayed in this production are fictitious. No identification with actual persons (living or deceased), places, buildings, and products is intended or should be inferred.

Book Cover by Martha Ortman

Author website (Ryhntopia Writings.com)

Dedication

Thanks to Stephen King, who unknowingly shaped my voice,

Andrea Luhman, who **very** knowingly shaped it,

And my love to Martha, who indulges my authorial neediness.

Foreword

There are writers of classic literature, like J.D. Salinger or George Orwell. I would equate them to a four-course dinner at a favorite steakhouse. A grand event and wonderfully fulfilling.

Then there are writers of incredible fiction like Stephen King or George R. R. Martin. I would equate them to a Sunday night chicken dinner with all the trimmings. A big meal that is fun to dig into and so satisfying.

I see my writing as a simple fast-food chicken sandwich—perfect for an on-the-go lifestyle, an easy little snack. It's fun to eat and quick to digest. I never saw myself in the first two groups, and I'm okay with that. If readers enjoy my writing, that is all I hoped for, and I'll call that a win.

Thanks,

Steve

Sunday — Late Afternoon

"Come on, Emma!" Elmo muttered, snapping his fishing rod forward. Men, in general, tend to give their possessions names, fishermen doubly so. Though he couldn't know it at the time, that would be the last cast he would ever share with Emma. The red and white bobber soared out over the water's reflection of the sunset and autumn colors, becoming part of the picture with a small splash and a few ripples. The scarlets and yellows of the maples flowed into the pink and gold of the sunset, but while he could appreciate the scene's beauty, the water's mirror-like surface was where his attention was focused.

Elmo Baalsen had been fishing on Turtle Lake for the better part of fifty years, so he felt entitled to a full stringer whenever he eased his canoe out. While it has been said that still waters run deep, still waters also signal a lack of fish interested in one's bait. "Another damn cold front..." he grumbled, willfully ignoring the beautiful cloudless sky. There had been an unusual number of cold fronts moving through the area this summer, at least according to Elmo.

Since the fish were not doing their part to occupy his time, he mulled over the slang his grandsons were trying to teach him. Apparently, now if something was "sick", it meant it was terrific. Describing someone as "turnt" meant you viewed them as a drunkard. And calling someone a "ferger" was a gross insult, reserved for special occasions only. None of it made a lick of sense, but Elmo wanted to maintain a good relationship with the boys, so he tried to use the slang they sent him in their endless text messaging, at least as often as he remembered.

The increasing roar of an outboard motor echoing over the water pulled him out of his reverie. A large deck boat raced across the lake, no doubt scaring every fish around. Elmo raised a fist and shook it at the speedsters before realizing that the blunt bow was coming directly at him and was not showing any signs of slowing. He hurriedly began waving his arms, but there was no change in the boat's speed or direction.

Realizing a boat that size would smash his canoe to splinters, he dropped Emma in a rush to grab his paddle and frantically backpaddled, straining and swearing. The canoe responded slowly to his efforts. He only made it a few feet before the big boat screamed past, a mere foot off his bow. From that distance, there was no missing the wording on the side of the boat: Bloomington Mayor David Deakins.

"Deakins, you addled thunderpate!!" he bellowed, relishing the punch of a classic insult, something that the grandkids' slang could not hope to match.

As the canoe heaved and bucked, Elmo held on to the sides and prayed not to capsize. After dismissing his wife's admonishment that afternoon to 'take a damn lifejacket with you!', he knew he would never hear the end of it if he went into the drink. Fate favored him on that front, and he managed to avoid capsizing. But on a less lucky front, the speeding boat's propeller ran squarely over his bobber, sucking up the fishing line attached to it like his grandsons at a spaghetti dinner.

To his horror, Emma leapt out of the canoe and began skipping over the water's surface, catching up to the speeding boat's engine. Not even thirty yards after vaulting into the water, Emma caught up to the hungry propeller and was promptly chopped into pieces. The cork butt of the rod floating on the water's surface was the only evidence of what had just happened; the other parts sank out of sight along with his reel.

Elmo cried out with a voice filled with more anguish than his wife would have been comfortable hearing. As the waves smoothed out, he stared at the boat that had cost him the finest rod he'd ever known and noticed something odd as it sped away; there was no one at the wheel, or onboard at all. As he continued to watch, the boat headed into the far shore with no decrease in speed.

The boat screamed up onto the shore, tearing completely through the Johnson's new dock (Bob's, not Doug's), launching itself up into the yard, then falling over sideways. Thankfully, the engine had stopped cold as the propeller snapped off against the ground. Elmo fumbled in his pocket for his cell phone, dutifully called 911, and began telling the operator what he'd just seen.

On the opposite side of the lake, beyond Elmo's view, a body floated face down, bobbing gently.

A casual observer would have noticed that the body was wearing a suit, and with the sides of the jacket open, it looked like wings had spread out in a failed effort to fly away. A tailor looking at the scene might have commented on the stitching and the material used in the jacket and pants, noting that the outfit was top quality and not off-the-rack. At this point in the game, comments of any kind would have only fallen on deaf ears; Mayor Deakins simply continued floating, waiting for the authorities to arrive.

Monday — Early Morning

Walking into the Ramsey County Sheriff's building, Detectives Johnson and Ollig were arguing exactly where they had left off the previous evening.

"You can't possibly believe that pickle juice makes any Bloody Mary better!" declared Johnson, polishing and smoothly pocketing his prized aviator sunglasses.

"I wouldn't have believed it either, but after having one, it was amazing! Have you ever actually tried it or are you just looking for something to piss and moan about?" Ollig asked, his left eyebrow rising along the outside edge.

"I do not need to eat shit-covered tater-tots to know I would not like eating shit-covered tater-tots!! Jesus Christ!" Johnson shook his head. Was there nothing folks wouldn't screw with and make worse, he wondered?

Gail Peterson heard their Bloody Mary conversation as they passed through Reception (she waved from her desk, buzzing them through the doors) and it made her thirsty. "Can the swearing, please," she admonished Johnson, who turned his face so she wouldn't see his grimace. The only thing Gail enjoyed more than a Sunday morning Bloody Mary (or two) was spending quality time at the shooting range first. Gail enjoyed bettering herself in any way she could find. She had attended many classes in de-escalation, psychology, and even a class in hostage negotiation when an FBI trainer had been in town. Large sections of her day were spent calming down irate citizens and helping them feel "heard" (a word her reviews referenced often). In her experience, most angry people only wanted to rant and have someone commiserate with them. Gail excelled at that. As her husband often told folks, "My honey is a world-class placator."

She looked every bit the cheery middle-aged rotund Midwestern woman you might expect to see at a reception desk (usually with a nicely styled bob of some kind), but Gail Peterson could be a surprisingly formidable individual to be on the wrong side of, like a mechanical poodle that was paid no mind until those hydraulic jaws clamped shut. Calming folks down was not the only thing she excelled at. The range master had been sworn to secrecy by Gail, but she was the most accurate shot in the entire building, barring the range master himself. Sheriff Glenn Campbell might not have known that particular fact but did know she loved having a polished de-escalation specialist like Gail around. A reporter had once asked if officers ever worried about safety at the station. Glenn laughed and responded, "Of course not; we have a Gail!!"

The depth of Gail's recipe library was another reason to love the woman. People had taken to scheduling various potlucks around her vacations because a potluck without a Gail Peterson entry was no potluck at all. Gail loved puns, alliteration, and any other kind of wordplay. A pun around a potluck entry was a sure ticket to her good side.

Upstairs, the conference room filled steadily as officers trickled in to start the day. There was a great deal less chatter than on an average morning. The word was out; something big was going to be announced.

Tom Maki did not care about announcements. He was finally making progress on a case near and dear to his heart. He had been forced home the night before by the sheriff herself. "Goddammit Tom, everyone has to sleep sometime; this case will still be here waiting for you in the morning," she commented ruefully as she physically walked him out of the building and to his car.

Tom Maki was the senior member of the Sensitive Crimes Unit and Chief Deputy of the department. He had closed more cases than any other two members of that team combined. Though, to be fair, he had also been in the unit ten years longer than the next senior officer, Seth Brueske, and Seth was coming up on nine years with the team. The saying "slow and steady wins the race" was tailor-made for Tom. Maki would have been at home in the old west, with folks calling him Marshall instead of Chief Deputy. He was decent, determined, and deliberative. Laconic, laid back, and level-headed. Most of his co-workers would agree he easily fixated on things, but that was one of the things that made him such an effective detective.

He wore his hair close-cropped, just north of a crew cut. Publicly, he would state this was for simplicity's sake, but privately, he had noticed some gray last summer, and crew cuts were a lot cheaper (and seemed less pathetic to him) than dying your hair in your 50s. He had the lean muscled physique of a man who worked for a living, at least in his mind. Tom was a lifelong marathon runner and had a small dresser at home dedicated solely to the racing shirts he'd acquired from many races through the years.

Maki hushed both Johnson and Ollig, who were furiously whispering like an old married couple amidst yet another argument about nothing. Glenn came into the room, unusually somber, with no hint of the smile that normally played around her features. That was unusual and infectious, and within a minute, there was no sound in a conference room filled with cops.

"Alright people, we have a tough one today, "Glenn started. "It appears the Mayor of Bloomington may have drowned in Turtle Lake. This one will be in the public eye, so I want everything by the book, and those directly involved with this case will not just cover but armor plate their asses. Am I clear?" The room murmured assent as one.

 More than a few eyes went to a dusky-skinned raven-haired woman sitting in the front row. Her name was Carmen Shapiro; she headed up Aquatic Operations for Ramsey County and served as Glenn's Undersheriff. She swam three miles before work every morning and had been SCUBA diving before she could ride a bike. She had not only swum around the glass ceiling, but she also laid her towel over it and started tanning. Officers across the entire Twin Cities knew her by reputation. If there was anything to be found at a watery crime scene, Carmen Shapiro would find it.

"Any theories yet?" asked the newest member of General Investigations, Bill Larson. The question sent more than a dozen eyes rolling back into their respective skulls. Bill was new to the sheriff's department, having transferred only three months ago from the Oakdale city police. Everyone else knew what the next words spoken would be.

"You never start with theories; you start with the evidence," Glenn stated. It was practically her mantra, and due to sheer repetition around the station, a mantra for many others. "Once we get all the facts, *then* we start working on theories," she finished with a smile. That smile made Bill feel marginally less foolish, but not by much.

"Vadnais Heights is requesting more patrols along their Harvest Parade route, and North Oaks is having their Autumnfest this week, so let's keep on things there. Other than that, business as usual and let's be safe out there."

Glenn remembered 'let's be safe out there' from one of the cop shows she watched as a kid and liked it so much that it became her go-to closing line for almost everything, from station discussions to formal occasions to personal life. As she got older, it became more and more meaningful to her and seemed applicable to so darn many situations.

"Tom, please hang back a minute; I'd like to get an update on one of your cases." Almost every person in the room knew precisely which case she was talking about, and they all crossed their fingers that it would be closed soon. Thanks to a personal favor done for Tom by a member of his bowling league who worked in the Bureau for Criminal Apprehension, there would be evidence that day that would jump-start the investigation and tighten the suspect list down to a single man.

Monday — Early Morning, Continuation

Bill Larson was in his last month of ride-along training, which made him happy. He was riding with Lance Miller (a great guy and even better teacher), but he was eager to be running patrol on his own to prove he had value for the department. Hopping into their SUV, he turned to Lance and asked, "Do you know what the deal was with Tom's case and the sheriff?" Lance drew a deep breath in and prepared to unload some behind-the-scenes details.

"First off, I'm glad you're asking me and not someone else. Any case being worked by the Sensitive Crimes unit has names withheld for one reason or another. Age, type of crime, things like that. The general rule of thumb is, 'if you weren't involved at the outset, you stay uninvolved.' Without violating anything, I can tell you it is a rape case. I will also tell you this: do not get into a discussion around any kind of sexual abuse with Chief Deputy Maki. He has a hair trigger with those kinds of things, and the smartest play for anyone, especially someone new to the force, is to let that sleeping dog lie."

Deputy Larson logged that piece of advice away in his mental notebook. His trainer was filling that notebook full. Bill was not a man to let nuggets of wisdom go to waste. "So, are we going to take North Oaks or Vadnais Heights today?" he inquired, shifting the subject.

"In fact, both. Deputy White is out sick today. Since North Oaks is on the way to Vadnais Heights, we can start with the Richie Riches." The average family income in North Oaks was upwards of $300,000. It was a perfect example of a 'bedroom community,' having no business district, only residential housing. The typical call for the area was either underage consumption by kids or frivolous calls around noise violations. Larson could not recall a single felony call there in the past summer.

Vadnais Heights was a different story. A scant ten miles away as the crow flies, the average income was only $70,000, and there were a variety of felony calls every week. There was a modest business district (which is where most of the said crimes were centered). Jorge's, a small family restaurant adjacent to several big box stores, offered free coffee for law enforcement. The coffee was so good that officers from the neighboring five precincts regularly stopped by. On any given morning, the parking lot hosted anywhere from four to a dozen squad cars, resembling less of a dining establishment parking lot and more of a police-themed used car lot.

The restaurant quietly received monthly checks from the surrounding big box stores to help defray the "coffee expense." That was the doing of one of those big stores' managers who realized that having so many overlapping jurisdictions of cops stopping at the restaurant at all hours was a far more effective crime deterrent than any burglar system on the market. Depending on the customer traffic for the month, those checks could account for nearly a quarter of the restaurant's income and had enabled them to expand their hours.

This was a true win-win type of scenario for those involved. Sadly, the little restaurant was located at the far end of the business district, and the crime deterrence effect of police saturation faded exponentially with distance. Shoplifting calls were a rarity for stores near the little restaurant but a regular part of a business day for stores at the other end of the district.

The family that owned the restaurant was from Mexico, and every single item they served on the menu consisted of meals the family had been making for decades. Jorge Rodriguez had spent the nest egg saved up by his parents and his own labors to move his family to America.

Every member of the Rodriguez family was genial and pleasant, which meshed well with the demeanor of the locals. The Minnesota community had embraced them with a warmth and acceptance Jorge had not dared hope for when he dreamt of opening a restaurant in the US when his family was still living in Oaxaca. Scarcely an hour of the day passed that he didn't have at least six of the eighteen tables filled. Good food and smiling service were the kind of things that ensured repeat business, and neither was in short supply at Jorge's. The only thing Jorge lamented was that his skill with peppers was largely unappreciated in this new city. But if making your food so tame a baby could eat it and not fart meant that you easily paid your bills and could save for college funds, that was a small price he was more than willing to pay.

Thinking about the toasted tortillas at Jorge's started Lance's stomach growling with speculative hope. If it had been later in the day, he would have suggested patrolling the Heights first, since nothing in North Oaks would require them so early in the day. In fact, he could not have been more wrong.

Monday — Morning

April Davis wanted out of her marriage and reflected divorce or murder were her only obvious options. She admitted to herself that watching crime dramas did not actually prepare her to murder her husband, so it would have to be a divorce. However, she would shortly find there was a third option she had not initially conceived of. Walking into the garage, she hit the door opener and headed for her red Mercedes SUV, with only a minimal amount of weaving. The water bottle in her hand was filled to the brim with an exceptionally dry vodka martini (i.e., she merely looked at the bottle of vermouth). Lately, she never went anywhere without a nicely filled water bottle.

Turning the key, she held it forward a little too long, resulting in a loud screeching from under the hood. "Shut up, you," she mumbled, then threw her car into reverse and hit the gas. She rocketed backward down her driveway and into the street, narrowly missing two children so young they still had training wheels on their bikes. "Get on the damn sidewalk!" she yelled at the children, neatly ignoring the fact that North Oaks did not have any sidewalks. The SUV roared down the street.

Looking down at her phone to let her friend Debby know she was en route; she suddenly made the connection that the cell phone companies and the reading glasses companies had to be scheming together. Why else use such a tiny font if not to make people buy glasses? She could not wait to share this revelation online, demonstrating to those friends that she was not "dumb as a mule," no matter what her husband might say. Unfortunately, she was so lost in those imagined accolades that she never saw the Anderson girl run into the street; those little eyes focused on catching a yellow ball before it rolled down the hill.

She would say later there was less of a sound and more of a feel as the car hit something. Annoyed, April pulled to the side to see whose pet was running loose and got what it deserved. There were more and more animals running wild every day.

Getting out of the car, she started walking to the rear of the car but stopped short when she saw the spread of golden hair and the jumper in the middle of the road. The thought that she could have run down the child never registered in her head.

"H-honey are you okay?" she stammered. "You shouldn't play in the street." Suddenly a soul-piercing scream ripped through the quiet morning. A flaxen-haired woman sprinted across a yard toward the little girl. "Louise!! Oh God, no! Louise!!" Leaping from the yard and scooping the tiny broken body into her arms, the woman could only hold the golden-haired girl tight to her, rocking back and forth, keening.

Other residents emerged from their houses to see what the commotion was about, with reactions ranging from horror to anger. April suddenly felt the safest place for her would be in her car.

"Did you do this?!" a balding man yelled in her face. "You fucking monster! Burn in hell!!" said a voice directly behind her. Feeling panicked as she got in, she quickly locked the doors. Then, as more people gathered around the car, she dialed 911. Before the operator could finish her opening sentence, April interrupted. "I need help! There is a mob of people trying to get into my car. I'm at the corner of Waldorf and Carnegie in North Oaks. Tell them to hurry!!"

Not two minutes after finishing her call, deputies Larson and Miller made their way up the street, lights flashing. From their vantage point, the deputies could see an SUV surrounded by the alleged mob as well as a woman sitting farther up the street, rocking back and forth like a metronome. "You check the woman, and I'll check on the caller," Deputy Miller started saying before he noticed the front end of the SUV had been smashed in. "Ah shit," he amended, "call in for an ambulance first." He waited to head over until he heard his partner radioing for the ambulance, never taking his eye off the vehicle in front of him.

"Come on folks, give me some room. Knock off the rocking, please," he said in his most steadying tone.

"She's a killer!" cried a member of the mass of people surrounding the car. "She ran that kid down like a dog!" bellowed a bald man of considerable size. Hearing that, Miller's heart sank like a stone. Looking inside, he saw a woman who was obviously terrified. At that point, he would have attributed it to the angry crowd. As Miller was working to disperse the crowd around the vehicle, Deputy Larson walked up to the woman in the road. "Ma'am, for your safety, we need to move you to the side of the road." The words had barely cleared his mouth when he came around to the front of her, and anything else he was going to say dried up. Suddenly he found it very hard to breathe.

She was holding a child, but the arms and legs were bent in ways that were not normal. It looked like both arms had two elbows and one leg had three knees. The gold hair was flecked with blood and brains. The entire front of the woman was soaked in blood. The autumn flies had smelled this bounty and were happily walking around in their new find. The woman was ignoring the world, rocking back and forth with eyes locked shut, murmuring a child's name. It was the most soul-crushing thing Bill Larson had ever seen. He began directing everyone back from the scene and radioed for additional backup.

Miller had correctly assessed that the safest path forward was to get the woman into police custody and out of this area. The anger in the air was palpable.

"Ma'am, I need you to step out of the car. I am going to put you in the back of my vehicle. Do you understand?" he asked. April looked at the hate-filled faces surrounding her car and rapidly agreed with that course of action.

"Back them away first!" she bleated. "They all just want to hurt me!" Moving the crowd back, Miller was starting to form a dislike for the woman's barking attitude.

Once the crowd had moved back, she opened her door and sprinted to the cruiser, whipping the rear passenger door open and jumping inside with a speed Miller could scarcely believe. Robbed of their original prize, the mob began kicking the red SUV, a lackluster runner-up for their anger.

"Knock that shit off; we need the car unspoiled if it is going to be evidence." The kicks stopped almost immediately after the crowd heard the word "evidence," with its association of consequence.

When the door opened, the woman was not the only thing that had departed the confines of the car. The smell of alcohol (and plenty of it) also exited the vehicle. Noting it, Miller's face lost its good-natured appearance, brow furrowing, and mouth drawing tight. Going into the back of his vehicle, he retrieved his Breathalyzer from the back and then let the woman know she would have to blow into the tube, just to rule out alcohol as a factor.

April hadn't had much schooling past getting her GED, but she had a five-star bullshit detector. It was going off full blast after hearing the deputy's words. "I am not doing that! I know my rights!" she exclaimed.

"Ma'am, everyone with a Minnesota license signed off, granting implied consent for this. If you still want to refuse, we will take you to a clinic and draw your blood there," Miller recited patiently.

April heard this and figured refusing a test to confirm she was drunk would be better than agreeing to a test that would confirm she was drunk. At this point, she was still only thinking of herself; the child she had run over was nothing she remembered.

"I won't do it. I know my rights," she repeated in a tone that was beginning to stretch the deputy's patience. Avoiding confirmation of her drunkenness was now a bright banner that hung in the front of her mind, and she could not focus on anything else.

"Alright, we will wait until the ambulance gets here. Then, if you still refuse a breathalyzer, we'll take you to the nearest hospital, get a warrant for the blood draw, and do it there," Miller said with his most logical tone.

Predictably, April screamed, "I know my rights! You can't do that!" Running a hand down his face in frustration, Miller began to wonder if he could get away with asking the nurse to miss the first couple of times. As fate would have it, April was going to take care of that for him.

Monday — Late Morning

Detective Maki was surprised when he felt vibrations on his wrist. Looking down, he saw that he had reached ten thousand steps by 11 o'clock. He hadn't realized how often he had walked down the hallway to peer out the window, checking if the mail truck had arrived. As he went down the hallway to check again, Carmen yelled from her office, "Christ man! Sit your ass in a chair and stay there! I don't know what the hell you're doing, but you're making me nervous, Finnegan!"

Although her words sounded mean-spirited on the surface, the inclusion of a nickname was a giveaway as to her real feelings. Being hailed by a derogatory phrase of some sort was a sure sign Shapiro viewed you as at least competent. To have been given a unique nickname was indeed a badge of honor; few were given out. That kind of behavior was a far cry from "Minnesota Nice," but the Undersheriff was not from Minnesota.

Eventually, the white mail truck turned into the parking lot, and Maki was down the stairs and even had the front door held open before the mailman started opening the back of his vehicle.

"Anything from the BCA? Bureau of Criminal Apprehension?" he asked hopefully.

"As a matter of fact, there is this cardboard mailer with that logo addressed to 'Gutterball Maki.' Would that be you?" asked the mailman with a grin. Maki admitted he was, and the mailman admitted that a man with that kind of nickname would be the only kind of opponent he would bowl against anymore.

Pleasantries fulfilled, the mailman left the plastic basket of mail on the lobby table for Gail, taking the previous day's basket in its stead. "Tom, you can bring that mail in through the door, but don't you dare dream of taking any away before I log it," Gail said with a scolding tone.

Sheepishly, Tom's hand stopped inching toward the mailer, and he grabbed the whole basket, bringing it through the buzzing and now unlocked door to Gail. "Looks like this is yours, eh 'Gutterball'?" she asked, holding the mailer out. She loved teasing the old Finn, but she could tell by his eyes he wasn't in a joking mood this morning. Grabbing the mailer from her hands, he sprinted back up the stairs to his office and ripped it open.

On BCA letterhead was a series of fuzzy bar graphs with a paragraph under each one. In fact, these were apheresis gel DNA tests gathered from several rape victims. All the graphs looked identical, a conclusion that the final paragraph attested to.

Flipping to the second page was a similar-looking graph. But this last one was from blood collected at the last crime scene. The writing under that graph emphasized the odds of it not being the same man's semen and blood was one in four hundred quadrillion.

With eyes wide and a hungry look on his face, Maki went striding down the hallway with a stiff walk that resembled a rooster ready to fight any and all challengers in the barnyard. Offering a perfunctory knock, he burst into the sheriff's office. Glenn's hand was already at her side before she recognized who had just burst into her office. "Goddammit Tom," she said while starting to smile. "If you are going to bother to knock, how about letting me respond before storming my office like the beaches of Normandy?"

"I was right—it's been the same guy this entire time!!" Maki exclaimed, not even hearing her protest. "It's been the same guy for the last six rapes we have, and who knows how many aren't reporting," he repeated.

"Tom, is that something we know, or is it something we believe?" Glenn interjected.

"We know it now! BCA report came back on all six. Perfect match on all semen samples, perfect match on the blood from the scene on the last one. All we need is the actual guy who matches the pattern, and we have the evidence to convict on six rapes for sure, possibly more."

Maki's eyes were wild and slightly unfocused. His hands were clenching and unclenching. Noticing this, Glenn walked around her desk. She leaned back against the front of her desk and looked directly into her Chief Deputy's eyes.

"Tom, we will get this man. He will not escape justice." Those words penetrated the fog of thoughts swirling in his head.

"Let's go through the reports again and make a list of questions that are focused on what we know now. The victims could have the answers that will help us find this man."

"I must have missed something before in the cases." He offered. "I'll find it."

"I doubt you missed anything, but now we have an additional set of facts to work with; that means we will get new answers. We know more. Hopefully, something will stand out now." Glenn knew that giving him something to focus on was the only way to get him back from this fervor.

Pausing for a moment, she asked, "How did you get this? BCA is backlogged six months."

Maki's breathing slowed to a much less alarming rate. "Joel Lindstrom is a BCA lab tech in my bowling league. I showed him three ways to correct a problem he was having on the lanes. The payment was running the DNA samples that night. I probably screwed myself down the road in the league finals, but if we get this POS, it's gonna be worth it."

Glenn laid a hand on his shoulder, anchoring him. "Once you know the new questions to ask the victims, get out there and ask those questions. This guy won't stop."

"I won't fail you." Maki's eyes were slightly unfocused as he looked through her, and the moment stretched out. She wondered if he was thinking of something else. His eyes still seemed unfocused. Then he spun on his heels and was striding back down the hallway so fast that he did not hear Glenn's soft reply, "I know."

Monday — Lunchtime

Carrie Weber had been a nurse for 16 years. She had seen her share of crazy behavior even out in the suburbs; unhinged behavior was not exclusive to the inner cities. So, when she saw Deputy Miller and another deputy walking a woman into the clinic, she already had a pretty good idea of why.

As the trio came through the door, Deputy Miller said in a loud, clear voice, "Will you take the breathalyzer now?" The woman between the deputies yelled, "I know my rights!" Carrie was shocked to hear both deputies say it along with the woman, in a passable three-part harmony.

"I'm guessing you had more than a little time to practice that trick," she offered, unable to help a wry smile from spreading across her face.

"Way too much," said the second deputy with an unhappy expression cemented across his face. Neither deputy was smiling, so Carrie simply directed them to the closest exam room, letting them know she would be in shortly. As they passed her, Carrie smelled alcohol so strongly that she half-wondered if the deputies had decided to drink their breakfast that morning as well.

"You can't do this! I know my rights!" April was screaming in panic now. A DUI conviction now would be a huge wrench in the monkey works of the profitable divorce settlement she had been dreaming about. "I know my rights!"

"Jesus Christ! Enough!" shouted the older officer. "You were not only driving drunk, but you also ran down a little girl. You have committed murder. The warrant to draw your blood came through on the drive over. If you still refuse, that is now a crime of its own, a gross misdemeanor.

"We will still draw your blood. We will prove you are drunk. You will go to prison where you belong, you over-entitled, murdering waste of space. As I told you before, anyone with a driver's license in Minnesota already gave implied consent when they signed their name. Save yourself the third charge and cooperate," Miller said with a terse voice and stone face.

Predictably, April countered this with another chorus of "I know my rights!" but this time, even louder and with tears of fear as the accompaniment. She had not registered anything the deputy said and was still only thinking of a way to escape a DUI charge. Not seeing a clear path out, she sagged into the padded chair in the center of the room. As though on cue, the nurse knocked on the door and entered, carrying a white plastic tray filled with vacutainers and needles.

April began drawing deep, ragged breaths that were not entirely dissimilar to a cow who had darkly realized the new metal-walled building it had been shipped to didn't smell like food because it had no need to provide any food. Having seen that kind of reaction many times before, Carrie said in her most soothing tone, "There is nothing to worry about. I've been doing this for a long time and haven't lost a patient yet." She offered the woman a comforting smile. The words did not have the intended calming effect, and the woman's eyes bulged as they swept over every corner.

"The deputies will hold your arms for a minute," she said in a saccharine sweet tone, nodding to the deputies. Bill took his cue from Lance's grip and held the arm on his side of the chair, gripping the bicep and forearm. The woman began to scream in fear, a desperate high note that unsettled every person in the waiting room and a few nurses too.

"Please be still for a moment; this will just take a second," Carrie began. Then, as she brought the small butterfly needle closer, the woman jerked her elbow upwards, snapping it into the needle. The needle completely disappeared into the elbow; only the nylon wings on the needle stopped it from disappearing altogether. Screaming in pain, April twisted against the deputy's grip, which pulled the needle sideways across her elbow, tearing the skin. Aghast, Carrie pulled it out and away from the now torn elbow. Blood welled up, and April's screams went up an octave in pitch and managed to increase in volume as well. Tears flowed in earnest now, leaving shiny tracks down her face.

Carrie expertly wiped up the blood with a gauze square before using a Band-Aid to hold another square over the top of the wound. "Guys, this isn't working. Hold the other arm tighter. We are going on the count of three." Carrie then whispered the needle into the vein before counting *any* numbers, just to avoid giving notice of when the needle was on the way. She quickly popped a vacutainer onto the other end of the tubing. April looked down and saw her blood flowing into a tube and realized that the slowly filling tube was the death knell for her lucrative divorce fantasy. "Noooo!! You can't do this! I know my rights!" she howled. April began shaking as she sobbed, but not one person in the room felt so much as an ounce of sympathy for her at this point.

Monday — Early Afternoon

Carmen walked into Turtle Lake and slipped on her wet suit, the water supporting her and helping the neoprene slide into place. Then, snapping her BCD vest into place, she waited for her dive buddy, Steve Ballard, to gear up before swimming out to the orange Sheriff's float that marked where David Deakins was found.

Ballard was a sound diver and a quiet man; both qualities she appreciated. Once they were out at the float, they swam down, anchored two stakes, each with twenty-five feet of high visibility polypropylene rope, then began swimming in circles, paying out line as they swam.

The resulting spiral pattern ensured every inch was scanned, nothing was missed, and there was no duplication of effort. The polyurethane rope floated above the bottom, avoiding snagging on any hazards.

The visibility was low, nothing like the saltwater diving that Carmen loved. Every spare dime she made went into her Dive Trip account. Down at the Caymans, her favorite getaway, you might find 120 twenty feet of visibility on any given day. Twenty feet of visibility was standard for most fresh water on a good day. Snapping out of her tropical daydream, Carmen noticed something glinting in the silt halfway through her first sweep. Grabbing it off the bottom, she saw it was a pen. The initials "DD" were adorned on one side. It promptly went into a Ziploc bag and slid into a pocket as she continued with the search.

Ballard had brought his own underwater metal detector and was delighted whenever he could use it on the job. Anyone who met him would be treated to the story of when he found a diamond ring at Square Lake and then reunited it with an owner who reported it missing. The woman had showered him with tearful accolades and still made a tray of cookies for him every year on his birthday. He had never found anything pertinent to a case with his toy, but the diamond ring story ensured he never entered the water without it.

After an hour and four spiral searches, they headed back to shore. "Didn't see much," Carmen lamented. "Just a pen with initials on it."

"Didn't find anything for the case but look at this!" Ballard held out a small silver coin, grinning from ear to ear. "1962!" he pointed excitedly at his hand.

"Is it valuable?" Carmen asked with genuine interest, seeing the ordinarily stoic Ballard now elated.

"Quarters from before '65 were made with silver, so collectors go nuts for them!" he replied with unmistakable excitement.

"So, are we talking early retirement money? Is this my last dive with you?" she asked with a sideways look and a grin.

"Well… no…not really," he fumbled. "Cleaned up, it could go for fifteen bucks. But this is the first coin of any value I've ever found! And the visibility was shit! I would never have found it without Old Billy here." He gave his detector a friendly shake while sporting a double-barrel grin.

"Do you know anything about pens?" she asked, holding the silver pen out.

Ballard's eyes widened. "Holy shit Carmen! That is a Montblanc pen! It's worth at least a couple hundred bucks. You found *that* down there?!" Carmen nodded. Ballard responded, "Well, it would fit with what I've heard about Deakins. Well off and liked to flaunt it. Nice little confirmation for this being the spot he went in."

Throwing their gear into their trucks, Carmen suggested celebrating with some jalapeno poppers at Jorge's before dropping off the pen at the lab. "Thanks to my new quarter, drinks are on me," laughed Ballard. Although they didn't know it, beer was about to become a central clue in the case.

Monday — Afternoon

Bent over a microscope, Josh Dubrik was lost to the world. Only his hand occasionally moved, bringing different areas of a slide into the field of vision. His thin red hair hung down enough to block outside light from the viewfinders, and gold wire-framed glasses rested on the table; glasses were a standard lab room accouterment. Looking through a microscope was the only time the glasses came off. When the Evidence Collection team came by with a bag filled with beer cans, they had to practically pry him off the scope in order to get his signature on the receiving forms.

"The beer cans were in the boat. Looks like somebody was having WAY too much fun out there! Photos will be over in the morning. Don't have too much fun without us!"

Laughing less than charitably, the EC team headed out for the day, clearly not extending a happy hour invitation to someone they considered to be the sheriff's pet. Josh was okay with that turn of events and welcomed silence back into the room like an old friend.

Receiving a diagnosis of Asperger's in his younger years had not stopped him from chasing his dream of solving crimes like the forensic techs and investigators from the TV shows of his youth. In his current role, it really was an asset. He never had a problem focusing on cases. Cases were interesting and solving them was a thrill.

People and their emotions, however, were neither interesting nor thrilling for him. He was better at reading social cues now than when he started eight years ago with the department, but he was well aware he was no one's choice to grab a drink with after work.

It might have surprised many people that Josh was the only person in the entire department Glenn regarded as genuinely indispensable. Just this year, Josh's analyses resulted in four high-profile cold cases being resolved and closed. He was methodical, meticulous, and motivated. Glenn was never afraid a detail would be missed if Josh had been assigned.

In one of the cases she frequently trotted out to showcase her prize lab tech's prowess, Josh had found fingerprints on a bottle under the seat of a burned-out car that had conclusively identified the kidnapper in question. In another case, he had determined that a rug brought in from a crime scene had traces of a machine oil used by only one company in the entire metro area. The prime suspect had worked at that very company in their maintenance department and had confessed when confronted with that evidence.

The fact that Glenn and Josh were both Trekkers certainly helped provide a basis for their social interactions. Whenever she stopped by the lab, Glenn always threw out a hearty "Qapla!!" Puzzled looks were a common reaction to that yell, but it always put an ear-to-ear grin on Josh's face.

There was a soft knock on the door, and Carmen Shapiro came in with something shiny in a baggie in her hand. "Not much found at the site except this monogrammed pen. If it really is Deakins', it could establish where he went in."

Ballard found a quarter out there. He was thrilled, but nothing for the investigation but the pen."

"How valuable was the quarter?" Josh asked, looking at the floor. Josh avoided eye contact with most women, and Shapiro was at the top of that list. She had a confidence and a self-assurance in social interactions, something which he could not conceive. When he did make eye contact with people, he tended to lock eyes to the point others might feel uncomfortable, so with women, he had learned to avoid that kind of interaction entirely.

"About fifteen bucks, so not super valuable. He was just thrilled to find something worth more than face value. As if he needed another reason to bring that detector with him on every dive. Did you know he named it?"

Given that Josh had named his mechanical pencil of sixteen years, he met this question with a non-committal grunt. He made a mental note not to bring up Gertude in conversation with the Undersheriff. "Men!" he said loudly, with an overly wide teeth-baring grin, "Am I right?" This rote response resulted in the intended effect of generating a chuckle and moving the conversation to some other topic.

Carmen enjoyed the company of the red-haired tech. He never tried to make inane small talk, never eyed her up and down, and didn't attempt cheesy pickup lines. She had several cases closed due to trace evidence he had discovered or theories he spun based on evidence he had found. He might be awkward personally, but she recognized the value that he brought to any investigation.

"If you come up with any ideas, I'd love to hear them. I cannot conceive of why a mayor from a major southern suburb would be up in a scrunty north metro lake in a whale of a boat. Anything you come up with would be welcome. Take care, Ace," she said with a smile and disappeared into the hallway. The fact that an autistic lab tech had earned a Shapiro nickname might have dropped a few jaws, but anyone who paid attention to how many cases Josh had helped close would have understood why.

Looking at the bagged beer cans, he counted only ten instead of the expected even dozen. Every can had been crushed, so he began inserting balloons into the cans. Inflating the balloons would force the cans to expand, allowing for printing off the now-exposed surface. Before pulling out the helium tank used for that purpose (as well as birthday parties and work anniversaries), he went to the door and pulled the shade down over its window. Then he turned off all but one of the banks of lights.

Josh counted Glenn as a friend, but she did have an annoying habit of forcing people home if she caught them working late. This looked like it might be a puzzle to keep him up for a bit seeing what he could find, so Josh was taking no chances of being interrupted. He moved through the now darkened lab like a red-haired hamster in a beloved habit trail, the layout memorized long ago, and began processing the beer cans.

Tuesday — Morning

Tuesday morning saw almost everyone coming through the department door in high spirits, particularly for a weekday. Part of that was due to it being Deputy White's birthday. More to the point, there was a potluck in his honor, and with the weather starting to turn cold, that meant Gail would likely be bringing in a hotdish of some sort. Maintenance had already set up a chain of outlet strips in the breakroom to accommodate all the crock pots. Two of the three folding tables set out were already filled up by 8 am.

Brad Knutson stormed through the front doors in anything but a good mood.

"Why am I being targeted by the sheriff's department?!?" he demanded in a strident voice. "Every time I drive anywhere, there's a damn sheriff following me! This is bullshit!"

"Brad, the sheriff's department does not remotely have enough resources to assign one to a specific member of the public," Gail offered smoothly. "If you are seeing our vehicles behind you, it would just be a mere coincidence." The fact that Brad was well known for not paying tabs or renewing his license couldn't be a factor, she thought to herself, surprising herself with the snark.

"I'm just saying it better goddamned stop, or there'll be consequences!!" he declared angrily, slapping a palm down on the counter. A stranger taking that action might have triggered a different reaction, but since Gail had dealt with the man on many an occasion, she knew it was just an empty display. Once he felt like he made his point, he would make his exit.

Brad did indeed head out towards the door. Unaware of the outburst that had just taken place, Carmen was just walking through the front doors carrying her embroidered crockpot carrier, a gift from her family out East. She held the door open for the exiting gentleman.

"I don't need a damn door held for me, and not by a woman for damn sure!" Brad barked. It was so unexpected that Carmen could only stare at the angry old man as he trundled out to his rusted-out truck. She took little personally and had dismissed the incident entirely by the time she finished walking up the stairs and entered the break room. Given her Italian roots, it surprised no one that she inevitably brought pasta dishes to potlucks. Savory carb-heavy entrees of any ethnicity were always welcome at Midwest potlucks. Her crockpot went into a free space on a breakroom table, and she proceeded to her office.

Down the hall, Glenn was working on several annual reviews. Taking a short break, she reflected that the reviews went a great deal easier when there wasn't dead weight left in the department to deal with. She had been sheriff for 16 years and had cultivated a roster she was proud of. There had been some culling in the first years, but she hadn't had to let anyone go in the last six years. A few had left for larger forces, but most of the officers under her command had been together for at least five years, and she had never been part of such a tight-knit group. Coming to work was a great part of her day, and Glenn knew how rare that was.

A gruff voice from her computer suddenly barked "Captain, incoming message." Only a few visitors to her office had recognized the voice as a Klingon from the Star Trek series. That particular notification indicated an email from Josh had arrived. Josh's reluctance to engage with women where there was a significant power imbalance (or even where there wasn't an imbalance, to be fair) had long ago led to Glenn telling the tech that using email to submit his findings in investigations would be sufficient, and that she would come to him with any subsequent questions.

Thinking back on that conversation, she had to chuckle at the results; Josh's analyses were extensive, encyclopedic, and exhaustive. Never limited to just the facts, he would also include many possible theories to explain the evidence. *Many* theories. Explained at great length. The record for these emails (so far) was forty-two pages. That case had been a theft ring that stole trailers of all sorts, reselling the contents and then repainting the trailers themselves for resale.

Looking through the report now residing in her inbox, she noted that only a single can of the ten collected had the mayor's fingerprints; the rest of the cans had no fingerprints at all, a strange thing to be sure. A firm knock on her door shifted her attention. Carmen stood in the doorway.

"I couldn't help but hear Josh's email notification. Was that his prelim on Deakins?"

"I am just starting to read it. I'll forward it to you when I finish. There were only prints on a single can. Doesn't that strike you as odd?" Glenn asked with a puzzled tone in her voice.

"Looking forward to reading it," Carmen said, heading back to her office. She hated people reading over her shoulder and was not about to do it to Glenn, no matter how curious she might be about the email.

Shifting attention back to the report, Glenn noted that Josh had called the mayor's and coroner's office this morning; the former was able to confirm David Deakins did indeed have a monogrammed Montblanc that he cherished. The latter reported that the cause of death was drowning, with both lungs filled with water. The only other noteworthy detail from the coroner was that the fingernails on the first two fingers on the right hand had peeled back. Not terribly surprising for someone trying to claw their way back into a boat, she reflected.

Josh's sole speculation in the email suggested that with only one beer can out of ten having prints, it could be that the cans were part of a plan to make the death of the mayor look like a drunken accident. He was holding off on proposing other theories until he had more evidence. Surprised that was his only speculation in the email, Glenn let out a heavy sigh, ran a hand over her face, and wished she had visited the potluck before reading this report. Her run-of-the-mill day had suddenly taken quite a downturn with the thought of a mayor being murdered under her nose.

Tuesday — Lunchtime

Potlucks at the station were one of the few times every folding chair in the building could be found in the breakroom. It was not only an opportunity to enjoy great food (Gail was far from the only wonderful cook in the department, although many agreed she was the *best* cook), but it was also a time to catch up with co-workers both personally and professionally. Glenn's intolerance for keeping assholes on the roster went a long way towards ensuring that potluck conversations were usually engaging, and the laughter was hearty and frequent.

Sitting under a huge banner that read "Happy Birthday Dave" was a small man wearing a huge grin. Dave White was a deputy with gentle instincts. If a position for community liaison or mental health officer ever opened up, Dave was an absolute shoo-in, based on his co-workers' opinions. He was also an avid hunter. He had not one, but two chest freezers in his garage for all his wild game. Cookouts at the Whites' were a summer staple on the department's after-hours calendar and one of the best chances to sample over 50 kinds of BBQ sauce. Dave firmly believed that two dozen sauces were simply not enough when company was coming over. "Variety is the spice of life," he often said. "I used to think it was paprika," was his obligatory follow-up.

His favorite birthday present from last year's birthday party (his all-time favorite present he admitted to everyone but his wife) was sitting only five feet away on the first table, a roller grill, which would let him cook 15 brats to perfection in only fifteen minutes. Every officer in the building had chipped in, knowing the resulting payback that would follow a gift like this. It might have seemed altruistic on the surface, but practically speaking, a gift like that guaranteed that every potluck Dave was part of would have an ample supply of wild game brats.

Usually, they would be venison, but there had been elk and even bear brats one year after a trip to Alaska. Not a single bear brat went home with Dave that day. After the day shift was over, a 200-foot daisy chain of extension cords allowed the relocated roller grill to keep grilling in the parking lot until well after dark. A neighbor down the block from the station had followed his nose to the source and was delighted to be given a bear brat for his efforts.

"Holy shit, that's good," the man said after the first bite. "Who do I have to do what to, to get another one of these?" he asked before taking a second bite. Several deputies had wild spit takes on that line. The neighbor's name was Bryce Miller, and he turned out to be a second cousin to the department's trainer, Lance Miller. Bryce was a naturally funny man and based on the fun and laughter from that evening alone, he was now regularly included in happy hour invites.

Up in the breakroom, Dave was chatting with several other deputies when Carmen came in, eyeing the other offerings in the potluck. "Thank you for remembering!" he yelled to her, pointing at his plate that still had telltale remnants of several helpings of her chicken pesto alfredo. One thing Dave knew was that cooks loved to be complimented on their efforts, and that giving them that praise made them much more likely to want to repeat the experience of sharing. It was certainly the case for him. Everyone won in that kind of scenario.

Carmen smiled and replied loudly to the room, "I'm counting on you all to help me avoid bringing anything home but an empty crockpot." Several people raised their forks and voiced their support towards this noble goal.

Over in the far corner, Tom Ollig was deep in conversation with Gail. "I have pulled recipes off the web, but they never measure up to your cooking. I swear to you, I'd take any secrets or hints you might share with me to the grave. I just want to wow the wife and kids once." That hit Gail right in the heartstrings. Family was everything to her.

"Whenever you are going to brown some burger, always start with a chopped onion in the pan," she began. "Start browning those onions with enough water to cover the top of them and let them simmer until the water is gone so they caramelize. When the water is gone, throw in chopped garlic for a minute and stir. Then add the meat. Season it with cracked black pepper and your favorite seasoning salt. The kicker is to put in six or seven liberal shots of Worcestershire sauce while the meat is cooking. That gives it a built-in savory quality. You try that and let me know how it goes. I'm going back for another brat and some of Talya's potato salad."

Talya Cetin was Turkish and a member of the Sensitive Crimes unit. Though English was her third language (after Turkish and Kurdish), she spoke it like a native, albeit with a fairly thick accent. She was currently listening to several younger deputies trade stories around failed sobriety tests.

"So this gal falls on the line three times in ten feet, cannot stand on one foot for longer than two seconds, and blows a zero on the breathalyzer. She had the worst sense of balance of anyone I've ever seen, and my mom is in a nursing home, so I've seen plenty. It was unbelievable!" exclaimed one deputy.

"I had the opposite end of the spectrum," said a second deputy with a baffled tone. His nickname was 'Bricks' and no one referred to him by anything else. "I make the stop, and the guy says he's had too much to drink and didn't want to risk falling and scuffing his fancy suit, so could we just do the breathalyzer? He blew a .28 and was happy to go to jail as long as his suit was fine. Damnedest thing."

Talya reflected that back in Turkey, drunk driving was seen as a moral failing, and that being forced to walk ten miles was a lenient punishment. She was now edging towards forty years old and still felt that being able to help people every day was the best part of this job in the States. She had transferred into the department twelve years ago and still enjoyed her job every single day. She was the only person in her friend group who could say that, and she was very proud of that fact.

She had a classic Eastern European build, wide and well-muscled. Tales were repeated endlessly about her willingness to get into physical confrontations, a rarity in the department. Her face was broad and plain, but her blue eyes were piercing, and she appreciated the pun when people called them arresting. On the job, she wore her dishwater blonde hair tightly braided to her skull. She looked like a Viking warrior from days gone by, and that look, combined with the lower register of her voice, made her quite imposing. She was deceptively intimidating (Talya was really the type of person who released spiders outside, even the scary ones) and was happy to encourage that daunting image while on the job, especially when the end result was almost universal compliance with her wishes from almost every member of the public she came into contact with.

Her fellow deputies regarded her with respect and joked with her regularly. She had a loud laugh and never tried to reign it in. If she found something amusing, she was not afraid to let those around her know how she felt. She was regarded as "one of the boys" and liked it that way. Growing up with four brothers had resulted in little being able to offend her, although in the rare case something did, she was not shy about calling that out loudly and immediately as well.

Tuesday — Late Afternoon

Officially, David Anderson was currently working on three cases. Truthfully, he had been diligently working all day on a single domestic abuse case. He had read through the case report, and although it was outside his purview, he also examined the victim photos. Though her assaulter had not used a foreign object, her injuries were extensive. The broken shoulder and cracked ribs were appalling, but it was her face that haunted him. Both eyes were swollen shut, but the shape of her head was just… wrong. That was what his eyes told him. The report detailed why she looked malformed. She had been punched in the face repeatedly, hard enough to break her cheekbone and her jaw.

Despite the injuries, she had refused to press charges, worried something even worse would result. Her partner was apparently quick to anger and openly antagonistic, a bad combination in anyone. She had told the investigator on the case that he had found her diary and had been outraged by the way he was described in it. He had shown her his addition to the last page: "I will teach Judy not to talk shit behind my back. Then he threw the diary into the fire and tore into her.

David had requested the burnt remnants of the diary be collected and sent to the lab. It had finally arrived this morning in a brown paper bag (to avoid condensation). The bag had been securely packed in a heavy cardboard box. His idea was to see if infrared photography would capture the image of the ink, even though on burned paper it wouldn't be visible to the human eye.

In his mind, this was going to be a straightforward process. In the real world, the ashy pages crumbled to dust when they were touched in attempts to wrangle them into position for photography. Josh came over to see what the whispered stream of epitaphs was about. David shared what he was trying to do. Hearing the plan, Josh made an impressed duck lip face. "Good thinking; that should work. Try putting the pages inside two panes of glass to handle them without disintegrating the evidence." Having offered his advice, Josh went back to his desk. Letting people run their own projects was his default mode. Micro-managing didn't make the least bit of sense to him, as he resisted anything that would cut into his own time for his analyses.

Even when the pages were safe and sound inside their glass sandwich, David found a problem he had not foreseen. The diary had close to a hundred pages. He had started with the pages from the back, but he was getting page after page with nothing showing up on the monitor connected to the camera. He was uncertain whether that was because the burned pages had not been written on, or because the ink used was invisible to infrared. The thought of his brilliant theory dying on the vine was frustrating and it was cause for more hissed invectives.

He decided to test his theory by trying to photograph a page from the beginning of the dairy, as that should surely have some writing and prove or disprove the validity of his plan. When he got to page four in position for its close-up, he saw handwriting show up on the screen. He shot a few frames to establish the results and realized that it was now only a matter of time before he found the page with the boyfriend's handwriting. The good guys were going to win.

David was not one to needlessly hurry things. If a page from the burned diary was damaged due to rushing, there would be no do-overs. As a result, he had been prepping pages and looking at IR images for the last hour, with no results to show for his efforts. He decided to skip back ten pages to dodge unused pages. Unhappily that page was as blank as those that had come before it.

Sweet Jesus, if this a brand-new diary... he mournfully thought to himself. Even with that thought bouncing around his head, he did not despair. He came to the conclusion if he didn't run this down, no one would. This case was going to be open and shut ONLY if he found what he was looking for. One truism applicable to many of the people in law enforcement is that they want to be a tool of justice. That was applicable to the Ramsey County Sheriff's Department in particular.

Steeling his resolve, David continued his work, examining every tenth page. The third page he put under the camera showed a woman's handwriting. *Pay dirt!* he thought excitedly. *I'm in the ballpark. Time to bring this one home.* He carefully prepped the page next in line and put it under the camera. From top to bottom, there was only the same rounded handwriting as the previous page.

That could only happen seven more times, worst case, he consoled himself. He prepped the next page. Only female handwriting was revealed. He got the next six pages carefully ready and got them in the camera frame. The same result. *Just my luck,* he thought as he prepped the final page that was going to put the kibosh on the boyfriend's continued freedom. He slid the page under the camera, and the screen showed… nothing. No ink of any kind. He could only stare straight ahead at the empty screen with an uncomprehending horror.

He couldn't understand it. The incriminating evidence should have been looking him in the eye, but it wasn't. He recounted the pages scanned; they were all accounted for. He grabbed for the case notes. Maybe he had read something wrong. When he pulled the sheet to him, several pages he didn't need came with it and almost caught on the diary, threatening to send it to the floor. Alarmed, he dropped everything and stopped moving. Standing up, he moved to gently release the case file. Irritated, he berated the case file, "You sticky shit! Look at what almost happened!"

He heard his own words and shocked himself silent. He put the next page in the diary between the pieces of glass and put it under the camera. He gasped as the image became clear. The top third of the page was filled with the same feminine handwriting he had been expecting. The rest of the page was taken up with crude printed letters, spelling out exactly what the woman said they would. David made sure to take plenty of photographs and detail how the evidence was found. This was the kind of thing that eradicated "reasonable doubt" from potential juror's minds.

Tuesday — Evening

A single extension cord snaked out of the building and into the middle of the parking lot. There were 100 more feet left on the extension cord's spool, which was sitting next to Dave White's roller grill. The new extension cord had been a birthday present that Dave had not waited to try out. As soon as he unwrapped that present at his potluck, he started to tear up over the thoughtfulness. Several heartfelt thank-yous later, with a half day of vacation hastily submitted, two-thirds of the spool had been rolled out to the parking lot, and he started grilling then and there. The smell of wild game brats filled the entire area, and folding chairs of all types formed a semi-circle around the grill. Officers from every shift and department were there, including several who had been off duty. There were even a few civilians there, like Bryce Miller. Stories were told, and laughs were shared.

Bryce was talking to his second cousin Lance and Bill Larson. Both of them had tears of laughter flowing down their faces from the stories Bryce was telling. "To underscore how stupid I felt, I used a mentally challenged voice and said to her, 'Duuuhh, Bryce loves Gretchen.' I was trying to shift the attention away from me. The next night, I was feeling a little amorous. She responds to my advances with her version of the voice I used the night before. 'Duuuhh, Gretchen loves Bryce!' I explained to her that the voice is not only *not* sexy, but also libido-crushing. Feeling like I'm trying to get it on with someone who is mentally deficient wilts me like a butter sculpture on a car dashboard in July. So for the last two weeks running, any time I try to get anything going, she breaks out that voice.

She took my goofy get-out-of-jail voice and weaponized it! Where's the justice?!" he asked in a loud pleading voice, arms open wide, an incredulous expression on his face, all exaggerated for comic effect.

Lance and Bill were both bent over at the waist, crying from laughter at this point. Several deputies who only heard the tail end of the story were laughing as well. Bill was trying (unsuccessfully) to regain some composure by stomping one foot. Each time he tried to talk; he would only get a few syllables out before collapsing back into inarticulate laughter. Every married man in earshot thanked their lucky stars their wives hadn't absorbed that little tale.

Dave White and his wife were sitting by the grill; both of them had their legs up on a four-foot-long cooler that his wife had brought with her upon accepting Dave's invitation to attend the spontaneous parking lot activity. When she had arrived at the afternoon's festivities, the cooler had been chuck full. At this point in the evening, it was close to empty, but the demand for brats had dropped off dramatically. The number of distended bellies now occupying folding chairs went a long way toward explaining both the blistering demand earlier and the subsequent slowdown as people finished gorging on the grub.

Dave assessed the condition of the folks in the parking lot. He swelled with pride, once again being able to feed everyone into a stupor. He wordlessly slid one of his legs up and down against his wife's legs resting on the cooler. This not only put a smile on her face; it earned him some thoughtful thigh rubbing. They were an understated picture of love and contentment, sitting and smiling with each other.

Across from them, in sharp contrast, Ollig and Johnson were sparring over whether giving baby back ribs a vinegar wash halfway through the cooking and then applying a tinfoil hat to keep the fumes in with the meat just made good sense or was an act of blasphemy. Ollig offered again that the vinegar, being an acid, meant the muscle would be broken down for optimal tenderness. The resulting tanginess was an incidental bonus. Johnson countered by offering that properly prepared ribs would already be tender, and only rotten meat was expected to be 'tangy.'

"Ribs should taste like ribs for Chrissakes! Why would anyone screw with that?!" He remembered so many afternoons spent standing around his father's grill as a child, stomach growling at the smell of slow-cooking meat. The final product was always worth the wait, one of the only things that every one of his siblings always agreed on.

Wednesday — Afternoon

Tom Maki had been visiting a select group of women in the last couple of days to go through a new series of questions relating to a common trauma they had all shared. So far, nothing had jumped out, no common experience that every member had shared. He was with the last woman on the list now, going item by item down his new questionnaire, with precious little to show for it.

"So can you think of anyone that paid unusual attention to you or seemed odd at all in the week before the attack?" He was having trouble looking at the woman, though not for the reason most would. Both of her eyes were still swollen, though much less than the first night Maki had met the woman. Now, the bruising was clearly evident, with most of her face green or yellow. This did not revolt the Chief Deputy; it enraged him.

She had not submitted meekly and had fought back. She was confident she had broken her assailant's nose with a spinning back kick but at the cost of enraging her attacker and being beaten to within an inch of her life, and then raped as well. She thought hard about anyone at all being odd in the week preceding the attack, but nothing stood out.

"I'm sorry, nothing comes to mind," she sighed. "Can I get you something to eat?" She slipped into the kitchen and went to the fridge despite his protests. This cop certainly cared, as his actions showed the night of the attack as well as today, and she felt like letting him know it was appreciated.

"Would you like some chicken cashew salad? It's really good," she commented as she opened a fridge that was almost entirely populated with take-out containers from almost all of the restaurants in the neighborhood. She pulled a small grocery deli container out of the fridge and seeing the logo on the lid dredged up a memory. "Oh my god, wait! There was a guy at the deli. He was totally staring at me and totally creepy. I had forgotten all about him!"

She suddenly heard a little bit of swearing and a lot of activity from the living room. When she came back, the cop was whipping through the pages of his journal so fast that she doubted he could even see what was written down. "Was this the store on the corner of Rice and Hwy 96?" His voice was much louder and more demanding than when he first greeted her this morning.

He suddenly came to a stop in the journal, fixating on something written there. "The first victim made a comment about a supermarket guy, she saw him looking at her in several different aisles! This is exactly the kind of thing that seems like a small thing but turns out to be huge. Thank you so much; this might be what cracks the case.

Hopefully, even wider open than you cracked this asshole's nose!" Then in a softer voice, sounding like a proud coach talking to a star player, he said, "The blood you spilled will put him away for several lifetimes. He cannot hide from us anymore; you marked him for us, and we will find him."

His voice and words were clearly for her, but he was now looking through her. Then he turned and headed for the door, talking to himself, too low for her to make out any words. One last 'thank you for your help' and he was gone, the door locking shut behind him as he closed it firmly from his side.

Thursday — Morning

As Glenn pulled up to the station (early, as usual), she noted that her Chief Deputy's car was already parked in his usual spot. With a resigned look settling on her face, she headed in, knowing that something must have happened with the serial rapist case to bring him this early. Sure enough, she had barely cleared the stairs before Maki set upon her with requests for her signature on several forms pertaining to someone named Bruce Swanson.

"Tom, why do you need the records for a grocery store employee?" knowing the answer was coming, whether she asked the question or not.

"I think we've got him. The new questionnaire had two of six victims referencing odd behavior from an employee at the same grocery store. Victim 6 broke the rapist's nose, and the store's manager confirmed that the next day this guy showed up for work saying his bandaged face was from stopping an assault. But there were no reports of assaults that night. He's sly, but so am I. I want to bring him in and blood type him. Then send him away for the rest of his life, which will hopefully be filled with many painful, humiliating, and endless shower rape situations so he has a long taste of the helplessness those women felt." The last sentence was delivered with more venom than she recalled ever hearing from him.

She would have been doubly surprised to find a pair of Army-issue tactical gloves in his desk, waiting to accompany him on the arrest. They had been purchased after the second reported rape, and Maki prayed that when they found him, the suspect would resist so that he could use them. He was not typically an eye-for-an-eye person, but this was not a typical case.

The day certainly seemed to be promising a satisfying conclusion, and Maki could not hide his feelings around finally closing this case, as a smile (that no one would describe as jovial nor genial) spread slowly across his face. Bruce's shift started at noon, and they would take him into custody shortly thereafter. At least that was the official plan that the Chief Deputy laid out to the department. His outline had no mention of the special gloves that were waiting in his car.

From Glenn's office, a deep voice announced "Captain, incoming message." Glenn had been waiting for that email, knowing that Josh had to have more thoughts about the case than his succinct initial email had suggested. She ducked into her office to see what Josh had come up with on the case. Carmen happened to be walking past the door at that moment and came to a stop. She was well aware of who the sheriff had assigned custom notifications to.

She thought of stopping in to find out what Josh's report had to say. Then, after reflecting on how much she disliked when a previous boss had started referring to her as "hoverfly" for exactly that kind of behavior, she instead continued the rest of the way to her office. Though she didn't want to, she could surely wait until Glenn forwarded the email, as usual.

Reading through the email, Glenn thought this second email was much more in line with Josh's typical style. It was twenty pages long and detailed some unusual findings. Part of the reason for the delay in receiving it had been that

Josh had visited the morgue to check on the mayor's body and personal belongings. He had found that the mayor's suit had been altered to include a slim pocket that would nicely fit a Montblanc pen. The fit was so snug that Josh estimated there could be zero chance the pen simply fell out after the mayor went overboard. He surmised it would take a fair amount of force to dislodge the mayor's prize pen from its custom pocket.

Josh had also investigated the mayor's past and discovered he was a captain of his high school swimming team. Since it made little sense to Josh that a former swimmer would be panicked enough to peel back the nails of his hands trying to get back into a boat, he suggested a theory that the mayor had struggled with someone in the water. If that someone was wearing neoprene, a struggle could certainly provide an alternate explanation for the torn fingernails.

He then speculated that anyone would notice a trail of bubbles following their boat, so a scuba diving attacker seemed unlikely. Possibly, the killer had actually been in the boat, and a subsequent struggle had taken them both overboard.

His final notes were centered around the coroner's findings. Toxicology showed a blood alcohol of only 0.02. At most, the man had a single beer. The other nine cans took on new significance and now screamed 'Red herring! Misdirection!'

The mayor's lungs had been filled with lake water. Since many drowning victims do not actually have water in the lungs (the larynx slams shut after a little bit of water goes down the pipe, and it is suffocation that kills the victim), both lungs of a former swimmer being completely filled suggested something other than a drunken fall into the water. Josh's speculation was that the mayor was held down and then inhaled lake water, which led to his death. It was certainly a wild theory, but as usual for Josh, his theory left no piece of evidence unexplained.

Glenn had never met David Deakins, but the thought of someone deliberately drowning the man chilled her. If it did turn out to be the case, she was going to make sure whoever was responsible was nailed to the wall for it.

Friday — Morning

Bruce Swanson's day started out on a good note. He had found a twenty-dollar bill in the parking lot, and Megan (the new deli assistant) was wearing black lingerie under her white uniform, leaving little to the imagination. The girl was always pleasant, and occasionally flirty in a way that he felt young girls tended to play at without understanding what stakes others might see on the table.

Ever since the story about stopping an assault to explain the nose brace, Megan had nothing but doe eyes for Bruce any time she was around him. If he wasn't such a believer in the rule of 'you don't shit where you eat,' Megan might have gotten a clearer picture of who and what he really was.

He had picked up an early first shift from a (now brutally hungover) friend who had planned on doing some serious drinking the night before. The money from those extra hours would pay for a little mid-month party of his own. That cash would bring home plenty of his favorite edible, Thunder Bear. He was down to his last handful of them. A friend of his in Kansas City made them and bragged their potency "would knock even Snoop Dogg's dick in the dirt." That friend was making a killing in the recreational pharmaceuticals market and had a standing invite for Bruce to stop by anytime. In truth, he had no plans to stop by ever, but there was no denying his friend's gift and commitment to his craft, and friend prices from a cutting-edge lab was a major plus no matter who you were.

He was restocking produce (a job that was easy to do and to look busy while doing it) when he saw a sheriff's vehicle pull into the lot through the wide front windows. He might not have thought anything of it but then he noticed a second police vehicle pull in right behind the first. Bruce was inherently suspicious of everything. Without a moment's hesitation, he headed for the back entrance, stopping to tell Megan that he'd be back shortly after a visit to the restroom. Once in the restroom, he removed the nose brace and walked out of the back exit to his car. So far so good. He got in, started it up, and headed out of the parking lot. He passed a third police vehicle coming into the parking lot. He saw a fourth on the way down the main street just outside the market. He knew it was time to get out of Dodge. Maybe a trip to Kansas City was in the cards after all.

With that many cop cars for one person (he had zero doubt they were there for him), he reasonably figured law enforcement would not be giving up easily, just because he had slipped the noose at work. He would have to go to ground for a while, and just not be seen. With that thought in his mind, he called his best friend Kevin, who he prayed was home.

Kevin picked up on the second ring. "Hey, hey-hey…" *Always the same stupid greeting* thought Bruce. "Kev-mo. What would you say to an afternoon gaming session? I'd like to park in your garage too, just to stay off the streets."

"Oh, need to get off the grid? Don't forget to turn off your cell phone, man. Is there any chance you can bring some Thunder Bears to the party? I'd never kick them out for eating crackers in bed."

"As a matter of fact, I have some with me now. Go ahead and open the garage door and power up the PlayStation.

Papa gonna knock you out!" It was utterly unfounded shit-talking, and they both knew it, but Bruce's experience had proven that Kev could not tolerate any kind of challenge to his gaming prowess. Now Kev would not ever be tempted to cut the festivities short.

Bruce knew that the intensity of a search was at its height in the first few hours and would then fall off. His plan was to chill with Kev and head out after dark. Kev regularly slaughtered him playing console games (the reflexes of youth, he griped to himself), but it beat being arrested and brought up on charges any day.

Friday — Afternoon

"Goddammit, where is he hiding?" Maki hissed under his breath. His office now felt small and confining, and his breath was starting to hitch. Tom Maki was beside himself. His team had come in a good hour before the suspect's shift was supposed to have started, only to find when they got to the store that the man had started over six hours before that due to shift swapping. The suspect had been working that morning, must have seen the team arriving, and headed for the hills. Maki's tactical gloves sat alone and unneeded in his glove box. Bruce had no idea what kind of bullet he had dodged.

APBs had been put out to the State Patrol as well as every neighboring jurisdiction's police force. So far, they had come up with a sum total of jack shit. The suspect's cell phone was not pinging any cell towers. His home remained unvisited. The man had simply disappeared. "GODAMMIT!" Maki suddenly roared. It was so out of character for him that not one head dared pop out to see what was happening. However, that shout did pull Glenn from her desk. She walked down the hallway, turned into her Deputy Chief's office, and in a calm voice, asked, "Tom, what the hell is going on? This isn't like you, and I want to know why my Deputy Chief is scaring everyone in the building."

Maki turned his chair around, and Glenn saw tear tracks streaming down Tom's face. His eyes were still watery and filled with sorrow.

"We should have had him. Goddammit, we should have *had* him!" Maki's voice was quivered with emotion, and the knuckles on each clenched fist were white.

"Tom, you need to tell me what this is to you. Clearly, it's more than just another case. I need to know that you are okay." Sheriff Glenn Campbell was well-versed in reading people but was reluctant to try and read her own staff, preferring them to come to her with any issues. She saw the anguish spelled out on her chief deputy's face and knew she could no longer let this sleeping dog lie.

"Tom, this must stop. I have given you latitude around this area for a long time; silence is no longer an option."

Tom Maki looked into Glenn's eyes, walked to the door, and quietly shut it. "This never leaves the room, then, okay?" Glenn gave her absolute word. "Way back when I was in eighth grade, I was picked on a fair bit by a kid new to our school. I don't know why he settled on me, but he did. It started out with name-calling and making up stories about me. I paid him no mind, and that just made him angrier.

One day, he pumped himself up and decided he was going to beat the snot out of me. Then after he finished exactly that, he told me that every day after that was going to end just the same way. And if I tattled, it was going to be twice as bad. I went home and just cried because I didn't see any way out of the situation.

My older sister, a senior then, heard me sniffling and came in to see what the fuss was. Well, when she saw my face, her face turned so angry it scared me into tears again. She demanded to know who did that to me, and I told her without a second thought about the tattling warning; that's how scared I was of the face she had made.

"The next day, I was running for the sanctuary of my school bus. The boy saw me running and tripped me. He moved in to give me another thrashing when somebody tripped him. It was my sister, Mabel. Mabel was a big girl. She hauled that boy up by his hair. 'You get home now,' was all she said to me, and she dragged that kid behind the school. I got on the bus as I was told. Mabel got home that night just before dinner. 'He won't bother you again,' was all she would say. I loved my sister so much. She always looked after me.

"Several years after that, I was a senior. Mabel had finished college and was working a job she loved. She was walking to our house to have dinner with the family and was attacked, beaten, and raped. I was powerless to help her. I could not protect her. I could not punish her attacker. I could do nothing. I felt worthless for not being able to right that wrong and make things right for the sister I loved so much. She killed herself a week later over the shame of it. I can never get her back. This case was a way I could honor her and give these victims some kind of justice. They deserve that. And this raping piece of shit deserves what's coming to him, and I want to be the one that makes sure he gets it."

This was the most Glenn had ever heard Tom Maki talk about anything, especially his own feelings. She could only sit in her chair, stunned by this personal revelation.

"Tom, I am so sorry you went through something like that. I am sorry you felt you had to keep a secret of that magnitude for so long. All I can say is I will try to get you to where you need to be to arrest this man when we find him. Maki's eyes locked onto hers.

"Promise me that. I need you to promise me that."

"You have my word." Glenn understood how cases became personal and the steps that people took when that happened. It didn't make her feel good about lying to a close friend, but that was a better choice than ending up with a dead suspect and a prosecuted chief deputy.

Friday — Night

Bruce left that night after giving Kev-mo a decent run for his money. Kev may have had the quickness of youth on his side, but no one was going to be very quick at anything with a few Thunder Bears in their system, and Kev had devoured all of the remaining bears Bruce had shown up with (except for the two Bruce had left in the car, he reminded himself, smiling slyly). Those two went down the hatch as Bruce got in and prepared for a long drive to Kansas City. He pulled out of the garage and started putting the lights of the Twin Cities in his rearview.

Driving along a frontage road circling one of the many metro lakes, Bruce figured he better call ahead to his friend in Kansas City to announce his impending arrival. He powered his phone on when a stop sign suddenly appeared, obstructed until just then by a huge bush on the roadside. Seeing lights behind him and not wanting to get stopped for something as trivial as a traffic violation, he stepped hard on his brakes, stopping fast. His phone shot out of his lap and landed on the floor.

Then, something unexpected occurred. The lights behind him did not stop. They didn't even slow down, instead running square into the back of his car with a full head of steam. Having never been the kind of sucker to mindlessly follow seat belt laws, Bruce was then pinballed around the inside of his car, his already broken nose delivering a painful reminder that, yes, it was indeed broken and not afraid to call attention to the fact. The coppery taste of fresh blood filled his mouth, and he heard a high-pitched noise as his world spun like a crazy top.

As coherency returned and things began to make sense again, his rearview mirror revealed that someone was exiting the car behind him. Opening his door and stepping out of his own car, Bruce saw an old woman exaggeratedly stepping through a carpet of broken glass, teetering toward him. He looked at his car; the entire trunk had been folded up and the lid sprung. The exposed trunk looked like a screaming mouth, outraged at what had just occurred. The contents of his trunk were scattered across the road, like vomit from this open mouth. He could almost hear the outraged howls coming from that jagged mouth. Yes, the thunder bears were already doing their job tonight.

Unfortunately, his car's quarter panels had also borne a significant amount of impact. They now resided four inches from their original location, in firm contact with the rear tires. The trip to Kansas City was unlikely to happen tonight (at least with his own car), and that thought enraged Bruce. His jaw clenched tight, and his hands balled into fists.

That was exactly the wrong moment for the woman to exclaim, "What the hell were you thinking, stopping in the middle of the road? What kind of idiot-"

With his judgment of what was appropriate dulled by both the edibles and by being tossed around inside his car like a pair of dice at a Saturday night craps game, Bruce's base instincts came to the forefront. He delivered an uppercut to the old woman's breadbox, intending to shut her up and give her some medicine for spouting off like that.

She folded in half at the waist, and then dropped to her knees, her eyes wide and unseeing. At that moment, her face and the immediate area were suddenly illuminated with bright light. Every wrinkle on her face (and there were more than a few) stood out in stark relief as a white pickup truck drove past the scene, its headlights flooding the area. Its brake lights flashed, and it pulled over on the far side of the road.

Inside the truck, a ball cap with LEDs decorating the bill was switched on and firmly adjusted. The man got out of his truck, crossed the road, and walked up to the vehicles, the lights in his hat so bright that it hurt Bruce's eyes. *Jesus, some do-good Samaritan asshole. Just what I goddamn need,* thought Bruce. He was already working on a story when the man drew even with the old woman trying to breathe on her knees.

Before Bruce could even begin the first part of his lie, the man gloated loudly, "Opened your big mouth around the wrong guy, didn't you, Helen?" Then wordlessly delivered a rabbit punch directly into the back of the old woman's skull. She fell to the pavement and stayed there, sprawled out as though she had been long lost in space and was now gratefully hugging terra firma. The man then turned to Bruce, whose jaw had dropped open. "Glad you helped her understand how the world works," the man said with a toothy smile. "She's been running that mouth of hers way too often for way too - aww shit pal, the old bitch cracked your tank."

Bruce whipped around, panicked. Driving with structural damage to the rear of a car might be doable, but driving with a cracked gas tank was not. Bruce looked under his car. He didn't see any drips, and the pavement under his car was bone dry. Who knew what Captain Flashy-Hat thought he saw? Bruce was so intent on looking for drips that he didn't notice how close the other man had moved to him. Looking under his own car would be the last action Bruce would ever take as a free man. There was a crackling sound, his muscles convulsed, his head smashed up into the bumper, and Bruce knew nothing more.

Friday — Late night

"Holy shit, his phone just pinged a tower by Valentine Lake! He must have turned it back on again; that's not even three miles from here!" exclaimed Tom Maki. "Let's go!" Without the calming presence of the sheriff at the station, the cops that had gathered in the breakroom were anything but calm. Most had been assigned to a suspect apprehension team that had thus far come up empty-handed. The sense of anger and frustration of being thwarted all day in the room was palpable. To a man, they were keyed up and ready for something (anything) to happen as the night unwound.

Hearing the Chief Deputy's words, six deputies sprinted into the parking lot, and the lights from that chain of speeding vehicles screaming down the highway certainly grabbed attention. Luckily, there was little traffic at that hour because Chief Deputy Maki was treating the stoplights as mere suggestions, so desperate was he to get to the location of the phone pinging on his tablet sitting beside him in the passenger seat. The pulsing dot in the center of the screen had not moved in several minutes, and as he came around a curve on Valentine Road, he saw a car accident that probably explained that lack of movement.

He had slipped on the tactical gloves while driving, and as he parked behind the rearmost car in the road, his expression hardened as well. While he did not recognize that vehicle, he immediately recognized the lead car that had been rear-ended from the paperwork he had been obsessively re-reading all day. A grim smile spread slowly over his face as he thought about how easy it might be to apprehend and "process" the suspect after all. He exited his vehicle quietly and cautiously moved forward towards the accident.

As he drew even with the rear car, he could see there was someone in the driver's seat. "We got one driver! Check it out!" shouted Maki. While normally he would have stopped to check on the driver's condition himself, nothing was going to slow him from finding this suspect. He scanned the seats of the other car as he edged forward, looking for any movement. As his feet crunched through broken glass, his hand slid to his sidearm. While he didn't want to let this shitbird off with a simple gunshot death, he also did not want an unexpected gun in a suspect's hands to end his night. Better safe than sorry was his line of thinking at that moment.

Moving forward to where he could see in the car, he saw there was no one in the vehicle. The only trace of the driver he could see was the driver's blood all over the steering wheel. "He's out and he's hurt! Look out and spread out!" The two youngest deputies immediately jumped into the high weeds on the lake side of the road and began high-stepping through it. With the ripples of energy surging through him as he looked at the bloody wheel, Maki felt like joining them despite being twice their age. Knowing he was the lead investigator and was expected to delegate and coordinate was the only thing that kept him up on the road.

Looking further inside the car, he spotted a cell phone in the driver's footwell, up behind the gas pedal. Seeing that the suspect's phone had been abandoned deflated the hope he had been feeling. Bruce had lit out on foot or gotten himself a ride. It seemed unlikely that they would find him yet that night. With a gloved hand, he retrieved the phone and tried opening it. The passcode screen wordlessly let him know this night would not deliver a surprise happy ending.

"Bag this phone and get it down to Josh's desk. The damn thing's locked. Hopefully, Josh can get it open, and we get some answers." Maki handed the phone off to a deputy, then slammed one gloved fist into his other palm hard enough to sting. The sour expression on his face had nothing to do with the pain in his hand.

Saturday — Early Morning

The view from the penthouses of the hotels near the airport was spectacular. The man in the Armani suit had been enjoying the sun rising over the Mississippi River for most of the morning, with orange juice and croissants. Strains of classical music filled the room. Rays of sunshine streamed in. From this vantage point, he could easily see where he wanted his new hotel to be built. The hotel room's desk was entirely covered with blueprints and cost estimates.

A layman looking at the blueprints would have been able to deduce they were for a ten-story hotel. A mason looking at those plans for the first time might have been a little puzzled by the foundation plans. Ten feet of concrete under the ground level might be a standard foundation for a 30-story building, but these plans indicated the same amount of concrete (and heavily reinforced at that) for a 10-story hotel. On the surface, it simply did not make sense. Additionally, the plans showed several rooms inside that massive foundation.

An environmentalist would have pointed out that the intended site of this hotel was not zoned for commercial or residential use. The man in the Armani suit had bitterly reflected that the initial solution he came up with to deal with that wrinkle had not been accomplished by the city mayor. 'Two people can keep a secret if one of them is dead.' This was a favorite phrase of the man in the fancy suit, and it turned out to be quite applicable to the mayoral situation. The bribe money had been wasted, and the promised rezoning of the nearby area for a new hotel never materialized.

All that was left to do was wait and see if Mr. Deakins's replacement was open to profitable business ventures. Another hotel in the area might appear to be oversaturation, but a hotel that offered off-the-books storage so close to an international airport was a market that had not even begun to be explored. Safety deposit boxes would range in size from five by five (large enough for rifles or other bulky items) down to a foot by a foot (which was more than enough space for any variety of contraband items.)

Contents were strictly the customer's purview – 'no questions asked' would be the motto when it came to the boxes. Explosives were the sole item not allowed, although the amount of concrete used in the level's construction would have allowed for several detonations with minimal effect. Rates for the boxes started at ten thousand a week and went up from there. Shopping the mere idea around revealed great interest in the business community. Conservative cost models showed breaking even after the first year and then, bolstered by safety deposit box income alone, an annual profit of seven million dollars.

A knock on the door broke his reverie. Moving across the floor, he glanced through the peephole and opened the door. Standing in the hallway was someone who looked like he could have been a movie stunt double for several different European action stars. Balding and fit, the man simply stood there, motionless.

"Come in, my friend." He had not known the man in the hallway for long (a mutual acquaintance had made the recommendation), but he enjoyed the dry sense of humor exhibited in the man's infrequent comments. The man's name was only given as 'Jan.' "Have you eaten? There is orange juice if you like." Jan nodded once and poured himself a glass.

"Anything else for me to do?" Jan asked in a surprisingly melodic voice. That voice belonged in an opera house tenor, not a killer, thought the man in the suit, and not for the first time.

"Not right now. But let's see how the cards fall before you head home if that would be acceptable."

Jan offered another brief nod. "You know how to reach me." Cocking his head sideways, he asked, "Are you listening to Van Eyck?"

The man in the suit raised an eyebrow. "You know Van Eyck?" he asked, visibly surprised. Van Eyck was rarely found on any list of great composers and was considered small potatoes by most critics.

"Of course. He is considered a national treasure in my homeland. Did you know he was born blind and still became a master of both the carillon and the recorder? A perfect example of the power of the human will." Jan offered a salute with his glass, drained what remained in a single gulp, and then left.

One thing about professionals, reflected the man in the suit, is they never overstay their welcome. He ordered more croissants and went back to the view to reflect on his next courses of action and their next steps.

Saturday — morning

Bruce awoke with one hell of a headache pulsing under his entire scalp. Opening his eyes, he saw a large mirror standing in front of him. He did not like the reflection in the mirror. That man in the mirror was naked and bound to a large wood-framed chair sitting on a metal grate. The man's nether regions hung through the seat of the chair in a way that rendered them anything but private. Even more alarming was the sight of a 'U' shaped piece of metal pipe bolted to the back of the chair, circling the man's head, with barely an inch to spare between it and his forehead. Pins had been screwed down from the pipe to the man's skull, rendering it immobile.

Looking around (as much as he could, at least), he was able to see the room was large, brightly lit, and the walls were concrete block. It was large and stark, anything but inviting. Although he could see straight ahead and behind himself using the mirror, he was unable to turn his head or move his arms or legs due to the pegs screwed down to his skull and multiple Velcro straps circling his torso, arms, and legs holding him firmly to the chair. In the reflection, he could see several stacks of green plastic bins, each one as high as a man. There was a 55-gallon drum and something that looked like a four-foot cube next to the drum.

Although he knew he was looking at himself in the reflection, something seemed off with that reflection's appearance. Bruce could not put his finger on it. The heavy chair reminded him of pictures he had seen of electric chairs. He was more than a little relieved to see no wires leading to the chair, and his mind took the opportunity to cross something (anything) off the list of things to worry about.

The sound of a door opening broke the silence and the man from the night before walked in. Without that ridiculous ballcap with the lights, Bruce could now see the man's face clearly. Light sandy brown hair framed a nondescript face. A total and complete pussy would have been Bruce's typical assessment, but these circumstances changed things completely. The man's eyes were beaming, alive with mirth and joy. That was even more alarming to Bruce than waking up strapped to a chair.

"Probably wondering what is going on by now," the man started, eyes sparkling. Disturbingly, he seemed as happy as a kid at Christmas with this scenario. "Let's start with introductions. My name is Peter Lewis. And your name is…?"

"Fuck you! Let me outta this chair, now!" Bruce snarled.

"I understand that you might feel you don't deserve this. That is an error on your part. You absolutely deserve this." Without a change in expression, Peter slapped Bruce so hard across the face that he would have fallen out of the chair without the restraints that held him tightly. The pins holding his head in place felt like they dug through his scalp and into his skull.

"Let's try again. Your name is…?"

"You fucking psycho! I get outta this and you are dead!" Bruce's tone was pure anger, but there was a simultaneous analytical voice inside his head that whispered that the fact this man wasn't hiding his face and even announced his name indicated that he did not expect Bruce would be able to reveal that information to the authorities. That analytical voice was absolutely correct.

Peter's good cheer remained unaffected by the outburst, like a patient schoolteacher with an ill-behaved student. "Let's try again," he said after another teeth-rattling slap was delivered.

"Go to hell, you fucker!" Bruce growled.

Somewhat surprisingly, the continuing venomous comments made Peter laugh. "Just checking your resolve, Bruce. I went through your wallet earlier. You're here with me because someone like you, a man who feels it is okay to sucker punch old women in the middle of the night is not someone we need roaming free among the masses."

"You punched her too, you fucking hypocrite! You even knew her." Bruce spat, even as he internally thought, *"You don't know just how badass I really am…"*

"My punch was to keep her from being able to identify her rescuer and to confuse you. That was easier than I thought it would be on both counts. I have no idea who she was. Although once you were safely in the truck bed, I did put her in her back into her car before we left. Nice try though. Out of curiosity, do you smoke?"

"Who the fuck cares!?" Bruce rasped. "If you didn't find either cigarettes or a lighter in my clothes, what do you think the answer is, genius?"

"Maybe this will help you understand what's going on right now." Peter patiently explained. "You might think that the concept of good vs. evil is a single line, with good on one side and evil on the other and you are currently the victim of evil actions. That is simplistic. Using only that as your definition of behavioral guidelines, I would seem evil. Now imagine a second line going up and down through the good vs. evil horizontal line, making a crosshair. This second line's label would be lawful to chaotic. A classic lawful evil would be the devil or a vampire. They might be evil, but they must follow set rules. Vampires must be invited in; devils can't just take souls; they have to buy or bargain for them.

"I would be an example of a chaotic good. Rules or laws do not limit me. I may do bad things, but only in the name of a greater good."

"Kidnapping someone isn't a good action, Mr. fucking boy scout!" Bruce yelled. This situation was already damn weird, and looking in the mirror again, he suddenly realized why his reflection seemed so off. His eyebrows and legs had been shaved. Bruce didn't know what that meant, but he correctly assumed that it was not a good thing.

Peter chuckled. "Oh, I don't fancy myself a boy scout. I'm a killer. I have no illusions about my trajectory in the afterlife. I'm on the supersonic plan to hell. If you died right now and I lived to be a hundred years old, I'd *still* beat you to hell. This isn't about me earning my way to heaven; heaven was never in the cards for me. This is about making bad people suffer in the here and now. It's for my own personal sense of justice."

"Who gave you the right to make that call, to do this?!" Bruce screamed, sweating and starting to be truly frightened about where this was going.

Slapping him hard enough to make Bruce cry out as the pins dug into his skull again, Peter responded, "The same person that told you it's okay to be a lady-punching shitsack. The self. *I* told me it's okay."

Peter bent down close enough for a kiss. Instead, he ran his tongue along the bony ridge where Bruce's left eyebrow would have been if it hadn't been shaved off, the salty taste of the captive man's skin inducing a shudder of pleasure. To Bruce, it felt like a warm wet slug was sliding above his eye. Suddenly, the tongue retreated, and Peter bit down hard on either side of the bone. The freshly denuded flesh pinched up into his mouth. Bruce's pain was white-hot, blinding. Bruce screeched, the sound bouncing off the concrete walls. Peter stood up, teeth still locked, neck muscles straining. The remaining tissue strands holding the eyebrow in place gave up their struggle with a small popping sound. Hot blood poured down into Bruce's eye, obscuring any vision on that side.

Through his right eye, Bruce was revolted to see Peter had not spit out the eyebrow but was placidly chewing it, eyes closed like a man enjoying the first bite of a nicely seasoned steak. A Mona Lisa smile played across his face as he continued chewing.

"You fucking psycho! You cocksucker!" shrieked Bruce.

"Yes on one, and no on two" Peter responded. "I tried explaining this to you with words, but experience has taught me words can't bring the situation into focus nearly as well as a single bite. Speaking of which…"

Peter leaned down again, and Bruce tried to shy away, muscles tightening into cords that stood out up and down his arms and legs. The straps and the pins afforded him next to no movement and held him inexorably in place. Anyone seeing this scene from the back could mistake this for a tender moment as one man bent down to kiss the other. That illusion was quickly shattered as the standing man bit the sitting man's right eyebrow off. A second torrent of blood poured down Bruce's face, the agony he felt was blinding, consuming. His screams of pain now had a tone of hopelessness and the room filled with the sound of them.

"I hate the feel of hair in my mouth, hence the shaving…" Peter said around his mouthful of flesh, shrugging as he mentioned it. Bruce did not even hear the words. He was consumed with the agony pulsing through his face. Peter swallowed and then finished his thought with a smile. "Let's stop that bleeding. We don't want dehydration to cut our time together short."

Reaching behind Bruce, he brought a small propane blowtorch into view. "Jesus Christ! Don't do this!" Bruce screamed, eyes wide and bulging. His former bravado had disappeared. His anger had likewise fled. All that was left was pants-wetting fear. Peter brought a torch igniter up in the other hand, and with a scraping sound, the resulting sparks turned the gas into a hissing flame. Moving the igniter to cover Bruce's left eye, Peter commented, "Don't want the flame to affect your vision. Seeing your progress in that mirror is the reason it's in front of you. It is part of your punishment."

The flame then moved over the bite, cauterizing it with a crackling sound. Bruce screamed and shook in the chair, moving not even an inch. The inability to get away from this was almost worse than the pain. Knowing that the flesh he smelled burning was his own added another layer to the psychological horror of the situation. He actually swooned; the room spun around him. If he had not been so tightly restrained, he would have fallen out of the chair.

The igniter moved to cover his right eye. "Let's balance you out now." The flame began searing the flesh around his other bite. Bruce cried out, weaker now. The pain was overwhelming, and his brain was retreating, refusing to process any more input. Peter noticed the change and said with a smile, "Let's hold off any more for now."

Looking at the thick black char marks over the man's eyes, Peter reflected that his captive's appearance now resembled some sort of gruesome Groucho Marx homage. Chuckling to himself as he thought of some of Groucho's better routines, he left Bruce limp in the chair for now and headed upstairs.

Saturday — late morning

"Goddammit, this harassment stops now! I've had all I'm going to take! Mark my words!" Brad Knutson's reddened face was quite a sight: eyes bulging, veins distended. His fist made vague threatening motions at the end of an arm outstretched so hard it almost bent backward at the elbow. Gail reflected that this was almost certainly the face of a man within spitting distance of a coronary event of some kind.

Making a mental choice on how to best calm him down today, she leaned forward and, in a conspiratorial whisper, told him that no deputies were following him, but there was a person of interest in several investigations a few doors away who was generating all the police traffic. Brad was simply an inadvertent bystander in the observations of the area. The entire scenario she was inventing was total and utter hogwash, but it seemed to produce the desired effect. He took several deep breaths and muttered, "All I needed was the goddamned truth. All this time they've been beatin' me around the goddamn bush. Shit!"

He exited the building, muttering unintelligibly to himself. Gail worried a little bit about the increasing frequency of the man's outbursts and wondered if he had found a new pharmaceutical hobby that was amping up his paranoia.

"He seemed more than a little off-balance" a quiet voice observed from behind her. Callie was the summer intern and was at the end of her program. She was a small woman, and Gail had found her to be exceptionally intelligent and well-suited to the job. She took her job seriously and had not missed a single day of work the entire summer. Gail had written several glowing letters of recommendation for the intern with a heavy heart. She would deeply miss having such a competent co-worker to lighten the daily load, but she understood the desire to travel around the country, especially when you were young.

"He shows up every week or so to act outraged about something or other," Gail replied. "I think, at this point, it is more about having human contact of some sort than anything else. That said, I would agree that he did seem rather lathered up today. I'm sort of wondering if he stopped taking something he definitely should be taking…" She trailed off, offering Callie a non-committal shrug to finish the thought. Gail had no idea that her little white lie to Brad was going to turn exceptionally ugly.

The outside doors opened, and the pair of Johnson and Ollig walked in, arguing about whether Irish whiskeys had better flavor than Kentucky whiskeys (with Johnson extolling the virtues of classic American whiskey). While they waited for Gail to buzz them though, she couldn't help but stir their pot by relaying that there were now several Japanese whiskies that had many American whiskeys beat hands-down before immediately ducking into the ladies' room to dodge any returning outcry.

Through the door, Gail could hear Callie's laughter, muffled as she tried to use her hand to conceal the laughter sneaking past her fingers.

"You can come out," the intern stage-whispered to Gail a few minutes later through the restroom door.

Stepping out with an ear-to-ear grin, Gail noted she could still hear the argument continuing from the staircase.

"You are so mean! Why would you do that to them?" Callie asked with a smile. With her head tilted in curiosity, she reminded Gail of dogs from the dozens of videos that her sister would continuously forward, no matter how often requests were made to stop.

"Deputy Johnson is the kind of person that is only happy if he has something to bitch about. The old saying, 'If it were raining gold, you'd complain about a headache' was tailor-made for him. Those two have so much fun arguing with each other that I feel obligated to do my part by winding them up whenever I can," Gail finished with a chuckle. "And at this point, I understand their dynamic well enough that I know I can interject a comment and avoid the subsequent argument entirely by ducking into the loo for a minute or two. Listening to them, on the surface, it sounds like they can't stand each other, but if you pay attention, they always eat together and sit by each other whenever we have any kind of meeting. Their actions really do speak louder than their words if you can pay attention to those noisemakers' actions instead of their constant snipping at each other."

Callie listened and tried to nod sagely, as though she also had come to the same conclusion. Never a dull day, she reflected. She would sorely miss working every day with Gail after the internship was over. The woman had become a second mother to her. What she did not know is that Gail felt equally strongly about their relationship from her own perspective and regarded Callie as family as well.

Saturday — early afternoon

Tom Maki was beside himself. Incensed, infuriated, inflamed. Bruce's cell phone lay open on his desk. Josh had come in that morning as a favor and had been able to unlock it in just a few seconds. "Totally predictable. My first try for a lock code, based on the suspect profile, was 696969. It opened right up. Didn't even need to hook it up and break out the tools." With an eye roll, Josh went down to the lab without another word. Since Glenn was not in today, he knew he wasn't going to get kicked out. It was a perfect chance to get ahead of cases he had been thinking about over the last few days.

The phone was open to a messaging app, and the text it was displaying was from Megan, the young girl who had worked at the same grocery store as Bruce. It had been sent the previous afternoon and read simply, 'The cops are here for you - run.' Reading it again, Maki's teeth began grinding. It had not been a good morning for his dental work.

A call to that grocery store provided the information that her next shift was on Monday. Truthfully, he knew this was the action of a girl barely out of her twenties, young and dumb, and not any kind of accomplice. Nonetheless, accomplice or not, he was consumed with the likelihood this girl's text had given Bruce the heads-up that had allowed him to avoid being brought to justice.

Maki's shoulders were a constant source of pain from being tensed and knotted for almost twelve hours straight. From the base of his neck to the small of his back and shoulder to shoulder, there was no way to sit that did not hurt. The thought of letting the memory of his sister down had not left his mind for two days, and he could not think directly about that without feeling hot tears of shame starting to well up. The chance to redeem himself, as well as her memory, appeared to be shrinking faster and faster. At this point, the only chance he could see for apprehension was a random traffic stop catching Bruce in whatever vehicle he had forced his way into.

The notion that, given a choice, Bruce would have willingly submitted to several of the tactical gloved beatings Maki's hands yearned to deliver in order to move to the safety of a jail cell was not something the detective could have ever imagined. Yet, to escape his current predicament, Bruce would have readily taken as many punishments as Maki and the justice system might have been inclined to dole out. That was not a choice Bruce was going to get; he was going to be offered a choice a great deal less pleasant. Things for him were about to go from (very) bad to (even) worse.

Saturday — afternoon

Bruce jolted awake from a sleep just deep enough for him to escape the reality he found himself trapped in. The pain in his face, the inability to move at all, and the horrifying reflection in the mirror all quickly reminded him that this was not a dream he could simply wake up from. His captor was in front of him with his back to Bruce, working on some unseen thing. The metallic sounds coming from it provided even Bruce's limited imagination with plenty of fodder for his panicked brain to create a variety of nightmare scenarios to explain what he was hearing.

In the mirror, he could see Peter sitting at a folding table, working on a medium-sized green metal box. The lid was standing upright, obscuring any view inside. Peter was intent on whatever the box was. Peter's eyes suddenly shifted from what he was working on, and he looked up at the mirror and met Bruce's eyes. As that happened, a wide grin spread across his face. Most smiles produced an effect in the recipient somewhere along the lines of warmth or affection; this one chilled Bruce to his core.

"Glad you're back," Peter exclaimed with a jovial wink. "I have something for you that might help our conversation." He scooped up a pair of syringes that were resting on the edge of the table. As he moved closer, Bruce could now see the table around him. The metal box was an old Coleman camping stove, the kind his family used on camping trips when he was a kid. Bruce felt no sense of nostalgia upon seeing one on the table.

"Get the fuck away from me, you fucking psycho!" Bruce barked, as he tried to lean away with no success.

"That's no way to talk to someone who's going to help you," Peter chided. "Just a little something for the pain. I know I find it hard to concentrate when there's an itch you can't scratch." Peter placed one syringe sideways in his mouth to free his hands. He proceeded to make a series of small injections around the burned flesh where Bruce's right eyebrow used to be. When that syringe was empty, he took the other one from his mouth and began the same process on the left side.

"What the fuck are you doing?!" Bruce cried out.

"We're going to have a conversation, and it's important to me you can focus. I have just given you something to ease that pain for a little bit while we chat. You're welcome." Bruce's mind spun at hearing this. The same man who bit his eyebrows off was now stopping the pain? It made zero sense to him. He didn't understand it, and he didn't like or trust things he didn't understand.

"I want you to understand what lies ahead of you," Peter began. "You seem like merely a run-of-the-mill shitsack, so I haven't bothered setting an IV to keep you hydrated. Given that, dehydration will be the limiting factor in how much time we have together. With IVs, I have kept people alive for over a week. There was very little left of them at the end of that time, but they were alive. My plan is to eat you alive. You will be given plenty of time to reflect on the life choices you made that led you to my chair. You will be able to see the results of our progress in the mirror."

"What the fuck?! Let me go! I swear I won't say anything at all about you, to anyone, ever!" Bruce knew he was pleading for his life and could only hope Peter would respond to the fearful sincerity in his voice.

Peter continued, "I know you won't tell anyone anything. I want you to understand the bigger picture that you will be part of. I am tasked to keep the area roads in three counties free of roadkill. I take that job seriously. I use that roadkill as part of the food for my vermicomposting - composting using worms - specifically Red Wigglers. The worms don't care for bone, so I boil the carcasses I collect for twenty-four hours in the 55-gallon drum behind you. That does two things. First, it separates the meat from the bones. The next day, I can just scoop the flesh right out. The bones settle to the bottom. Secondly, it cooks the meat, so after it goes through my grinder and then gets spread into the tubs, it won't stink. Boy, until I figured that out, you couldn't stay down here more than a few minutes at a time without losing your lunch." Peter thought back on those early days and couldn't help but chuckle at how inexperienced he had been.

"Back in the day, I read an article about a church lady down in Rochester who was using vermicomposting for her church. The soil was then used in the church gardens. As an aside, there are only a few ways to reliably get rid of DNA. The movies show bleach as an end-all-be-all, but it isn't. Gasoline isn't. Do you know what it is? Soil bacteria. That fact was my driving force in wanting to learn more about the process. I drove to Rochester and met with that church lady. It was amazing. She was amazing. Her eyes were piercing, and she just seemed so… vital. So alive. I've been asexual my entire life. I never felt urges along those lines. That gal was 60 years old when I met her, and just talking with her was electrifying. Maybe it was arousal. I don't know what it was. I do know I have not felt anything like that with someone before or since."

Bruce listened along in a stupor of indifference and nodded when he heard the talking pause. He could not have cared less about what was being said. He simply knew that if this nutty fuck was busy talking, then he was too busy to do things that hurt. Given that as a starting point, Bruce was happy to sit there and fake interest in whatever was being said, even if had been as pointless as whether Jesus Christ himself would have worn socks with His sandals.

"The bones go through the grinder and the resulting powder fertilizes my garden. It is just under an acre. The veggies love that, the tomatoes and peppers especially. I use some of the worm dirt for the flowers as well. The rest I bag and sell under the name Garden Gold. It's insanely profitable. Fifty dollars a bag for something that comes from my garbage. Naturally, the dirt that comes from people is only used in my garden. There is no sense in tempting fate. As my mom always said, you don't poke God in the eye. Of course, she would never have applied it to a situation like this, but I say, 'If the shoe fits…' You'll be helping me get one last round of garden goodies before the weather gets cold."

Bruce looked up, eyes wide. "You want me to pick things in your garden? No problem!" Bruce was already thinking about ways to escape once he was outside. Finally, things might be going his way. Peter looked at him with a sad smile. "You misunderstand me. You're going to help by giving the garden one last dose of nutrient-rich soil."

That clarification dashed Bruce's hopes of escape. He thought of what he could do to buy some more time. "So, you have done this before?" he asked, hating the quiver he heard in his voice, hoping for a lengthy answer to a question he did not care about.

Peter just smiled. "Do you think a chair like the one you are in now is sold in stores? No, it takes time, practice, as well as trial and error to find what's needed and what works best. Although it would be hard for you to see it, your chair is sitting over a 150 cubic-foot cistern. The cistern then runs out into its own private drain field. I am not interested in carrying bodies that are shit-caked to the boil barrel. This way, when they shit themselves or piss themselves, it all drops into the cistern - no muss, no fuss.

"I've been harvesting shitsacks for more than a decade now. Over that time, there have been months at a time when I didn't run into anyone who deserved time in my chair. My busiest year ever had a baker's dozen. That was the year I had to add two more stacks of worm bins. You are the fifth shitsack for this year. The most important thing to remember for work like this is you never force anything. All things in time."

Bruce heard this with a growing feeling of sick panic. He tried desperately to think of any other questions that might hold off any kind of action and keep Peter talking. "How have you not been caught? Are you just that smart?" He hoped the flattering tone (insincere as it was) would keep Peter talking for at least a while longer. "To be honest, I would have to credit my selection process for keeping me off the radar. I only take people who are shitsacks. Shitsack isn't a race. It's not a gender. It's not an age. As such, there really hasn't been a common demographic to track. If you know what to look for, when you look at missing person cases in the metro area, it's clear there are at least two other people doing this kind of thing. One is in the northeast suburbs of St. Paul, and one is in the western suburbs of Minneapolis. The one to the east favors twenty-something girls, the other favors young children. The fact that those two have trackable appetites will be the thing that gets them caught. I drive all over as part of my job, so I'm not leaving a geographical pattern either. There would be no reason to suspect what really happens in this home." Peter threw Bruce a cheery wink, one which was not reciprocated by the restrained man.

"Now, at this point in my time together with someone in the chair, I like to let them know they have a choice. What lies ahead of you is terrible. I will eat you alive, in front of you. You will be able to see in the mirror exactly how much of you is disappearing as we continue. This is the punishment you have earned. If you admit what you are, I will give you a quick and painless death. You just have to say, 'I'm a worthless shitsack and the world is better off without me in it.'

"You psycho fuck! You won't get me to say anything for you. Suck your own cock, fucker!" Bruce spat his opinion with venom; he was still operating largely pain-free thanks to the earlier lidocaine injections, so the bravado came easily. Peter simply smiled. It was always the same with guys, no matter their race or age. Women took that option as soon as it was articulated. Telling men what was coming never changed things. They inevitably thought there would be a reprieve, a rescue, an escape. A single day of suffering was usually enough time to convince most of them to opt for 'the phrase that pays.'

There had been some unusual characters throughout the years. The third person to occupy the chair this year had been astounding. With an IV keeping him hydrated, the man had lasted eight days and, towards the end, had been little more than a talking skeleton. Peter found the man's will to live to be a true inspiration. Of course, things ended with the grinder as always, but the veggies that got that batch of bonemeal seemed to boast the same zesty flavors that the man himself had boasted.

Bruce was still trying to come up with questions to keep Peter distracted. "If you've been doing this for so long, you must have found some tricks to make the whole process easier?" He was proud to notice his voice still had a quiver to it but sounded less like a crybaby than before.

"Well, I do have one superpower" Bruce explained. "I am able to project an air of weakness."

Bruce couldn't help himself. "What kind of lame-ass power is that?!? Is being a psycho douche with an underbite another one of your 'powers'? Being nuttier than a squirrel turd? Christ!"

Peter's eyes sharpened at the outburst. "Projecting weakness takes people off their guard. The lower the target's IQ, the easier it is. It certainly worked like a charm with you." he said pointedly, cocking an eyebrow at Bruce. "As soon as I got out of my truck and saw you standing there like a schoolboy caught picking his nose, your goose was cooked, and you didn't even know it. It was child's play to get close to you and give you a shot from my cattle prod. It's half the length and has twice the juice of a normal prod. It would knock down an Angus bull, and they run over 1000 pounds. It's perfect for rendering humans limp and easily manageable."

Peter straightened up. "I need to get a few things done around the house like mowing the lawn and getting a few items from the store. I'm going to leave you a while, but I do want you to look in the mirror and reflect on the kind of person you are."

Peter leaned in close. Bruce instinctively tried to shy away again, eyes bulging in naked fear. The pegs screwed down onto his skull kept him from moving away at all. Peter's mouth slid over Bruce's nose and then bit down Bruce screamed, the sound was nasal and muffled. This time, Peter shook his head from side to side, tearing cartilage and tissue free. Hot blood poured over Bruce's mouth. In the mirror, he saw that half of his nose was gone. Where it should have been, there were now two bloody holes. It effectively made him look like pictures of skulls he had laughed at every Halloween. He did not feel like laughing now. Looking at the grim remnants of the face he had loved, he wailed, as the hopelessness of his situation came crashing in on him.

Peter was chewing his crunchy prize and watching Bruce in silence. He leaned in, reaching over Bruce's shoulder, and retrieved the blowtorch and igniter. He twisted the knob, and in quick succession, Bruce heard the hiss of gas, the scrape of the igniter, and then the tiny roar of the flame.

Without a word, Peter delivered a punch straight to Bruce's solar plexus, driving the wind out of him. Peter then moved the flame to the bloody ruin of Bruce's nose, listening to the crackle of flesh. Once the holes had been well seared, he explained, "I didn't want you to inhale the flame and accidentally sear your lung tissue. That's not how you're leaving the world."

He then turned off the flame with a small popping sound, and went upstairs, leaving Bruce to catch his breath and wallow in pain. Staring straight ahead, Bruce saw a reflection that was now barely recognizable to him staring straight back.

Saturday — late afternoon

Carmen stopped by the lab to drop off a collection of pills in various baggies, the evidence collected from a successful drug bust. She was not surprised to see Josh pouring over several books sprawled open in the conference room. *When the sheriff's away, the lab rats will play,* she thought to herself with a smile. If Glenn didn't regularly force Josh to go home, Carmen believed the tech would live in the lab. Personal time really didn't matter to him; solving mysteries was how he measured his happiness.

David Anderson was the active tech for the day. He asked her for her signature on the chain of custody forms, and when she replied, Josh's head snapped up at the sound of her voice. He bolted out of his chair, came running over, and, as he got within arm's distance, dropped his eyes. This surprised neither Carmen nor David.

"Just the person I needed," he informed the floor. "If you were diving, could you hold your breath long enough that someone on a boat wouldn't know you were down there?"

Carmen would happily have dive-related conversations all day, every day, if she could find them. "If the boat were moving, I could hide my bubbles in the prop wash. If they were just floating there, no. You'd hear the bubbles, even if I was directly under the boat and the bubbles weren't visible. Why do you ask? Did you finally get certified and want to branch into aquatic police work?" Carmen was always encouraging everyone to get dive certified and was always ready to help a fledgling diver. "You will never regret getting certified; it's as close to flying as people can get!" was her stock response when asked the question, 'Why?'

Josh's brow furrowed as he answered, "I'm trying to figure out the Deakins case. I feel confident now that all those beer cans were just attempts at misdirection. The mayor was a medal-winning swimmer. It might be possible he could have been held under the surface, but I'm at a loss to explain how a man who spent a great deal of time on or in the water could be taken by surprise and drowned. The coroner's report showed his lungs were filled with water. I would expect that from someone who was terrified of the water, flailing and gasping if they went in. It'd be kind of odd for a lifelong swimmer, don't you think?"

Carmen agreed and then offered a thought on the original question. "You could stay undetected using a rebreather. No bubbles at all. It's the size of a backpack. I use mine when I'm doing underwater photography because the lack of bubbles lets you get much closer to your subjects. They don't get scared off by the weird sight and sounds of bubbles that regular SCUBA gear produces. Seems like one of those might fit a theory like yours. You could check with local dive shops to see if any of them rented out or sold rebreathers that day. Hope you find your answer, Ace." With that, she departed. Although it was a throwaway thought for her, the idea was already stuck in Josh's mind like a Velcro-wrapped potato at a fuzzy sweater contest. It was going nowhere.

Saturday — early evening

Tom Ollig stood in his kitchen, biting his lower lip almost hard enough to make it bleed. Though he could hear the turmoil his sons were up to, he chose to believe his wife (Gwen) had it handled and did not need him out there. His eyes never left the oven's timer display. This was going to be his test hotdish implementing Gail's suggestions, and he made sure every suggestion was adhered to. He had opted for tater-tot hotdish (the kids' favorite) as the vehicle to try the advice out. The timer finished, and he dutifully removed the pan and placed it on top of the stove.

"A little bit of butter over the top really browns things up" had been her last piece of advice. Tom now misted the top of the hotdish with a melted butter sprayer he bought just for this purpose. Once topped, the hotdish went back in the oven for a 10-minute browning adventure. Sure enough, when he pulled it out ten minutes later, every tot was golden-brown and nicely toasted. With his hopes high, he brought the entire pan into the dining room and placed it on the table.

Gratifyingly, the sight of the steaming hotdish waiting to be dished out had an immediate calming effect on the children. "Wow, does that smell good!" his oldest declared. "Did you buy it? It looks like all the pictures online," his youngest inquired.

"How *dare* you!" he exclaimed in mock outrage. "Well done, hon," his wife offered with quiet approval. She was well aware of how important this hotdish was to her husband's ego. No matter how regularly she complimented him on his cooking, he never seemed to internalize her praise. Only praise from the kids or guests at the table seemed to make it through her husband's mental filters.

The hotdish was plated out and Tom waited to see if the feedback would be any different. His oldest offered the first reaction - eyes widening as the first bite was shoveled in. "Dad this the best one yet! It's awesome!"

Not to be outdone, his youngest piped up with, "Yeah, Dad, you really nailed it! I could totally sell this to the kids that have to bring their own lunch!" Then he realized he may have said too much as every eye at the table suddenly swung around to rest on him. "Not that I'd ever do that," he added, with a muted and unconvincing tone.

"I've never had better!" Gwen proclaimed loudly, partly because it was true, and partly to see if her comment would register with her husband. It appeared to have done exactly that. Both boys had already finished their first helping and were scrambling for second servings. Tom uttered a choked 'Thank you' and suddenly got up from his chair and headed into the bathroom. The glint of tears in his eyes alarmed her and instantly shifted her from general annoyance to actual concern.

Trying the bathroom door, only to find it locked, she said soft enough that the kids couldn't hear, "Tom - open this door. You are scaring me now." The door opened a foot. Tom's voice told her to come in and his arm reached out, gripped her arm, and pulled her in, the door closing quietly. Inside, she saw her husband's eyes with tears welling up. Alarm now pounded through her, capsizing her earlier sense of well-being. "What is it? Are you okay?" Not hearing any response at all was starting her down a panic spiral. That was when Tom said, "I can't tell you what it means to hit the bullseye for everyone with a meal. I'm just so happy!" he said with an embarrassed grin.

"I only ever saw my dad cry once. It was after Mom served him with divorce papers. It was one of my most awkward experiences, holding my dad as he cried and trying to comfort him. I was not ready for that role reversal back then. I did not want to make the boys feel uncomfortable, so I came in here to get ahold of myself before coming back to the table, that's all."

Gwen took this in, pulled him into her arms, and told him, "Well, in the future, please give me a sign or something. This scared me." She was surprised to see her arms were now trembling as if to physically support her words.

"Well, I never meant for that to happen. Hearing your praises about my hotdish was the grand slam of the evening. Let's go back to the kids." They both let out a little self-conscious laugh and headed to the table. When they turned the corner to the dining room, they were both stunned at what they were looking at. Not only were there not going to be leftovers for anyone's lunch, the baking dish had no scraps of any kind in it. There was no sauce on the sides of the pan. An open loaf of Hawaiian bread had been used to squeegee every trace of the meal into eager mouths.

"Can we have this every week?" The boys asked in unison. Gwen saw Tom's eyes starting to fill again and promptly asked him to get in the kitchen and she would bring the dirty dishes to him. Grateful for the excuse, he hurried in. She asked the boys what they should say after a meal like that. This prompted a series of 'Thanks for the delicious meal, Dad!' Yells that she was sure were making her man tear up in the kitchen. She loved that he always tried to keep his strong side showing to the world. It was her secret knowledge that he was as soft as a marshmallow on the inside.

Saturday — evening

The pain in Bruce's face had settled down to a throbbing ache, and his breathing had grown less raspy when he heard the door open, and Peter appeared in front of him. Disturbingly, there was a knife with a long thin blade in his right hand. The other arm swung a tote bag onto the table. In an attempt to stave off the inevitable, Bruce asked one of the questions he had thought of that afternoon that would hopefully take some time to answer.

He started by asking, "Does anyone stand out in your mind of people you've had here?"

Peter smiled, knowing exactly what Bruce was hoping to accomplish with the question. He was happy to play along. Time was certainly not scarce, and he was willing to help construct an illusion of hope. With a glimmer of hope came the possibility of its opposites: disappointment and despair.

"There was someone a few years ago that sticks in my memory. Let me preface it so you understand. As you no doubt have grasped by now, I do not believe in the sanctity of life. Everyone has life, even shitsacks. What I do believe in is the sanctity of innocence. Murder is a crime, but one where the victim's suffering stops. It ends. Contrast that with rape. With rape, the victim goes on suffering. Emotionally broken, sometimes they can never connect with anyone. I've known people like that. I find rape to be monstrous and the epitome of selfishness. That is why I regard rape as a far worse crime."

Bruce was focused on every word Peter said. He reflected that holding his tongue instead of bragging about his badass status had already paid dividends, and it sounded like it would be a correct choice going forward.

Peter continued, "I was going through a parking lot by a city lake. There were a pair of cars, but no one in sight. Most of the time it's just horny kids, but it's always worth checking out. As I got out, I could faintly hear a muffled voice cry out from down a trail, and a sharp, angry voice commanding, 'Shut up!' Well, it sounded like something worth checking out. I turned off my hat and went quietly down the trail.

"Sure enough, in the first campsite, there's some big guy with no pants putting the wood to a little crying gal he has bent over a picnic table. Blood's all the way down her leg, so it doesn't seem terribly consensual to me. The possibility of consensual activity was the only thing that delayed my taking action. With that possibility gone, I was free to move in and take him.

"He's so focused on what he's doing that he never notices me come up behind him. Behind is the operative word; the prod goes right up his bare ass, and he gets the shock of his life. I did feel bad for the girl because she took some of that hit as well since they were in physical contact.

"It was like the off switch tripped for both of them. He fell forward and then sideways to the ground. Her legs went limp, but she stayed on the table, face down and not moving. On the plus, that meant there was no issue of her identifying me. He woke up in the chair like you did: unclothed and shaved. The difference was I set an IV in his shoulder. I knew from the giddy-up that we would be spending plenty of time together, so I wanted to keep him hydrated, with enough energy to stay alert so he could understand what was happening to him and why.

"He clearly took good care of himself. His hair was not greasy, and he was quite fit, muscles bulging and no fat on him to speak of. The first thing I asked him when he came around was if he smoked. He replied with nothing but curses and insults. I was excited to think this would be a chance to try someone in shape without the taint of cigarettes coloring their taste. At the same time, the man's actions repulsed me, so I saw no need to be kind to him. As soon as he came to, I took a pair of garden shears and clipped off his left little finger without a word. His screams assured me I now had his full attention. I put the jaws of the shears around his right thumb and asked again if he smoked. To my delight, he indicated he did not. He then told me he wore women's underwear on occasion."

Bruce's eyes swiveled and met Peter's. That last part was certainly not something he expected to hear. Weirdly, Peter laughed and winked at him.

"Just a joke. It's an old movie reference I threw in to see if you were staying with the story. Anyways, since most men judge themselves by their penises, that was where I started the show. When I reached between his legs, he let loose with a flood of expletives and insults that made his earlier outburst pale in comparison. He had a fairly thick cock, at least compared to others who'd been in the chair. I could understand why the girl had been bleeding when I had found them.

"I pulled his cock forward and used a serrated steak knife to saw it off at the base. It was shockingly easy to do. Six sawing motions were all it took. Impressive as that was, I don't see that fact making its way into a commercial anytime soon." Peter's voice took on the tone and cadence of a 1940s radio announcer. "It slices! It dices! It circumcises! Truly a dream machine! Order yours now! Operators are standing by!"

Peter lost his composure and descended into giggles. Bruce came to the conclusion that the man who had kidnapped him was not remotely sane. He saw no chance for escape or even survival. Depression and sorrow wrapped tightly around him, and he felt nothing but self-pity.

Peter finished his giggling fit (with a few laughing aftershocks) and continued his story. "After cauterizing the wound, his cock went right into a beaker of watered-down sulfuric acid in front of him so that he could watch it dissolve into sludge. That evening, I cut off his balls and cauterized the hole. I strung them on hemp twine and tied them around his neck so he could see his former manhood had not just been taken away but was now mocking him.

"The next day I read a news story about a junior in a local high school having been raped in a park. I went to the man and told him that he had made the news. He seemed proud of it; there was not one iota of remorse. I told him I was going to eat the face off his screaming skull. That is exactly what I proceeded to do over the next hour. When I finished, his eyelids were the only pieces of skin left on his face. The reason for that was so that his eyes would not dry out and he would see the horror show he was becoming with perfect clarity. A faceless skull with his balls hanging on his chest.

"Over the next week, I ate him to the bone. He did not get your choice to opt out. I will say, shitsack though he was, he was delicious. When he finally did shuffle the mortal coil, the worms didn't have a lot of flesh to compost; most of what went into the bins was organs."

Horrifying as this story was, Bruce now saw a way to get the last laugh. The best part was that this psycho was going to help him do it.

"Okay Bruce, story time is over. Time to eat." The Velcro strap across his right thigh came loose with a loud ripping sound. Peter then slid the thin knife through the leg just above the knee. It went under the muscle and emerged on the other side. The pain drove every thought out of Bruce's head. Then the knife began sawing up his thigh, working the big quadricep muscle free. Bruce screamed so hard he felt like his throat would burst. The knife angled upwards by the hip and emerged like a schoolboy tunneling out of a snowdrift. Peter grabbed the loose end and raised the slab of muscle at a right angle from the leg and gave the small strip of flesh still holding it to the knee a practiced flick of the knife. Freed, the strip of meat went into a five-gallon bucket, splashing as it did.

The blowtorch's quiet roar grabbed Bruce's attention, the sound cutting through Bruce's agony. "Jesus please no…" was all he got out before the flame began kissing his bloody thigh, cauterizing the massive wound. Screaming until every vein stood out, Bruce had never felt anything like this; the pain was overwhelming, all-consuming.

Once he finished cauterizing, Peter turned and used the blowtorch to light the camping stove. He brought out a small container from the bag and from it, put several pats of herbed butter on a griddle and began spreading them. The butter melted and then started to brown. The aroma was mouth-watering to Peter, not so much to Bruce. Ignoring Bruce's screaming (not unlike a parent with a perpetually wailing toddler), he hauled the now-rinsed muscle out of the bucket and slapped it on the griddle, savoring the sizzle.

The smell of searing meat was anything but enticing to Bruce. His empty stomach heaved but there was nothing to come up. The heaving did nothing to help, and just left him exhausted. He shut his eyes and tried to tell himself this wasn't happening. With his eyes shut, he didn't have to look at his ravaged face in the mirror or see the look of naked anticipation on Peter's face as he hovered over the grill. The sizzling stopped for a second as Peter flipped his thigh over on the griddle. Then it started again in earnest. That sound had the effect of loosening Bruce's grip on reality, like prying the fingers up of a person hanging from a tenth-story window ledge. His mind spun, and he felt like he was floating.

"Dinner is served!" Peter's delight was unmistakable. As ghastly as those words were, given the situation, they did tether Bruce to the real world. His eyes opened in time to see the first bite disappear into Peter's eager mouth. The look of contentment on his face was sickening.

"Everyone says wild game tastes amazing," Peter remarked after swallowing the first bite. "Venison *is* delicious, no doubt. Elk doubly so. Still, there is no animal that compares to the delicate taste of human. Human is also easier to chew. We are so tender. It is interesting how much diet affects the taste of the meat. You see it in lots of animals. Corn-fed squirrel tastes considerably different from acorn-fed squirrel. I'm sad to say that most shitsacks have a poor diet, so they don't taste as good as they could. Still, given that, shitsack is still going to beat almost any other meat out there.

Bruce did his best to ignore Peter's words and instead shape his idea for getting the last laugh. With the earlier story clearly demonstrating Peter's feelings around rape, being able to ask for a quick death and then confessing his many rapes just before he died, he would leave this psycho frustrated and outraged. There would be nothing to do to a dead man, and the psycho would know he was the one who let a badass escape punishment through his own stupid offers.

Sunday — Morning

Driving to the office, it seemed as though the sparse morning traffic was deliberately trying to drag her down to a crawl. Talya gritted her teeth and turned up the volume.

Dinner seemed forever away. She had made some brats with classic Turkish seasonings - thyme, cumin, and sumac. They would spend the day in the fridge at work, wait for the end of the shift, and then accompany her to Dave White's house for a grill out. She had promised him Turkish brats after they started talking about Turkish seasonings at his birthday potluck. Dave loved to hear about world cuisine and the differences from his own cooking. The fact that he was also happily married meant his attentiveness was never misconstrued. Time spent talking with him was just that and nothing more. In every way, it was obvious that he doted on his better half. Talya enjoyed conversations with his wife as well. She was not shy with opinions and not afraid to give someone the boot from their grill outs if her lines were crossed. She was quick to love and was already calling Talya her 'Turkish sister.'

Never having had a sister, Talya was quick to accept the title. Trying to open the road up for herself to get back to the office, she started firing her radar gun at every car in her lane, hoping someone (anyone!) would move to the right so she could fire through any opening that might appear. Because she was shooting every car in her way, her radar gun let her know there was not a speeder within range. The cars in front of her were moving at a gentle five miles under the speed limit. *Oh, for the love of God, thank heavens the roads this morning are perfectly safe from the scourge of speeders.*

"RS-14, please head to Shoreview Village Mall for a code 621." Talya rogered the call (giving thanks for the deliverance from the convoy of grandmothers on the road as she did) and turned off the highway. Public drunkenness was an unusual call for a Sunday morning, but anything that got her away from this morning's vehicular frustration was welcome. Pulling into the mall parking lot, she immediately hit her light bar as she pulled up to a knot of people, making them aware of the police presence. The flashing lights resulted in almost half the people suddenly remembering they had business to check inside the mall, and they scurried back inside.

Stepping out of her cruiser, Talya was greeted with the sight of a teenage boy, naked as a jaybird, waving his fists at anyone coming close to him. Judging by his pubic hair, Talya surmised he was no more than sixteen (having several brothers growing up gave her a great deal of experience to draw from). She strode up to him, looking him in the eyes as she approached.

"Good morning. How are you doing?" she started.

"I'm naked in a parking lot on Easter. How do you think I'm doing?"

Given that Easter was more than four months ago, new questions formed in her mind. "Why do you think it's Easter weekend?"

"Are you blind? I don't have my burial robes and I just walked out of my cave after resurrecting. How could it be anything *but* Easter?" the boy asked, outraged and surprisingly articulate.

Immediately, Talya thought this was not someone drunk, but someone having a bad trip of some kind. "Can you show me where this cave is? I think that would help me to help you and maybe there is a clue to find there so we can solve this mystery." Her blue eyes stayed locked with his, wordlessly suggesting working together was the best choice.

The talk of clues and mysteries to be solved had the intended effect. His combative stance softened, and he motioned for her to follow as he started off through the parking lot towards a distant trailer park. He marched like a parade marshal, excited to be part of a team solving a mystery. He was unclear what mystery they were solving, but he had a good feeling about this Viking woman.

Two blocks into the trailer park, the boy executed a crisp ninety-degree turn, marched across a yard, and through the open door of a double-wide trailer decorated with many crucifixes and a wide variety of Christian symbols. Talya cautiously walked up to the door and knocked hard.

"Ramsey County Sheriff! Is anyone home?" Her voice left no room to doubt she expected anyone inside to promptly answer her.

The boy bounded back to the doorway. "I'm here! I think I found a clue in the living room!"

Entering the trailer, she saw a low table in the living room. It had several empty plastic bags on it, and a glass with a remnant of what looked like filthy water. The boy pointed to the glass. "Here it is. Our clue!"

The reek of what must have been pounds of marijuana smoked in the trailer was so strong, it hurt her eyes. A large pool of vomit on the floor didn't help.

"What do you think is in the glass?" she asked innocently.

"I would bet that someone made some super strong mushroom tea here." The thought that he was the one who did the brewing did not remotely occur to him.

"Are these your clothes, do you think?" Toeing the pile of clothes next to the wall, an image of events was starting to coalesce.

"Yeah! That's my favorite shirt!" The boy held it up for Talya to read. 'I don't always roll a joint, but when I do, it's my ankle.' Talya couldn't help but chuckle at that. Then she asked, "Do your parents live here?"

The question was met with a scoff, and a head shake of dismissal. "Mom's long gone. Dad's only home to sleep then back out selling. I think someone used some of his stash to brew that tea. I remember drinking it, feeling sick, barfing, and dying. When I came back to life, I knew I had to tell people about the miracle. I started at the mall, but they wouldn't believe me. I was starting to lose hope, and then I found you!" A beatific smile spread over his face, and he gave her an enthusiastic thumbs-up.

Talya nodded and turned away. She quietly said into her radio, "RS-14, I'm going to need someone from child protective services at 1645 Dellwood in the Woodlawn Terrace trailer park." Looking at the boy, she asked, "Do you have a name?"

"Aidan" was the prompt response.

"Aidan, why don't you put on those cool clothes and come with me outside?" The smells in the trailer were getting to be a bit much and she was starting to feel a little high herself. "I want to run a theory past you and get your thoughts."

Aidan thought this might be the best day of his life. First, he had been resurrected, and now a Viking was asking for his help to solve a mystery. He felt tremendously important and now people wanted his opinion. It was glorious.

"Here's what I'm thinking. Tell me if this sounds right to you," she asked Aiden. "I am thinking that you made the tea, but it was a little strong. You threw up and then passed out. You woke up and were still tripping. I have no idea why your clothes were off. Regardless, it really doesn't seem like this is the best environment for you, with almost no parental supervision and illegal drugs laying around. If you are okay with it, I would like you to go with friends of mine."

Although there was no legal way she could have left a boy she had just met a half hour ago alone and on his own, just providing the illusion of choice was enough to help him think he was doing a favor. "If they are friends of yours, that's good enough for me!" he stated, confident he sounded majestic. Happily, a county van pulled right up so they didn't have to wait around and give Aiden time to change his mind. Hopping in, he waved goodbye to Talya through the window. Smiling widely, she waved goodbye.

Saving a kid from a terrible home life felt a lot better than navigating through the road sloths on Sunday morning. Being able to take one more drug dealer off the streets was icing on an already delicious cake. Talya radioed for backup and sat on the steps, waiting to see who would show up first. Her money was on Deputy Johnson, who seemed to harbor a special joy for busting drug dealers. If it did end up being him, she knew he would happily collect and catalog every piece of evidence to be found inside the trailer and in the yard, too.

Sunday — Late Morning

Bruce hurt everywhere, and his leg felt like it was on fire. Every time it moved, it was fresh agony. He had been awake all night, fixating on his plan for a final 'fuck you' for Peter. When he finally heard the door opening, he immediately began shouting, "I'm sorry for being a shitsack!" over and over, eager to get his plan started.

Peter sat down in front of Bruce. "You know the world is going to be a better place if you are not in it."

"I do know that. You promised quick and painless. How are we doing this?" Bruce was cutting to the chase and felt in control of something again. That did feel good.

"You are quick to bring the curtain down this morning. Must have been a tough night for you, eh? I figured you were a four-day man for sure." Peter couldn't resist a little last-minute needling. Reaching into the tote bag still sitting on the table, he pulled out a syringe and a small straight razor. "I'll give you some lidocaine and then nick your femoral artery. No pain and it will be just like falling asleep."

That fit perfectly into Bruce's plan. There would be no stopping that kind of bleeding, so he wouldn't have to worry about being brought back once his secret was out. He looked forward to seeing the frustration on Peter's face when the dipshit realized he'd been duped and there was nothing he could do to keep his captive alive.

Peter made a number of small injections around the inside of Bruce's right thigh. Given what had happened to that thigh, Bruce didn't even register them.

"We'll wait a bit for those to take," Peter clarified. "As I promised, you stay whole from this point forward."

Bruce doubted that would be the case after he pulled his little trick, but he simply nodded his head in agreement. Knowing he had an ace to play was giving him something to look forward to. He almost felt giddy.

Peter leaned forward, as though sharing a secret. "You're going to be number 40. I went back through my calendar and counted. Quite auspicious, I dare say!" He seemed quite proud about that. Bruce had no idea what 'auspicious' meant, and he didn't care. "I know it's got to be hard for you to understand much from your perspective, but this is for the best." Peter's voice was low and pitying.

Keep it up, you patronizing fucker Bruce thought to himself. *It's all about to go tits-up for you.*

Peter reached between Bruce's legs, which made Bruce start. There was a feeling of pressure then the sound of liquid falling into the cistern. It sounded like Bruce was pissing like a racehorse after a long night of drinking. Peter returned the straight razor to the bag.

"That straight razor is from Solingen Germany. The craftsmen there have been making them for 200 years. Solingen is known in Germany as the city of blades. They have razors there made in the 1700s that can still slice tomatoes so thin you could see through them. This one has been used for shaving and cutting for over a decade, and I've only had to sharpen it twice in all that time. You have to hand it to the Germans; they make great razors."

Bruce started to feel a little lightheaded. He tried telling Peter that he had done much worse than punching an old woman, but his tongue wasn't working right. He couldn't form his consonants and all that came out was an unintelligible vowel slurry. Panicked that his plan was falling apart, he tried talking louder.

Peter stopped him with a hand on his shoulders. "I know that talking thing seems scary. You seemed so eager to go; I did a bit more than just nick. This should be quick."

Bruce heard this, and the bottom dropped out of his stomach. He tried to tell Peter again, but it sounded even worse. He didn't have enough breath to force out words, and he couldn't form any consonants. Knowing that his own behavior had led to his brilliant plan going right into the shitter was one of the last things that went through his mind before he passed out and passed away.

Peter watched the body for five minutes and then reflected it was too bad Bruce wasn't able to get that last comment out. The man died in frustration, which Peter did regret. Although if he hadn't been a shitsack, he wouldn't have been in the chair in the first place. Peter began unstrapping Bruce to move him into the boil barrel, never knowing the real truth about who was going in there.

Sunday — Evening

It was always easy to find the White's house. It was the one with all the cars in front of it. Talya found a spot on the street (almost half a block down), grabbed her cooler, and headed back. From a half block away, you could smell the food and hear the laughter. Talya had spent the majority of the day worrying about Aiden, the kid she had helped remove from his home that morning. On the way over to the grill out, she had finally gotten a return call from child services. Aiden seemed to be accepting things, but it was hard to be sure because he had fallen asleep after lunch and was still sleeping. Given what he had ingested, that news did not surprise Talya at all.

As she crossed the yard and people saw the latest addition to the evening, there was a rousing chorus of "Talya!", "Whooo", and other affirming shouts. She exchanged several high fives on her way to the grill, where Dave White was standing with a large pair of tongs in one hand, and a grilling spatula that could have served as a medieval axe in the other.

"Talya!" he said with a wide grin. "I hope that cooler of yours is toting your Turkish brats. Everyone I've been talking to is eager to try one. Your recipe is nothing I would have ever thought of, and I've been thinking about it all day."

Talya cautioned the grill master, "Remember that the meat is lamb, so that's going to be a different flavor from what you might be used to. Give them a couple of stabs before they go on, or they will split open on your grill. Lamb brats can be a little fatty. When the drippings are clear, grab a brat and a beer." Everyone in earshot grinned at that one.

Dave laughed at the fat comment. "You're singing my song! Fat equals flavor! Let's get those babies on the grill!" Dave reached down and swung her cooler up onto the grill table. The weight of it almost pulled him off balance. Looking inside, he was surprised to see not two or three brats (as he expected) but a cooler that was completely filled with them. There had to be at least twenty brats in there. "Talya, what gives with all the brats? Are you planning on feeding the neighborhood?" he asked with a typical smile in his voice.

"My butcher had a sale on ground lamb, so what we don't grill tonight will feed me for next week. The fact that Talya could eat the exact same thing for lunch and dinner for weeks was astounding to almost everyone in the department. No one was willing to ask if it was a Turkish thing or just a Talya thing. Her stretch of three weeks eating pickled red cabbage every day was an office tale of wonder (less so for the ladies who shared a bathroom with her during those three weeks).

Dave found room on the grill for three of her brats. Watching the grill, he had to dance the brats around to avoid burning them with flare-ups. The smell was certainly different. They had a grassy, spicy smell. Once the drippings ran clear, he called Talya over and nestled all three brats in toasted buns. Talya moved two onto her plate, leaving one for Dave to try. Eschewing condiments to match Talya, he took a big bite. He had been thinking that it wouldn't taste like a regular brat. Now, there were some general flavor notes that made him think of the Mediterranean, and there was a single note cutting through everything. He could only describe it as a kind of smoked lemon.

The sharp and unusual flavors evoked two memories in his mind's eye. The first was from a Mediterranean cruise he had taken as a young man. They had docked for two days in Istanbul. He had gone to the Spice Bazaar early in the morning of the second day. It had been mesmerizing. The rising sun's rays had painted everything in a golden haze. As the merchants began scooping spices for the day's customers, the motes drifting around lit up in the sunshine. The air was filled with warm but unfamiliar smells, smells you could almost see. He had been so excited to move through this alien culture, filled with wonder as he explored. The memory was so crisp he could still see all the wild colors in the vendor stalls and the elaborately styled mustaches of the shop owners. It had been nothing like Minnesota, and he had wanted to take every memory away with him.

The other memory the brat had dredged up was nowhere near as crisp, as it was an amalgam of so many hot summer days and the inevitable relief of an icy cold glass of his mother's lemonade. He could almost hear the clink of the ice cubes in those green glasses.

"Wow, Talya, that is sure a different kind of brat. Is it Sumac giving it that tang?"

"It sure is," she confirmed. "Sumac is a staple in many Turkish dishes. It's got a smokey citrus flavor. It pairs well with most meats and salads. It's gaining in popularity so much here in the States that I don't have to order through the mail anymore. I love it!"

Listening on the sidelines, both Carmen and Deputy Johnson began clamoring for one of Talya's special brats. As word spread through the party about 'the Turkish brats,' Dave found he was grilling little else. They certainly didn't taste like regular brats, but that was the point. Everyone was enjoying the opportunity to fancy themselves as daring explorers of world cuisine. Brats in hand, Carmen and Johnson moved to the side of the yard, out of the way of the grilling, and back into their previous conversation.

"Mugshot is a three-year-old American Bulldog. Out of the puppy stages, but into other stages." He rolled his eyes, and Carmen laughed. However, Carmen was laughing at something else. Mugshot, she thought to herself. Of course, Johnson would name his dog something like that. Being a cop was the man's entire self-identity.

"I had a gal over the other night. She says she's great with dogs, and of *course* Mugshot can sleep on the bed with us. He is fifty pounds of blocky muscle, and he loves meeting new people. He plunks down next to her on the bed. Par for the course. She assures me it's fine. I hook an arm around her waist and promptly fall asleep."

Carmen exclaimed with a big grin, "Typical man!"

Johnson offered a grinning shrug and upturned hands, as if to say, 'You got me.' Then continued his story. "Around fifteen minutes later, she scares me awake! She yelled, 'Jesus Christ! Your dog is licking the sheets so hard, the mattress is shaking like he put a quarter in it.'" Carmen let a belly laugh out at that. Johnson nodded his head. "Yeah, that was my reaction too, a big ol' laugh."

"I can't imagine that laugh made it all better," Carmen sniggered.

"Yeah, I don't think she liked dogs as much as she thought she did," he said with downcast eyes. "It's been over a week. She won't take my calls, she won't answer my texts. I really liked her. Maybe if I didn't have Mugshot..." His voice dropped on that last line, and Carmen was amazed to see he was genuinely distraught. Normally the expected emotion on his face would be some level of outrage. Now he just looked like a puppy whose favorite ball rolled under the couch.

"Let me share this with you," Carmen said in a low voice so only he could hear it. "You might be able to imagine a future with someone. That does not mean it will happen that way. No one can love enough to keep a relationship going if the other person doesn't want to be in it. One person just can't love enough for two and make a happy relationship. It sucks but it's true. Someone that fits with you and Mugshot would have laughed at that situation. I'm sure you're hurting now, but if you'd gotten six months or a year down the road and then she hit the silk, that emotional pain would've been so much worse. Cold comfort, I'm sure, but it is the truth.

"Giving up your dog for any woman is ludicrous for you to even consider. You love that dog, and he clearly loves you." Carmen had run into the pair on different running trails several times that year. Without exception, they always had matching outfits of some kind. Those were not the actions of an indifferent dog owner. "Together, the two of you make up Team Johnson! And that's awesome!" She gave him an exaggerated grin and threw up a high five. Hearing someone else mention Team Johnson, he responded with a delighted grin of his own and a crisp high-five back.

"Thanks for that, Carmen." With watery eyes and a smile still on his face, he mumbled, "I really needed to hear that. You are the very best." Getting things back on friendly footing and away from the sentimental morass it seemed they were on the edge of, she hooked an arm around his neck and steered them both back to the grill for another brat and another beer.

They arrived at the grill just in time to hear Dave's wife ask if a previous story's whole "guys' voices deepen when their balls drop" was seriously a real thing versus something made up to serve as a good punchline. Dave looked at his wife and stiffly said, "If I'm the one telling it, then of course it's true."

Without hesitation, she retorted, "In that case, you should sound like *Barry* White, Mister Low Riders!"

There was a moment of silence with people not knowing if laughing at the host was acceptable. Eyes were looking sideways, and then Dave let loose with a roaring belly laugh. He had to hold onto his grill's handle to stay upright. People started laughing at how hard Dave was laughing, which made him laugh even harder.

The entire grill out spiraled into a vicious cycle of hysterics, lasting well over five minutes. Every time it seemed to be winding down, someone would start laughing at someone else who was unsuccessfully trying to stop their own laughter, and the whole thing would repeat. Even though he was laughing so hard he was having trouble catching his breath, the one thought that stayed in the forefront of Dave's mind was that he had unquestionably married the right woman.

Monday — Morning

Gail had a morning routine that ideally ended with a cup of flavored coffee made from her personal Keurig. Having an intern this summer had been wonderful in a number of ways. One of the ways was that with Callie taking some of the load onto her slender shoulders, there had not been a single morning that summer that had been bereft of a soul-warming cup of joe. With a twinge of sadness, she reflected that losing Callie might mean winter days where the morning coffee might not get brewed until lunch.

As if on cue, Callie came smiling through the front doors. Brad Knutson followed on her heels. Gail saw him and began mentally preparing for yet another of the man's diatribes. She quickly genuflected before the ornate cross above her desk (it had belonged to her grandmother). She buzzed the door for Callie, and that was when everything routine about the day went right out the window.

Brad hip-checked Callie with the effectiveness of a ten-year NHL veteran. Outweighing the girl by a hundred pounds, she practically flew into the wall. As he slipped through the now open security door, he pulled a Luger pistol from his waistband and bellowed, "No more mister nice guy!" Gail could scarcely believe what was happening. Once she saw Callie was back on her feet, she hissed, "Get outside now!" She then retrieved her beloved revolver from its quickdraw mount on the side of her desk and moved to the side of the door, ready for anyone to enter the doorway.

She saw Brad's shadow move past the door and continue down the hallway towards the stairs. She moved to the doorway and glanced down the hallway. Brad was walking right down the center of it, his gun hanging at his side. She stepped one foot into the hallway and assumed a Weaver stance, left hand supporting her right, legs braced. With her rump against the doorway, she was completely balanced.

"It's all over now!" Brad yelled as he reached the stairs. Although she had never shot anything living, Gail now saw this situation's potential to change that standing. While she could have easily killed Brad with a single shot, she was hoping some other end would present itself. Then Brad made a move that changed her entire outlook on the situation.

Brad raised his gun straight up over his head, as though he were going to fire into the ceiling. It was exactly the wrong move for him to make. Knowing that the breakroom was above him, with any number of people ignorant of the danger they might be in, Gail's eyes sharpened. No one would hurt her family if she could help it. He was not moving forward anymore. "You won't hurt anyone here," she said in a whisper. She drew a breath in and at mid-exhalation, she squeezed the trigger.

The hand holding the Luger exploded in a shower of blood and gore. The gun flew to the end of the hallway, landing on its side at an angle, the finger that was caught in its trigger guard acting like a makeshift kickstand. Dumbfounded, Brad looked at his arm which now ended at the wrist, screamed, and collapsed on the stairs. "Why would you do that to my hand? Why not kill me?" he moaned, staring up the stairwell.

Walking up to him, Gail felt a measure of pity for the man, now that he was no longer any kind of threat. He screamed in the stairway, voice carrying through the first and second floors, and rocked back and forth. "It's two years today my Betty passed away. My life is shit without her. I miss her so much!" His voice cracked with emotion as he spoke. Tears poured from his eyes, though it was hard to tell if that was from emotion or the pain. Gail pulled off her belt and cinched it as a tourniquet on his forearm. She had never killed anyone and was determined to keep it that way. "Callie, call an ambulance," she instructed the intern, who was still standing there, staring horrified at all the blood.

Carmen had heard the single gunshot and subsequent caterwauling from her office and came hustling down the stairs carrying her EMT bag, ever prepared. Seeing no one else injured, she threw Gail an okay symbol and crouched by Brad, who was still wailing, a pitiful sound. After checking the tourniquet, she pulled a syringe and vial from her bag. She sucked up some of the vial's contents into the syringe and injected it just above the belt on his arm. Within a few minutes, his wailing tapered off. Gail stepped over Brad to see if she could help.

Brad looked up at Gail and mumbled, "I saw the guy you're tracking. He moved into the house next to mine. From my window, I saw him chase a woman and beat her, and I saw him knock down two different men on his porch. I understand now why there were always cops around."

This made zero sense to Gail. "Brad, what the hell are you talking about?" Her voice was colored with more than a little bewilderment.

"You told me about the guy, that he was the reason there were always cops around my neighborhood. That the deputies driving behind me was just a side effect of watching him. I got him for you. He's in the hospital."

Listening to him, Gail remembered the conversation from the week before and felt a growing sense of alarm around what her words had wrought. With a furrowed brow, she asked "Brad, what did you do? Brad?" Whatever Carmen had given him seemed to be taking effect. His eyes kept closing, and his head lolled from side to side.

With a groggy voice, he clarified, "I was driving here and saw him in his driveway, digging around in his trunk. I swung into his driveway and smashed into his trunk. He was still between our cars. Then I drove here."

Carmen heard this and asked the million-dollar question. "Why would you be driving here with a loaded gun?"

With the drug unquestionably taking effect, he slurred, "I wouldn't. Eeesh not even loaded. I couldn't shoot myself without ending up down below so I came here so someone else would."

Hearing those words, every smidgeon of pity and compassion Gail had been feeling drained right out of her. "You were afraid for your immortal soul, so you were going to damn one of us?!? You selfish, worthless old coward! I wish I'd blown both your arms off! I wish I'd shot your dick off, you useless waste of space!" Gail sputtered, looking for more words. Carmen admonished her saying, "He's not going to remember anything that happened after that shot I gave him. Save your energy."

Gail looked around and saw many faces looking down the stairwell at the scene. Those watching faces saved Brad from getting the kicks Gail felt he deserved. The gall of the man to expect them to deliver him to a better world at the cost of condemning their own souls. It was enraging.

Wisely, Carmen took Gail's arm and walked her back into the reception office and out of earshot of the second floor. She buzzed the waiting EMT team through the security door, then turned to Gail, who was still white-knuckled and red-faced. Carmen told her, "This job is not fair. Every day we put everything on the line. Most days, we get everything back. That is the job. Yes, selfish dickheads suck. That is part of our job. We won't let their shitty behavior change who *we* are. That is the realm of the weak, and we are *not* weak." Carmen concluded by saying, "As an aside, that was an amazing shot. I would have just gone for center mass, but you spared his shitty life. You might be the most moral person I know. And you're hell on wheels in a kitchen. It's a privilege to know you, doubly so to call you a friend."

Gail's eyes were a little teary, and her voice quivered as she answered, "Dammit Carmen! I want to be pissed, and you hit me with that?! Cripes!!" With zero warning, she pulled the bigger woman into an inescapable bear hug. Her chest started heaving, and then she could speak no more, and only choked sobs emerged. Carmen simply held her tight as Gail's legs began shuddering as well.

Weeping opening now, Gail tearfully confessed, "I almost killed someone just now. And while man's law would have called it justified, God's law has no loopholes. No matter what kind of life I've led, it could've been all for naught! I almost earned myself damnation!" With it said out loud, she began openly sobbing in earnest. Carmen (who was not at all religious) simply held her friend, whispering "I know… I know…."

Monday — Late Morning

The man in the fancy suit admired the skyline of Minneapolis, its sleek glass building reflecting the yellows and oranges of the morning sun. The sound of church bells coming from his speakers filled the room with music, as though Sunday had arrived a day late. A knock on the door shifted his attention away from the view, and put an anticipatory smile on his face.

With a glance through the peephole, he swung the door open wide. Jan stood in the hallway, not moving, patient as a sphinx. "Please, come in," came the invitation, and he moved inside. "Help yourself to orange juice and croissants. They are a little dry compared to the last hotel, but still decent."

Jan filled a glass and drained half of it in a single draught. "You said you had something for me?" Straight to business. No surprise there.

"Given our last conversation, I wanted to let you know there will be a concert featuring Minnesota's largest carillon this coming Thursday night. If you are still going to be in town, I invite you to join me. According to the carillonneur for the performance, Van Eyck will be prominently featured."

Jan grinned, and it was amazing how the smile changed his entire demeanor. From dour and taciturn, he suddenly seemed approachable, even friendly. Smile lines that had not been visible before unabashedly displayed themselves. "I would never turn down an invitation to such a concert, and I thank you for extending it." He straightened up to his full height and then bowed his head forward in a gesture of respect. Extending the arm holding the glass, he tilted it in his host's direction then finished off the remaining juice. "Just text me the address and time, and I'll be there." Then he headed to the door and left quietly.

Reflectively, the man in the fancy suit wondered how a prolonged conversation with Jan would play out and what topics might be addressed. Whatever they might be, he looked forward to an evening of discourse and insights. The dichotomy of the man was fascinating. He was capable of ruthless violence but also had an exceptional depth of knowledge regarding history and the arts. It would no doubt be an evening to remember.

He was absolutely correct, but not in the way he thought it would be.

Monday — Afternoon

Chief Deputy Maki grilled Megan in the grocery store's back office, hoping for some clue as to Bruce's whereabouts. Megan's face was shiny with tears, and the girl was filled with shame over being so easily duped and misjudging Bruce's character. Now that she knew the truth about how his nose had been broken, she was sickened that she had sent a text helping him, and Maki saw all of that on her face. Any remaining doubts about her being an actual accomplice had vanished in the first five minutes of the questioning. The only hope now was that some offhand remark Bruce might have made would give them a location to descend upon.

"It looks like he might have strong-armed his way into a Good Samaritan's car. He has completely disappeared from the grid. We can find no trace of him. Did he ever mention friends in other states?" Maki slid a hand firmly down his face, attempting to wipe off the frustration that was eating away at him. If he knew what really had happened to Bruce, he might have felt a kind of heavy-handed justice had been served, but that was not going to happen. He only knew that the man had almost been in his grasp twice and had slipped through his fingers like sand.

"He never really talked about other people, just himself." Megan offered. "He talked about all the times he screwed over people that were going to screw him over. He told those stories over and over." Megan wanted to help the cops. She did not like the feeling of being the stupidest person in any group, and it felt like she absolutely was.

Being so easily manipulated, it was hard not to feel like an idiot.

"This guy fooled a lot of people, so don't beat yourself over being suckered. Sounds like he had everyone in the store buffaloed, your managers included." Maki was torn apart. Part of him felt sorry for this young girl who hadn't known the full picture and simply tried to help a friend. The other part was still angry that her text might have helped this guy get a leg up on his pursuers. Regardless, it was still his nature to help the morose girl across from him feel better about the situation she was tangled up in. If he got something useful from the girl (now that she had stoppered her tear ducts), so much the better.

"Nothing is coming to mind. I'm sorry. I will call the number on your card if I think of anything." Megan was now feeling hot shame, turning her face red, and she just wanted to get out of the room and go home. A hot bath and an early bedtime sounded like just the ticket. A thought popped into her head. "Should I be worried about him coming after me?" Her voice was high and full of sudden fear.

There's absolutely no reason for him to come after you. As far as he knows, you are a friend who gave him a warning. Stopping at the home of someone we know he knows is the surest way for him to get caught now." And without knowing how correct he was, Maki followed up with, "I don't think you need to worry about him stopping by. He is long gone by now."

Even though the words were said with the intent of pacifying the girl, the fact that this human trash bag had given them the slip made those same words burn his throat to say out loud. The thought that he would not be the tool of justice bringing the guilty to heel had been gnawing at him night and day for days. He still hoped some miracle would drop this guy into his waiting clutches.

Monday — Late Afternoon

With the lab down by two techs for the day, Josh came to the inescapable conclusion that he would have to drive all the drug test orders to the Bureau of Criminal Apprehension himself. Unlike the other lab techs, Josh saw this not as a way to get home a little early, but as a distraction preventing him from getting real work done. But the orders had to be run, and someone had to transport them. If he was the only one who could make it happen that day, then that was how it would have to be. David Anderson was in the middle of several tests, so he started getting things ready to go.

The sheer number of tests going on this trip meant he would not be able to use the little locking lab bag, but he'd have to use the plexiglass box with a locking lid. That meant the two-wheel dolly would be coming as well. Thankfully, his car, Emma, boasted more than enough trunk space. He noted the job was getting less simple than a mere drop-off. At least nobody was trying to tack on food orders as well, he thought as he packed the box almost full. The many special orders his co-workers insisted upon ensured no meal run or even a simple driving errand (that could have food requests tacked on to it) ever took less than 30 minutes.

Wheeling the dolly out of the front doors, he headed to his car. Doctor Crusher was waiting patiently, an old tan Sonata with astounding trunk room. When he had first started with the department, he had commented he could stuff his entire staff in the trunk. Although true at the time, no one else found it amusing. It was another case of trying to socialize gone wrong. Nowadays, Josh didn't try anymore, and it seemed to suit everyone fine. He was happy analyzing evidence on his own, and the team was happy when he was doing that, leaving them to joke and laugh. He knew they were not being mean-spirited; everyone in the department had told him at some point how much they respected his skills and expertise. Leaving him on his own just worked better for everyone.

Settling into his seat, he fastened his seatbelt and re-adjusted all three mirrors for optimal coverage. The pride of his vehicle was his CD player. The current CD featured an Israeli techno band called Infected Mushroom. For Josh, featured meant the disc had a single song burned 15 times in a row. There were no lyrics to distract the driver. It was unadulterated musical enjoyment, with no need to think about what song was next. He could focus on the music and on his thoughts without commercials or yammering DJs disrupting his concentration.

On the road, Josh was the embodiment of a law-abiding driver. However, his adherence to speed limits was not appreciated by other drivers. Even staying in the rightmost lane, plenty of fellow drivers used their horns and wild gestures to suggest that a few miles above the speed limit would be appreciated. Josh paid little attention to anything but the road when he was behind the wheel, so efforts like that were uniformly ineffective.

Josh had not ever been in any kind of traffic accident in his life. He had a few close calls under his belt (Minnesota winters, after all), but nothing tainted his driving record after fifteen years. Despite that sterling fact, he was always the last choice if someone needed a lift somewhere. If others didn't prioritize an immaculate driving record the same way he did, that was their loss. With no ego in the game to bruise, he felt no need to try to actively campaign for a change of opinion. He was fine with things the way they were.

Arriving at the BCA, he unloaded the box and wheeled it in through the Evidence Intake door in the back. He waited to be buzzed through, fully expecting to see Carla or Julia at the intake desks. Both women were fixtures in the building, having been there for over fifteen years each. The door's buzzing sound was deep and always made Josh think of mechanical wasps. Going through the door, he was a little surprised to see that only one person was in the room to process orders. He was further taken aback when he noted the woman behind the desk was easily the most unique human being he had ever seen.

She smiled and waved him over. Josh had black friends growing up and had always been confused by the terminology associated with them. He would have described those friends as "brown" rather than "black." The woman in front of him was not just black, she was black-black. Her skin was almost the color of coal. Maybe it was the sharp contrast against her dark skin, but the teeth in her flashing smile were so white they seemed to glow. Her entire head was as smooth as an egg, with not so much as a suggestion of hair anywhere on it.

Josh felt an unfamiliar tickling in his chest and worried briefly about incubating some kind of illness and passing it on to the woman. He stopped five feet away and dropped his eyes, not wanting to seem confrontational. He opened the box and started pulling out double-bagged samples, leaning forward to place them on the desk barcode up for her to scan. Each bag had its own intake form specifying what tests were to be run. Josh pretended to look at each form intently as a way to avoid looking at the striking woman.

Her name was Agnes. She was originally from Uganda. In Ugandan culture, it was considered polite to avoid eye contact. In her time in America, she had found that was not the case at all for Americans. Although a friendly woman by nature, the amount of eye contact in almost every interaction here had been a little off-putting for her. When Josh dropped his eyes, she (mistakenly) thought this was an act of deference and was touched by the surprising consideration.

"Let's see what you've got. Show me everything," she said with a laugh.

"I will leave nothing to the imagination," Josh answered, missing her flirtatious subtext altogether, unaware his response suggested he had not.

His chest started to feel unusually tight, and his eyes felt a bit dry. He hadn't been sick in several years, which he attributed to ample amounts of sleep and a healthy, if repetitive, diet. He hoped that spending time around other people (or as he referred to them, disease reservoirs) was not a factor. *Play it cool, play it cool,* he thought to himself. Out loud, he inquired, "Are the regulars on vacation today?" That seemed a safe conversational road to go down.

"Are you saying I'm not enough?" That response illustrated that it might be a less safe road than he had thought. A quick glance up showed she was grinning, so she was not being mean-spirited. He answered, "Uhh, you are pretty. Plenty! You are plenty! I wanted to make sure no one was sick...." Even in his own ears, his reply sounded weak.

Josh felt a growing possibility of saying the wrong thing and derailing the conversation with her. He didn't understand what he was feeling, but knew it was tied to the woman. He just wanted to get out before he offended her somehow. As soon as the last package was scanned, he handed her the final intake form, locked the box, and headed for the door without a word. At the doorway, he realized that might be too abrupt an exit, he threw out a "It was a real pleasure to meet you!" combined with a backhanded wave. He could see her looking at him in his peripheral vision as he exited. He did not look up and kept his eyes on the ground all the way to his car.

Once everything was packed back in his car, the mirrors adjusted, and the seatbelt securely holding him, he replayed the events again in his mind. The good news was that her departing smile indicated she had not been offended by his verbal slip-up. The bad news was that he had no idea what she did think about him. Trying to imagine what other people thought of him was certainly not his forte. This was going to take some outside help. He checked all three mirror mirrors again, backed out carefully, and drove to the office.

Monday — Evening

With a firm knock on the door frame and a loud hello, Talya announced her arrival at the protective care unit. There were seven children watching cartoons and she was more than a little relieved to see a smile spreading across Aiden's face when he saw who the visitor was. It had been her experience that even in terrible homes, children hated the person responsible for taking away the world they knew. She did not expect what came next.

"Talya!" Aiden shouted and ran to embrace her, something she allowed reluctantly, and only for a moment. All she could think was that this was someone else's child and not hers. Saving a child from a horribly unsafe home environment was her job; she was no savior to be adored.

"Aiden, how is it going? I'm glad to see you are doing better than when I first met you." Aiden blushed, looked at his feet, and giggled. Talya continued, "I checked with the court, and your custody hearing will be Wednesday morning. How do you feel about that? Do you have any family nearby?"

His face showed almost no signs of emotion as he told Talya, "My mom left when I was a little kid. I didn't really know her. My dad has been selling drugs since I can remember. I've had to keep it secret forever. I don't want anything to do with him or that shithole trailer. The only family he had was a brother out East somewhere, but they didn't talk to each other, so I don't know where."

Talya heard that and her heart filled with sadness. "Well, Wednesday they will determine if it is in your best interest to be moved into the foster care system. Given that your father is facing felony drug charges currently, I'd say that is a foregone conclusion. Your days in that trailer are done."

Aiden's face now wore an expression of relief. "So after Wednesday morning, I'm free to choose a new home? I can be the one making the choices?" It hurt Talya to have to tell him that was not the way foster care worked.

"You meet with families, and there is an interview process where both sides decide if everyone meshes well. Only if both sides agree would things move forward at that point."

Then came the question she was hoping not to hear from him. "Can't I live with you?"

"No, you cannot. Not only would it be grossly unethical to remove a child from a home just to keep them for yourself, but it is also illegal. Additionally, I am not certified in the foster care system so I could not ever be a legal option."

Aiden barely reacted to her words and asked, "But couldn't you just adopt me? Then it wouldn't be foster care. You'd be the mom I never had!"

Jesus Christ, this kid is hitting every button, she thought. "That would be illegal to attempt. My apartment and my life could not handle a child. I'm sorry."

His eyes filled with tears. "What did I do? Why don't you like me anymore? Did I do something wrong?" *Oh God, this kid is breaking my heart*, she thought to herself.

"Of course not. I still think you're a good kid in a bad situation. But there are laws around this kind of thing for good reason. Kids *have* been stolen away from their parents and kept by the people doing the taking. You are a bright kid, and any foster family would be lucky to have you. It just can't be me."

Aiden seemed to perk up at the mention of being a member of a future foster family. "Okay, but you can still stop in and check on me every week, right?"

"This never ends." Talya was beginning to think stopping by might not be the best idea. "It might not be that often, but I'm sure I could swing by and check in here and there. Let's aim for that, and we will see how it goes." That was her best attempt at being honest without crushing his hopes with the truth.

He smiled forlornly and told her that he appreciated everything she had done for him. Talya was impressed to see a brave smile on his face this quickly. He must have plenty of emotional strength, she mused. However, there was a different explanation for his behavior, and Talya would discover it later in the week.

Monday — Night

Glenn was getting ready to head home, stuffing endless stacks of forms into her rhinestone-studded laptop bag (another gift from the previous sheriff). Given how late it was, she was surprised to hear a knock on her door. Looking up, she was even more surprised to see Josh standing there.

"Qapla!" she bellowed. The surprises continued, as this did not raise a smile on the tech's face. In fact, he looked morose. "Josh, what's going on? Why the sad face?" Josh looked her squarely in the eyes and simply said, "I need help and advice. I am hoping you can give both."

"Maybe you better sit." Glenn motioned to the rightmost 'comfy chair' as she sat in the other. She sat on the edge of the seat, leaning forward, wondering what would prompt an in-person visit at this hour. "Let's start with the background, please." Josh sat down with a heavy sigh and a furrowed brow.

"Well, it's about a girl…" he mumbled quietly, his body language spelling out how uncomfortable he was. Hearing the issue was a personal one, Glenn put a finger to her lips, then got up and shut her office door. Coming back, she reflected that this was the first time she had heard of Josh talking to anyone about something as intimate as personal relationships. He could speak intelligently about any number of work-related topics, she and he had discussed Star Trek matters endlessly, but this was brand new territory.

"Today I had to drop off the weekend's case tests at the BCA. Mitch and Becky were both out, and David was in the middle of testing of his own. Mitch was up in Cuyuna Lakes, mountain biking. It's up north by Crosby. He was competing in the Cuyuna Crusher race. He felt good about his chances to place in it. I'm not sure about why Becky took the day off, but she asked two weeks ago so it was planned."

"Did something happen at the BCA, Josh?" Glenn asked gently. From her personal experience, Josh's retelling of stories always benefited from innocuous questions that could steer him back to the central issue. She remembered one conversation with him before she had picked up on that truth. The conversation had started with discussing altruism and ended up being a twenty-five-minute digression around the intelligence of the squirrels compared to small breed dogs compared to wild rabbits. She was not about to go down that rabbit hole again (pun certainly intended).

"When I got there, neither Carla nor Julia were working Evidence Intake. I am not sure if they had vacation days as well. For as long as they have both been there, I would imagine they have enough vacation days to take off whenever they want." At that point, Glenn made a beckoning gesture with her index finger to head off another vacation digression. Josh noted the gesture and switched back to the Intake room.

"When I walked in, there was a black woman behind the desk. I have never seen someone so beautiful. I didn't embarrass myself, because I got out of there before I said something stupid. Remember how excited people were in Star Trek when they met someone special to them who had been replicated in the holodeck? That is how I felt when I saw her. I want her to like me, but I am afraid I will say or do something that offends her, and it will go swirling away and it'll be my fault. I don't know what to do!" He raised his hands and smashed his fists down hard enough on his thighs that Glenn felt obligated to raise a palm in front of her and say, "No more of that. We are going to talk this out. If you want to do more than talk, like that, I get it, but I will go home. Deal?"

Josh sheepishly nodded, his eyes on his feet. Glenn explained, "That is something that everyone in the world struggles with. 'I like them; do they like me?' Barring telepathy, no one ever initially can know for sure how the other person is feeling. There is one way, and only one way to know for sure. You have to ask. But, you don't ask that kind of thing right away. If you ask too soon, you come off as desperate and worse, creepy. Do you understand that just because you think someone is amazing, that doesn't mean they owe you anything? Josh, please look at me, this is important."

Josh looked the sheriff in the face, "Of course I know that. That's why I'm so scared about letting something like that slip through my fingers and go to waste. You might not know it, but my dating history is a little sparse. It's always my fault that things don't work out. I don't want to feel like this about her, but I do. I don't want to shrug and say, 'It doesn't matter' when something goes wrong again. It does matter. To me. That's why I'm asking for help. You always say the right thing, and that's why I'm asking you."

One thing about Josh, Glenn thought, you never have to wonder what he's thinking. He threw it all out there. Even in his thirties, he still was still a bit naive with social interactions. He was unjaded, unpretentious, and unsuspicious. Maternally speaking, she worried for him regarding that. He might not behave the same way as most people, but that didn't rule out the possibility he could still have his heart broken.

"Well, thank you for that," she said with a smile. "Flattery is never a bad way to start a conversation with a woman you like. But never make it about anything that could be considered taboo. Race, sexual matters, politics, et cetera. That's a broad rule but it's a good one. You can't go wrong following that rule. Second, while it can be scary to risk rejection, you can just try to talk to her. If she's a good fit for you, things will be easy. If she isn't a good fit, that's when things can go badly. When it comes to trying, remember this: every chance you don't take will always be a no anyway."

Pausing for a moment, she finished with, "Josh, you are attractive, you are incredibly smart, and you are funny. You have a lot to offer, so don't get down on yourself because you might not be just like everyone else. Confidence is a sexy trait for men and women alike. Even if you feel nervous inside, you can act like you are the king of the world. That's not lying, it's helping others *want* to get to know you. That is all any of us want, to be wanted."

Josh did not deal well with flattery. As soon as the word "attractive" hit his ears, his eyes went to the floor. Nonetheless, when Glenn finished talking, he looked up, met her eyes, and thanked her for her insight and advice. He had known she would be the right choice to have this conversation with; there was no one else he could talk to about personal feelings. One other thought suddenly popped into his head.

"I didn't see Gail this afternoon. Is she alright?" Gail was always friendly to him and regularly asked after him.

"She's okay. That woman is a tank. I gave her a gift card to a spa in Stillwater and warned her that she better not come back before Friday. She has a lot to process right now."

"Why Friday? Why not the whole week?" Josh asked, looking puzzled.

"There's a potluck Friday. A team of wild horses couldn't keep that woman away from bringing a dish to a potluck. It's for the best; I heard Bricks is bringing lingonberry troll cream again for his part, so it will be nice to have a savory Gail entry to fill up on." She accompanied that last part with a gentle foot nudge and an eye roll. They both laughed, and Glenn said, "It's time to head home. I'll see you tomorrow.

Remember, you need to be yourself around other people; if they don't like who you really are, things will never work out in the long run anyway. You are worth getting to know. Keep that in mind, and you'll be just fine." Hearing the unanticipated rhyme in her last line, she commented, "Oohhh, I'm a poet and don't know it." They both left that night with smiles on their faces and a lightness in their hearts, which was not how every night ended in their line of work.

Tuesday — Morning

"Hey there! It's a good day to go down!" This chipper greeting was delivered by a young smiling woman behind the counter of the dive store. Kelsey was trying out some of the greetings she had heard used by other staff members use to start conversations. It seemed like a dive reference to Josh's ears, so he ignored it.

"Hello, I'm with the Sheriff's office, and I was hoping you could answer some questions for me." That simple sentence and a flash of a law enforcement ID were all that was needed to melt the smile of the (formerly) smiling woman's face. Josh did not mention he had taken the day as vacation and was there unofficially.

"Questions for me? About what?" Not only had the smile disappeared, but her voice now had a slightly panicked tone. Josh figured that immediate clarification of what he was, and more importantly, was not, looking for would be the best way to achieve the cooperation he knew he would need if there were answers to be had. Then the woman asked an interesting question.

"Is this related in any way to that mayor that drowned?" Her voice sounded almost hopeful as she tried to transition to a topic that did not involve her off-duty activities.

"Why would you ask that?" Answering a question with a question came naturally for Josh, as he was always trying to ensure what he thought was being talked about was actually what was being talked about. The fact that such a thing could be perceived as rude never occurred to him.

"Everyone in the shop is talking about it. It happened only fifteen minutes away from here." Josh did not like where this turn in the conversation might be headed. His questions now might be remembered, repeated, and rumors created around them. But since he was not going to skip any dive shop in the metro area (especially one so close to the scene), he decided to be as honest as he could be.

"This is classified information, and I'm going to have to ask you to swear you will keep it confidential and not repeat it to anyone. This is for you alone." The thought of being part of the inner circle of an investigation was a fantasy come true for Kelsey. Most of the appointments on her calendar centered around various true crime podcasts. Without knowing it, Josh had stumbled into the single way to absolutely guarantee the woman would never utter a word about their interactions. "I absolutely swear not to repeat any of this." Her voice was solemn, and she raised her hand as though she was being sworn in before a judge.

She moved from a fear of being found out to an excitement of a fantasy realized before Josh had time to utter another syllable. "Oh wait!" she said in a breathless voice. "I'll lock the door!" She was not about to let a random customer derail the dream she now envisioned was speeding towards her. She raced to the front door of the dive shop, locked it, and raced back.

"Let's start with two questions," Josh started. "Does this shop have a security camera system, and do you sell rebreathers?"

"We do not have surveillance capability. We do sell rebreathers." Thinking about her podcasts, she tried to slip in a little crime jargon so the cop would know he was dealing with someone who was "in the know." Josh heard the substitution and understood exactly the kind of person he was dealing with. Someone with no training who still saw themselves as Sherlock Holmes. From conversations he had overheard in the station, the problem with people like this was not getting them to open up but getting them to shut up.

"In the last two weeks, have you sold any rebreathers?"

"I can look up past sales in the office. Follow me!" With a job to do before her, her tone suddenly took on a commanding tone. The thought that her dive shop might have any information that could help an actual investigation made her feel like she was receiving a low-grade electric current, and it affected her sense of propriety. Moving quickly down a short hallway and sitting down in front of a computer, her fingers danced over the keys. Josh was impressed by her typing. His words per minute speed was over a hundred, and she was typing at least that fast.

"We sold three in the last two weeks. Two were bought by Undersea Photos Inc. and one by... Hans Gruber." She groaned as she said the name, and Josh asked her why. "Don't you get it? Hans Gruber? Die Hard? It's a fake name and he paid cash, so there's no way to trace anything. Shit!" Her dream of being part of solving an actual case was drying up. Looking for anything else that could help, she saw a small pony bottle had been purchased as well.

"Whoever it was, they also bought a '6L Spare Air' canister. That seems like it could have been a paranoid diver," she opined, trying to sound knowledgeable. Josh heard her, and his mind started spinning.

"Why would they have to be paranoid?" he inquired.

"It's a tiny air tank with an integrated mouthpiece. They are meant to give you enough air to get to the surface if you are deep, and there's an emergency. Not a whole lot more air than that. But there isn't much call for them in freshwater. Freshwater visibility is so poor, there's no point diving deep enough to realistically need one, unless you were paranoid about running out of air. Hmmm, looking at this, Sandy was the salesperson. She is a bit aggressive, so the Spare Air could be her selling hard, and not the diver at all. I'll check with her and email you the complete details." Her voice now had a decidedly authoritarian tone as she viewed herself as part of the investigation team.

Josh absorbed the diving information and then thanked the woman for her assistance. "I will let you know if this information helps with the case. Again, this entire conversation needs to stay confidential." While case details in ongoing investigations were indeed classed as sensitive information, he was also aware that a lab tech like himself had no business in the field, and there would be a lot of trouble for him if anyone found out what he was up to. She would be protecting two secrets with her silence, but Josh didn't share the second secret with her. He was applying the hard-learned lesson that every truth didn't need to be told.

Tuesday — Afternoon

Steve Ballard knocked twice on the metal door frame and walked into the open hospital room. While he thought medicine was getting fancier all the time, he was surprised to see the man in the bed was wearing an old-fashioned plaster body cast that covered everything from his nipples to his knees. The nurse had told him the patient's name was Cliff Jackson, and he had broken both legs and his pelvis. She let him know the pain management drugs being given via IV meant the patient might not be able to answer any questions. Nevertheless, Ballard was going to give it the old college try.

The man in the bed looked at the entering deputy with unclouded eyes. He seemed attentive and stared his uniformed visitor in the face. "Hi there. I'm Steve Ballard with the Ramsey County Sheriff's Office. We are following up on the incident that landed you here. The man who did this has been apprehended. He is in the hospital himself and poses no threat to anyone. Did you want to press charges?"

Ballard expected the usual answer and had his clipboard up and at the ready when the man asked, "Does that old coot even have money to take? His house is run down, his car is run down, and he is run down. Is there even a point?" The question left the deputy temporarily flummoxed.

"Uuuhhm, I doubt it..." was all he could think to say. He had been utterly unprepared for that line of thinking. The fact that a guy on pain meds would be with it enough to ask a question like that was not something he'd have expected. Normally, these conversations would consist of mushy single-word answers. He started to wonder if a nurse might be siphoning off some of the medicine, but the guy didn't seem to be in any obvious pain either, so he dismissed that as unlikely.

"If that's the case, I'm not fucking around with charges and courtrooms," the man in bed said with more than a little annoyance. Ballard boggled at this statement. It was so outside his realm of experience that he had no response for it. After a silence that seemed like it lasted minutes, he finally asked, "So you're not pressing charges against a guy that broke both your legs and crippled you?" His voice sounded as confused as he felt.

"Again, there's no point. I won't waste my time if I can't get anything out of it. Fuck him. Someone that can get something out of a court case can have my time." Ballard was stunned. Not pressing charges against someone who took away your ability to walk didn't make sense to him, even with that seemingly pragmatic explanation. In the few minutes he'd been talking with Cliff, the guy did not give off the vibe of a person who would give a shit about wasting someone else's time.

The incongruity of the situation and the man's attitude made him think about Brad's rambling accusations. "That was a shitty welcome to the area. Sorry that happened. You're still pretty new here, right? This is far from normal in this area." Burying the real question inside running patter was Ballard's standard questioning technique. He was one of the better witness interrogators, and the responses he was getting right now were amping up his curiosity about ol' Cliffy.

No answers were forthcoming. The only thing coming from the man was a wordless stare. Ballard tried again. "Normally, Minnesotans are a friendly bunch. Did you know Brad well? We certainly knew him well." He paired those words with a head shake and a guttural throat clear. While that statement was not strictly true, he was hoping to get some back-and-forth going because loose lips sink ships. All he was getting was more wordless staring, although the man's expression and body language were now definitely not amiable.

"I'm the one who got fucked up! Why are you asking me questions? I haven't done anything but get pancaked!" he protested in a low tone that made Ballard think of his own cats, just before they pounced on each other.

"Just standard questions in any case involving assault," Ballard smoothly lied. An orderly knocked on the door and announced he was collecting the garbage. He swapped an empty plastic trash bag and headed out with the full one, the interruption further breaking any remaining tension. Ballard noticed a glint from the trash bag that was leaving the room. The abrupt turn in the patient's tone now had Ballard very interested in Cliff Jackson and it had nothing to do with Brad's case. For his part, Cliff noted the change in the cop's posture and didn't like that one bit. Growing interest by the authorities was the last thing he wanted.

"I have to use a bedpan and I need to sleep. Sorry," he said with a voice that indicated he was anything but. Heading out of the room before the bedpan could arrive, Ballard tossed out over his shoulder that they could talk later. Scooting down the hall, he caught up with the orderly.

"Pardon me, I noticed there was a glass bottle in the last trash you grabbed. I wonder if I might look at that."

"Do watchoo want," was the indifferent reply. The orderly took the moment to sit and stretch in the padded visitor's chair of the nearest room. He pulled out a cell phone, opened some game, and the world fell away for him.

Finding the bag in question, Ballard carefully looked carefully through its contents. The glint had come from a Miller High Life beer bottle. While hospitals had been updating their menus, a bottle of suds was still not something typically on the menu. He put a pen through the mouth of the bottle, and carried it out to his vehicle, where he bagged and labeled it. Hopefully Josh would find a print or two on it to run through the system.

Tuesday — Late Afternoon

Stepping into the interrogation room, Talya saw Aiden's father had been resting his forehead on his hands on the table. "So, I have some questions for you that revolve around your home life and your son," she began. "First, why are you dealing drugs from a residence you share with a minor? Your son?" She expected some sputtering, a denial. She did not expect a look of utter confusion, and then the reply, "Drug dealer? I'm Head of Sales at the Shoreview Kia dealership."

"You can prove that?" she asked with an incredulous tone. This was not playing out the way she thought it would.

"Of course. Call them and ask if Scott Jessup is head of sales. You have my ID so you know I am Scott." Tilting his head, the man then asked, "What would make you think I was a drug dealer?"

"We found a black lacquered box with dragon inlays under your bed. It contained a large number of illegal drugs." Those words seemed to hit Scott with the force of a sledgehammer. He rocked backward in his chair, then collapsed forward with his head in his hands. "Oh God. Oh God!" was all he said. He began to sob as though his heart was breaking, crying out Aiden's name. Talya started to suspect there was more going on here than an evil father and his angelic son.

"There's a devil in my son." He said, looking at her through eyes red and raw. "That box was a gift from his mother before she passed. I've been working extra hours to try and make enough to get out of that damn trailer. I thought Aiden would just play video games while I was gone. There have been problems at school and problems at home. I guess they were worse than I thought. Drugs? Lying to the police? He was raised better than that!" He laid his head in his hands and began crying anew.

What. The. Hell. The three-word vexation ran on a loop in Talya's head. Did I get played? By a kid? It was embarrassing to admit, but it looked like that was exactly what happened. That cherub-like demeanor might be only skin-deep, and there might be something a lot darker underneath. Best to check out every part of the story Aiden had spun for her.

"Do you have a brother living out East? she said, starting simply.

"My brothers live in Richfield and Bloomington. My sister lives in St. Louis Park. After my wife died, we wanted to be close to family." Another couple lies, she reflected. It appeared she hadn't gotten any true answers from the boy. "Have you reached out to any support systems around here? There are a lot of them."

Scott could not lift his face from his hands as he told her, "We tried the greatest support organization in the world: the church. I put crosses around the whole trailer. We said prayers before every meal. Despite everything, he was kicked out within a month. They caught him stealing collection money and drinking the Communion wine. I cannot tell my family of his shameful behavior. I don't know what to do. I am so alone and such a failure to my son...." He collapsed against the table. Without an ounce of strength to hold him up, his back sagged like an old prospector's mule. He was the consummate picture of paternal hopelessness.

Talya was beside herself. The pain and despair in his voice made her feel even worse about blindly believing the boy. "We are going to check everything out. We will get this figured out. We'll get all the facts verified and go from there." Which was exactly what she had not done earlier. She had let emotions get in the way of the exact fact-checking she was now promising the distraught father. "You fool," she repeated over and over to herself as she left the building.

Tuesday — Evening

Kelsey was bent under the counter stacking belt weights when the sudden perfusion of sandalwood wordlessly announced Sandy had arrived for her shift. Popping up from behind the counter like a jack-in-the-box (or jill-in-the-box, which was more accurate but less common), she got a glimpse of Sandy going into the breakroom, and headed that way as well. Kelsey had been practicing being nonchalant all afternoon. Shaking her hair to loosen herself up, she rounded the corner and walked into the breakroom.

"Hey there, Sandy. How's it going?" After pouring through internet articles on questioning, she figured she would start off with a friendly greeting, establish rapport, and move into the real questions. Leaving nothing to chance, Kelsey had a series of letters written on her palm to help her remember how the planned questioning would unfold. Each letter corresponded to a sentence in the mapped-out conversation.

Sandy favored blue mascara and feathered her hair. She fancied herself a Farrah Fawcett lookalike and saw that as her secret weapon in sales. The blue mascara was getting a fresh coat before her shift started. She had a bit of twang in her voice. She had grown up in Texas and was fiercely proud of it. "Not bad now, sugar. Ah'll be doing much better Friday night. Got a date with a fit bald guy. And his earlobes are *tight* to his skull, not hanging in the wind. Connected *all* the way down. You know what they say about bald guys with attached earlobes, right?" She was grinning like a Cheshire cat.

"I honestly do not know" Kelsy admitted.

In a saucy Texas accent Sandy teased, "Well, it's not mah place to spill those beans, but rest assured, ah'll be checking the accuracy of that one." Switching back to her normal voice, she offered, "Guy came in last week looking for a rebreather. Ahh almost thought it was Jason Statham, the movie star. We got to talking, one thing led to another, and he picked up the rebreather. Then he asked if he could pick me up too, for dinner this Friday. He paid cash for a rebreather! Said he always pays cash so his ex-wife can't track him down. He plays his cards right, and one thing might lead to another again, but in the bedroom this time…" She accompanied her opinion with a lively victory yip and a wink so lewd it made Kelsey blush.

This revelation rendered most of Kelsey's planned conversation and questions moot. Three hours of hard thinking for nothing. She hadn't maneuvered into any of her carefully detailed questions and already she had more information than she dreamed she could obtain. Imagining what the deputy from earlier would want, she decided he would want to set up a sting operation. "Where are you guys meeting? Anywhere fun?" She was trying her damnedest to sound nonchalant.

"We will meet at Ruth's Chris Steakhouse at 8 pm. Not bad, eh? Damn sight better than my last date, who took me to Arby's and then bowling." Sandy rolled her eyes thinking about the date. The guy had shown her no mercy, bowling a 257, and had high-fived everyone BUT her when he threw a strike. The entire evening had been a total gutter ball, and she had no interest in the proverbial ball return or picking up that spare. It had been a perfect example of the old "one and done."

Sandy noticed that Kelsey was now staring into her hand, apparently in her own world again. The girl was sweet, but bit of a spaz, Sandy thought, not unkindly. Trying her best to be casual, Kelsey commented, "I saw you sold another Spare Air. You're the best at adding those in. What is your secret?" Kelsey hoped the flattery would distract from the abruptness of the question.

It did indeed. "Shucks, I didn't have to do anything special for the last one. He knew exactly what he wanted. Well, I did get him interested a little something extra." Sandy shook her rump back and forth, grinning and cocking an eyebrow at Kelsey as she did. She'd had a string of crappy dates in the last month, but it looked like her luck was changing. Good looking, rich, and attractive! She had been smiling since last week, anticipating what Friday night would bring. Jan had also been thinking of Friday night, but in contrast to Sandy, he was not looking forward to what he *knew* the evening was going to bring.

Wednesday — Morning

Passing through the front doors of the Office, Steve Ballard noted Gail was still out. He missed her cheery greetings; they never failed to start his days off on the right foot. Double stepping his way up the stairs, he arrived at the break room without any outward signs of exertion and was disappointed there was no one around to notice. He took a big breath and exhaled, letting his belly drop.

He remained determined not to buy any pants with a waist more than four inches larger than he wore when he graduated from the academy years ago. Unfortunately, that meant his current wardrobe's pants were serving double duty as mid-body tourniquets. With a drop in the number of water-related cases causing a dip in his calorie-burning SCUBA work, he was finding himself drifting into an untenable position. He once again made a vow to exercise more, knowing all too well he would not be giving up Sunday morning coffee cakes, no matter how tight his waistbands got. As long as he could get the pants shut, he could put this off a little longer.

Sitting at his desk in the General Investigation room, he powered on his computer and fished a bag of bacon ranch cashews out of his top drawer to occupy his time as it booted up. "Nuts are good for you," was his response to any comment concerning his beloved snacks. In fact, his entire bottom drawer was regularly refilled with bag upon bag of flavored cashews, as well as the infrequent box of nut bars (those were kept out of sight in the back of the drawer). Lately, he had been favoring the dark chocolate and sea salt flavor.

The nut bars only came out when no one else was in the room. They had accompanied him on emergency snack trips to the bathroom stall, but he was set on not letting that become a daily routine. Weekly would be fine, but daily would just be begging for the shopping excursion he dreaded.

Opening his email, he hoped to find a fingerprint report around the bottle he had retrieved from Cliff Jackson's hospital room. He was a little surprised that there was no report waiting for him and even more surprised to find an email directly from Josh asking him to stop down. Finishing the bag of nuts and throwing the bag in the trash on the other side of the room (two points!), he headed down to the lab.

Entering the lab, he saw Josh's head down over some reports in the conference room. "I'm here." Ballard had a naturally carrying voice, but he had learned to turn up the volume to capture Josh's attention whenever he saw the lab tech focused on anything else. Josh looked up, saw it was Ballard, and motioned him into the conference room, pulling out a large manilla envelope from under the scattered paper covering the desk as he did.

Since they were the only ones in the room, Ballard didn't bother closing the door. Holding up the envelope, Josh started out saying, "The beer bottle you submitted had lots of prints. None of them belonged to anyone named Cliff Jackson. All the prints on it belonged to someone named Martin Marquez. He has been indicted on eleven felony charges. All violent crimes. No convictions because witnesses either disappeared or reversed their testimony. In all eleven cases. That is statistically impossible on its own. There would have to be outside variables involved."

He stopped speaking and looked directly into Ballard's eyes. "Known associates include members of the Chicago street gang Latin Kings, going back at least nine years. Living that long with those kinds of friends is not usual. This Martin individual would have to be exceptionally tough. If you visit him, I recommend bringing Bricks or some other backup with you, just to be on the safe side."

Ballard reflected on what he had just heard. Paired with the weird interaction in the hospital, he saw another visit with 'Cliffy' in the cards. He was glad the man was not whole and was bedridden with a pelvic cast. If the guy didn't have his plaster diaper, he felt there could have been real danger dealing with him. Ballard was exactly right on that note. What he was not right about was the thought that the cast removed both the possibility of danger and the need for backup.

Wednesday — Late Morning

Talya took several deep breaths in and out to calm herself before dealing with Aiden that morning. She had learned quite a bit talking with his father. The lab reports on the lacquered box revealed that it had held a greater selection of drugs than her favorite "variety" snack pack. She darkly recalled that every snack in her last purchase had been the exact same snack, and she was none too happy about *that* (Nabisco would be hearing from her on the matter). She snapped herself out of that line of thinking and focused on why she was there. Opening the car door, she unloaded her rolling cooler and headed in.

Walking across the parking lot, the cool autumn air felt like it was helping carry away the anger stemming from her last visit. Some of it was directed at Aiden, and she was successfully able to set that anger aside with a little effort. The remaining anger was directed at herself, being duped by a sixteen-year-old child. That was much harder to deal with, let alone set aside. Anger, shame, and guilt of your own over things you had done always seemed to be the hardest emotions to deal with and face. Talya knew this was not the time to agonize over mistakes made, so she did her best to put everything on a mental pause to keep her attention solely on Aiden and complete some evidence gathering of her own.

Knocking and walking into the room, she was greeted with a big smile from Aiden. This time, however, she did not allow the smile to penetrate her heart. Internally, she was staying aloof, waiting to see how things would unfold. Externally, she offered up an equally big smile and exclaimed, "Aiden!" He hopped off the couch where several kids were watching TV, almost skipped over, and held his arms open, clearly expecting a hug. While she certainly didn't feel like doing that, Talya embraced the boy, all the while wondering if any part of this performance was sincere.

To keep him thinking things were going his way, she passed along that a family had been found for him, and that there was an interview next week so they could meet each other. He did smile at that, but Talya noted that smile did not touch his eyes and it did not curl at the ends. The smile felt like part of an act. There was no denying the kid was good, but now Talya was looking for anything that seemed the least bit off. Unhappily, she admitted to herself that if she hadn't talked with the father, she would have been taken in again.

Out loud, she did say, "Time to celebrate!" She opened her cooler and pulled out a pair of well-chilled bottles. Ballard had mentioned bottles as a source of fingerprints last night and his story had not fallen on deaf ears. "Henry Weinhard. The finest root beer commercially made. I always have at least two six-packs of these bad boys on hand. It's mighty heavy, like Guinness. I order mine through my local liquor store. There is no shame if you can't finish off a whole bottle." She was counting on that comment to stir up his adolescent competitiveness, and it worked like a charm. He grabbed the offered bottle from her hand, twisted off the cap with a practiced wrist snap, and emptied half the bottle in one long swig.

"Are there more?" he gasped in an out-of-breath voice.

"All you want and more. Throw the empties back in the cooler; I recycle the glass." While Talya did indeed recycle, that was not the reason she had brought several bottles of her favorite root beer to share with a shameless liar. She needed a set of fingerprints to compare to the fingerprints on the black lacquered box. She could have simply arrested Aiden and gotten his fingerprints that way, but she didn't want to find out she was wrong and destroy an innocent boy's trust. Plus, she felt like matching wits with the little shit.

Aiden was already working on his third bottle and had obediently thrown his fingerprint-laden empty bottles back into the cooler. To allay any suspicion, she polished off her own bottle, threw it cooler, and grabbed a second one. With a popping noise as she pulled the bottle away from her lips after a lengthy guzzle, she sighed and said with honest satisfaction, "Oohhh, now that is the good stuff." She held her bottle out and clinked it against the boy's bottle. For just a second, she saw a self-satisfied smirk cross his face; then it was gone, replaced with guileless eyes. If she hadn't been watching carefully, she would have missed it altogether.

Holy shit, this kid is good. She felt less foolish about being suckered in; he was a born actor. None of her friends could boast this level of brazen self-confidence, and they were all in their forties. She could feel her anger trying to gain footholds and climb into the forefront of her mind. Before she could give herself away, she told him she would be back later (oh yes, she would), packed the cooler, and headed out to her car.

As she crossed the parking lot, her phone began chiming. *Another cutesy text chain, I'm sure.* When she got to her car, she checked her phone. It was a text chain alright. It was her brothers asking about everyone's Christmas travel plans. As she was the only sibling not living in Turkey, she sighed and put her phone away, feeling a little resentful. Standing at her car, she glanced up at the windows and saw Aiden looking down, watching her. She reflected that not bagging and labeling the bottles in the parking lot had been dumb luck, born more from distraction on her part than conscious thought.

She waved, and upon realizing he had been seen, a smile suddenly spread across his face, and he waved back. *I know your kind,* she thought to herself as she got the cooler into the back seat and then headed out. She had dealt with plenty of people who thought they were smarter than her. She had proven every single one of them wrong and the tight smile on her face as she thought about fingerprinting the bottles reflected her confidence that she would be victorious here as well.

Wednesday — Afternoon

Steve Ballard stopped at the nurses' station before going in to see 'Cliff'. He inquired if any of the nurses had seen any identifying features in their time with the man. One nurse commented that he had an 'L' and a 'K' stretching over his stomach and that he told her it stood Loraine and Karina, his daughters. Ballard knew what the letters really stood for. He emphasized the man was dangerous and should never be checked on by only one nurse from here out. 'Cliff' would be moved to a prison hospital inside the business day but would have to stay put for now. A uniformed officer would be posted on the door within the hour.

Finished with the conversation with the nurses, he walked into the hospital room without bothering to knock. 'Cliff' was on the phone, angrily barking orders in Spanish. As soon as he saw Ballard, he hung up in the middle of a word. Much like the first visit, he greeted Ballard with a wordless stare. Ballard was used to this reaction when talking to people in prisons. Not so much in hospitals.

"So, the guy who did this to you will spend what little remains of his life in prison. Small comfort, I'm sure, but we wanted to let you know." Silence. The man simply watched Ballard's face. "Nothing? I thought you would like to hear that. After he hit you, he made the mistake of carrying a gun into the Sheriff's department and lost his right arm from the elbow down. He'll be wiping his ass southpaw from now on," Steve finished with a grin.

Not even a ghost of a smile crossed the bedridden man's face. "Did you have a question for me, *officer?*" It was surprising how contemptuous he could make that last word sound. His flat eyes completely masked the anger that had been building over the last few days, and after that interrupted phone call, it was now boiling over.

"As a matter of fact, I have a few, Scooby-Doo." Ballard sat down and opened his case folder. As he was rummaging inside, 'Cliff' fished out the hypodermic needle he had swiped from a distracted nurse and had been hiding under the mattress. He swung both legs over the side of the bed and lunged at the distracted deputy. Several things occurred in the next few seconds with shocking speed. The first was with the power of the lunge, the pair of IVs in Martin's arms tore right out, spraying blood in a wide arc. Several of the drops hit Ballard's case folder.

The second thing was that the moment real weight came down on his lower body, a bolt of blinding pain fired into his brain, and he fell straight down, screaming the entire length of that short journey. The plaster cast around his hips cracked in several places as he hit the floor, sending plaster chips everywhere. The third and final action was Ballard's. He did not bother to ponder where a flying blood drop would have come from. He knew blood flying around meant something was wrong. His legs (toned from years of diving) shot his chair backward so fast it seemed like a magician's trick. For the first four feet at least, until his chair caught the edge of an aging floor tile and sent him flying to the floor, ass over teakettle.

Although the pain in his legs was agonizing, Martin was determined to make the smug cop suffer. He saw the cop's chair tip over, and immediately began commando crawling over to the fallen officer, intent on stabbing and stabbing until he was physically restrained. *The cop better have had a doughnut on the way over because he's never going to have another*, he thought maliciously.

Hearing the ruckus, a nurse stepped in and saw the man who should have been in the bed, on the floor. He was crawling like an animal, horribly fast towards the deputy, also on the floor for some reason. The deputy was on his back, like a turtle. The nurse's reaction to seeing the bizarre scene was to scream. But this was no breathy scream from a damsel in distress. This nurse had been active in the local musical theater scene for years. Her scream was like a firetruck siren going off inside the room.

The scream snapped Ballard to his senses, instinctively looking for the source of the scream. As he looked around the room, he saw Martin had almost closed the distance between them. Martin's face was sweaty from all the effort he was putting into the crawl. His mouth seemed like it had tripled in size and the lower half of his head appeared to be composed of a huge toothy grin.

Martin's usual victims were not people who regularly engaged in physical activity, which partially explained his overconfidence as he got into stabbing distance. The cop was already pulling his legs up, like a woman seeing a bug. *Wait 'til he finds out how hard this bug bites*, Martin thought to himself. However, Ballard had not drawn his legs up to get away or make himself smaller. He had pulled them up, so they had more power in a kick. Martin stretched the arm with the syringe up as high as he could, preparing to deliver a brutal first strike. It never happened. As his arm went up,

Ballard kicked out both legs as hard as he could. His right foot kicked through the evil smile, taking most of the front teeth with it. The left foot landed squarely on Martin's forehead, powering it backward with a deep crunching that sounded like folding an entire bag of celery in half at once.

Martin's hand spasmed open, dropping the syringe harmlessly on the floor. His entire body began shaking back and forth. Ignoring the movement, Ballard whipped out his cuffs, straddled the shaking man, and trapped the man's wrists behind his back. Ballard tightened the cuffs more than strictly necessary. He was not ruling out the possibility of Martin faking an injury to lure him in closer and was playing it as safe as he could. He suddenly felt the hairs on the back of his neck stand up, and he spun around, his stance low and ready to charge. The only thing behind him was the nurse who had screamed, now shocked silent, her eyes as big as saucers. Ballard relaxed his stance and stood up.

"Thank God for those pipes of yours! You saved me!" Silently, he admitted that statement might be an over-exaggeration, but without her scream alerting him, he would have been in a world of hurt. For that fact alone, she deserved to have a story where she was the hero of the day. It was no skin off his nose to say a civilian's actions had made a life-and-death difference for him.

Speaking of life and death, Martin had stopped shaking. His open eyes stared straight into the floor, his bleeding mouth wide open. Blood and saliva drooled slowly into a widening pool by his head. *Ah shit, that's gonna be a ton of paperwork,*

Ballard thought regretfully. His sense of compassion (normally expansive) had dissipated after being attacked with that kind of furious commitment. The nurse was still standing there, staring aghast at the man on the floor.

"Why don't you sit down for a minute, nurse?" Ballard picked up the chair and set it down for her. Since that would have taken her three steps closer to the body on the floor, she instead moved over to the bed and sat down heavily. The reality of what she had seen seeped in, and tears began seeping out. She started drawing in ragged breaths, faster and faster, unaware of her now shaking shoulders.

In three big strides, Ballard was at the doorway. "I need help now!" He was using his Josh voice, and despite the earlier scream, the surprise of a voice at that volume made every nurse on the floor jump again. Seeing several heads turn and head in his direction, he turned back to the nurse on the bed. "You are absolutely safe now," he said in what (he hoped) was a comforting tone. Hearing the tone, if not the words, the nurse stared at him, clearly needing him to make everything make sense.

A beefy security guard burst into the room, moving into some sort of martial arts stance as he scanned the room. Startled, the nurse put the deputy in between herself and the intruder. Then she recognized who the guard was, and relaxed, muscles unlocking, shoulders slumping. Ballard motioned for the man to sit on the other side of the nurse. "It's all going to be okay. You are okay." He repeated the words like a mantra, still using his comforting tone. Catching the security guard's gaze, he motioned to the nurse with a sideways shift of his eyes and then shifted them to the door.

"Let's get you out of here," said the guard, understanding Ballard's silent request perfectly. Ballard knew he would have to leave shortly as well; the emotions of the whole thing were no longer in stasis, but starting to creep in. He bent over the inert body and pressed his thumb into one of the open eyes. Only when he saw there was no reaction to that did he remove the cuffs, continuing to play it safe.

Using his radio, he called in the fatality and arranged for a scene investigator. Then he moved through a sea of curious nurses clustering in the doorway, and down the hall to the public restroom. He shut and locked the door and thought of how his wife would have reacted to never having him come home again. The thought of leaving her heartbroken and alone was more than he could bear. With no one to see, the emotions around what *could* have happened to him flooded his mind, bringing hot tears and muffled sobs along with them. Abandoning himself to his feelings, alone in a hospital bathroom, Steve Ballard cried as he thought of his wife's reaction to becoming a widow.

Wednesday — Late Afternoon

All three of the other lab techs boggled when Josh, of all people, volunteered to drive the BCA tests over to Saint Paul. Looking around the room, Josh could not understand why everyone was staring at him. He had never seen anyone get excited when anyone else offered to make the trip to the BCA, so it didn't make sense that they would take notice of his offering either. The fact that the senior member of the lab never volunteered for anything that took him outside was lost on him as a reason for their behavior.

Grabbing the locking lab bag, he started filling it with the testing samples and their respective forms. It took less than a minute. "Uhhh, Josh... there are only three tests. Normally, we don't make the trip for less than five. Is there something else going on?" David was hesitant to ask questions of his boss, but this whole thing seemed quite out of character for Josh, and he wanted to make sure everything was okay.

"There is someone that I want to talk to over there," Josh answered honestly. That single sentence was all the other three needed to hear. Once they could see the unusual behavior was explained by rational reasoning, their focus moved back to themselves and their own work. That suited Josh just fine. He did not feel comfortable elaborating on what he wanted to talk about over there or to whom. With no one paying much attention to him anymore, he snapped the lock shut and left the lab.

Once he had checked all three mirrors and fastened his seat belt, Josh began his drive to the BCA. Much like when he was working evidence for a case and wasn't sure where things were going, he felt a thrill of anticipation. He loved that sense of impending surprise. Although he had no idea where this conversation might go at the BCA, he didn't feel that same sense of anticipation a case brought. He would class his current feeling closer to a sense of impending disaster. The sheriff's advice had been perfectly logical; talk to the person you are interested in and map the landscape. That was exactly what he planned to do, dread be damned.

It was easy to *say* what you were going to do. As Josh walked across the parking lot, it felt anything but easy. *Look confident even if you don't feel confident*, he told himself. For Josh, this consisted of putting on a wide smile and adopting a ramrod-straight posture. Unfortunately, that smile seemed to project less of an air of confidence, and more a likelihood of gastrointestinal issues. The unnatural posture only seemed to confirm such a conclusion.

He hurried to the Evidence Intake door. That door had been catching the sun's rays all day, and that warmth had attracted dozens of boxelder bugs clumping and clinging to its surface. Although fully aware those bugs couldn't hurt a person if they wanted to, that many of them crawling around one spot seriously creeped Josh out. The upshot of this was that as he carefully opened the door and slid past the uncaring bugs, he forgot all about maintaining his phony smile and posture. As he stood in front of the glass window and waved, he looked relatively natural.

Walking through the buzzing door, he decided to follow the sheriff's advice to the hilt and be confident. The striking woman was the only person there, and without an audience to judge him, he felt his confidence growing somewhat. He was not so confident, however, that he would look this woman in the face, which again played to his favor. "Hi, my name is Josh. What's yours, lovely lady?" he asked as he began pulling the samples to be tested on the desk. He did not expect the answer he would get to that question.

The woman smiled and said, "My name is Agnes. I already know about you, Josh. You are well known over here. Well, known by reputation, at least." Josh was stunned into silence. Although it did not project the confidence he was striving for, he could only reply with a confused "What?"

Agnes explained, "There are no lab techs in the metro area with a close rate like yours. There aren't even many investigators with numbers close to yours. After your visit Monday, I asked around. The lab techs here knew your name from that close rate. They even knew other things about you. It seems no matter what continent you are on, I can tell you that people do love to gossip." She offered a conspiratorial smile to indicate she was on Josh's side in the matter, which Josh completely missed. Hearing that other people were talking about him, he flashed back to high school, a time that had not been good.

Agnes saw his expression turn dark, which was the opposite of the reaction she had hoped to induce. As a rule, Ugandan people are considered by most on their continent to be an exceptionally friendly people. Agnes was a perfect example of this. Additionally, she possessed a kind heart and a gentle disposition. Seeing Josh's new expression, she tried to imagine the next thing she would want to hear if she were a guy. "Everything I heard about you made me more interested. You seem to be an unusual character."

Despite the implicit compliments, remembering high school had knocked the wind out of his conversational sails. Josh figured he might as well ask about the subject he disliked discussing the most and sink the ship if it was going to sink. "Did they mention that I have Asperger's?" His tone was defiant, but he was feeling sad inside. Thanks to other people talking, he was going to lose a chance to get to know this woman before he said a single thing. It just wasn't fair.

"As a matter of fact, that did get mentioned. I was wondering if you can hyperfocus?" Josh simply nodded. "I cannot imagine what that must be like. I have ADHD, so I am on the opposite end of the focus scale. I walk into my kitchen to get a glass of water for the plants, see some dirty dishes, and the thing you know, everything in the kitchen has been washed, and I'm reorganizing the silverware drawer." Agnes laughed at her own story, and Josh realized that the chance to get to know her might not have flown away. In his experience, people didn't laugh at themselves unless they felt comfortable with the people around them. He did not understand why she would feel that way around him already, but he was not going to let that go to waste.

"Could I take you out for dinner sometime?" He blurted out.

Agnes looked him directly in the face. Josh looked up, felt the power of that gaze, and quickly looked back down. He felt lightheaded and simply waited for an answer.

"You may," she said with an easy smile. "Did you have a place in mind?"

Josh swallowed hard. "I don't. I didn't think about it before I asked. Do you have any food allergies? Is there anything you hate to eat? Do you have a food genre you prefer?" This was not where he expected the conversation to go, and he wanted to define where some boundaries (any boundaries) were. Playing things by ear was not his preference, and he wanted to get back to the safer ground of fact-based conversation.

Agnes' smile was growing. "No, no, and I like Vietnamese. I love those bean noodles they use as the filler in their eggrolls, versus cabbage in Chinese egg rolls." She opted to keep the other (gassy) reason she didn't eat cabbage to herself, for now. *A girl has to have some secrets*, she wryly thought to herself. She had not been on a date for weeks, and certainly had not expected that would change when she got up this morning but was pleased with this turn of events. "How does Friday night work for you?" Agnes was not a beat-around-the-bush kind of woman and was comfortable asking for what she wanted.

"Uuhhmm, that should be fine. Would six o'clock work for you? I can email you with a list of restaurant choices tonight, and you let me know your pick." The thought that he might want to go home and freshen up after work, or at least put on a different outfit never crossed his mind. He was thinking only about how soon after his shift ended that he could join her, wherever she decided they would meet. With an hour of possible driving time, he calculated he could make it anywhere on time.

Even though Agnes did not have to spend time on her hair, she knew she wanted more prep time than six o'clock would allow. "If you make it seven, you have yourself a deal!" She had a joyful demeanor, and her sparkling eyes showed it. Josh did not feel like he was sparkling at all. At this point, he was thinking of just one thing: making an exit before he stumbled all over himself and lost all the wonderful progress he was making. "Seven it is," he said as he walked to the door. He dared one final comment, "Looking forward to it," and he was out the door.

Walking to his car, the realization of what happened slowly dawned on him. He had not only talked to the woman, but they had also exchanged pleasantries, names, and compliments. She knew about his Aspergers and didn't seem to care. She was also outside the neurotypical spectrum in her own way. And he had a date with her. He tried to imagine how things could have gone better and couldn't think of any way. By the time he was belted in with the mirrors checked, he sported an impressive grin himself. If he had someone riding shotgun, they might have described him as beaming, which is just a hop, skip, and a jump away from sparkling.

Wednesday — Night

Glenn slogged through the paperwork she had been putting off for days. Since no one else was around, she had her rhinestone cowboy hat on, brim pulled low. Wearing it that way helped her concentrate by restricting her view of potential distractions. Privately, she felt the fancy hat functioned as her own stylish set of blinders. The report of Gail's shooting, the murder of a suspect, requests for updates on the mayor's drowning from news stations. Those were just the first few of the bricks in the wall of paperwork towering over her. She decided the evening needed a caffeine boost, and a cup of dark chocolate cocoa with a shot of Baileys felt like just the ticket. Unlocking her bottom drawer, she moved past the higher-proof options and retrieved a large bottle of Kirkland's Irish Cream. *Just as tasty at half the price.*

Like Gail, she had her own Keurig, a gift to herself many years ago. It truly had been a gift that had kept on giving. From her top drawer, she pulled out a brewing pod that had a top with no markings. She had a friend who reused pods and filled them with her own blend of ground vanilla beans and dark chocolate. A few years ago, that friend received several parking tickets in the space of two weeks, thanks to sheer bad luck. Mortified, she had come to Glenn and asked if there was anything the sheriff could do about them. Glenn let her know that she would take care of it, and then simply paid the tickets herself. The friend had been so grateful to have the issue resolved, Glenn had been receiving fresh pods for the Keurig every month since. While Glenn normally would have called it even-steven after a few months, the cocoa was so damn good she had not put the brakes on the situation. Glenn wasn't proud of that, but a mug of that delicious cocoa always washed away any lingering guilt. She told herself she wasn't demanding anything from anyone; she was only showing someone offering her a gift a modicum of courtesy, nothing more.

Thinking of creature comforts, she turned to her office stereo. Glenn absolutely adored ABBA and knew the words to every song in their catalog, despite not having a trace of Scandinavian in her bloodline (a rarity in Ramsey County). As far as she was concerned, ABBA was a lofty pinnacle of rock music. There was only one thing better than hearing the songs she grew up listening to, and that was hearing Cher sing them. The soundtrack from the second Mamma Mia movie started playing, and with no one on the second floor, Glenn began happily singing along. She had no illusions she was a great singer, but she certainly enjoyed belting out a good tune. Anyone who had ever been with the sheriff at a karaoke bar would attest to her enthusiasm.

With a steaming mug of cocoa at hand and tunes playing, she sat down and began slogging through the river of paperwork. She had been back at it for about fifteen minutes (long enough to get into an attention-absorbing groove) when there was a loud knock at her door.

"Shit-FIRE!!" she screamed, the surprise of an interruption elevating her voice and her blood pressure. Her hand instinctively dropped to her hip as her other hand batted off the hat to clear her field of vision.

In her doorway stood Josh, his jaw practically on the floor, shaking like a leaf. Seeing who it was, she exclaimed, "Goddammit, Josh! You scared the shit of me! What are you doing here this late?!" Josh sputtered but no complete words exited his mouth. His Adam's apple bounced up and down like a little kid on a trampoline and his eyes looked like saucers. Glenn saw that her vocal outburst had scared him even worse than he'd scared her. She turned off the music so they could hear each other and knew just what to say to calm him down.

"Hab SoSlI'Quch!" she uttered gruffly. Josh looked puzzled as he translated her words. Then he broke out laughing. "My mother *does* have a smooth forehead. It's been a family curse for generations."

Star Trek for the win, thought Glenn. "Sorry about scaring you. I thought I was the only one still here. Why are *you* here this late?" Glenn knew Josh had a tendency to work long hours, but when he did so, he sequestered himself downstairs. Now he had stopped by her office two nights in a row, a radical departure from his normal behavior. Looking at him, she saw he had stopped shaking, but he stayed near the open space of the doorway, like a skittish fawn. Thinking about their conversation the night before, Glenn made an educated guess and asked Josh if he had talked to the woman at the BCA.

That question was the key. As though a padlock had been removed from his mouth, words now flooded out. "I followed your advice. I acted like I was confident. I was not confident, but I acted like I was. Her name is Agnes. She asked other people about me. That seems like a good sign.

She already knew I had Asperger's and didn't care. She has ADHD. We're going on a date Friday night. This is making me happy."

Glenn tried to take in everything she was hearing. "Wow, that sounds like things really went well. I'm glad to hear that Josh. Where is your date going to be?"

"I don't know that yet. She likes Vietnamese food, so probably someplace Vietnamese. I'm going to get her a corsage. Should I get regular flowers too?"

Uh-oh, Glenn thought to herself. She reminded herself to keep her demeanor educational and avoid sounding judgmental. "Let me offer that corsages are normally for formal occasions like proms or weddings. It might be seen to be too much for a first date. The same for flowers in general. I would suggest holding off regular flowers until date three at the earliest. If you give flowers too early, it might come off as desperate rather than nice. When you do go with flowers, remember that red roses usually symbolize deep romantic love. If you both have not said 'I love you', I would suggest a bouquet of seasonal flowers instead. Chocolates are a safer choice of gift. Find out what her favorite kinds are and stick with those gift options. It not only helps you give a gift, but by picking what you know she likes, it shows you listen and that you are thoughtful."

I should charge for advice this good, she thought to herself, chuckling at the idea. Looking over at Josh, she saw he had tilted his head, and his eyes were looking into the ether. *I can actually _see_ him making mental notes about this,* she thought with wonder. She felt a tiny bit of jealousy at that kind of mental alacrity; she was getting to the point where she could walk into a room, and not remember why she had gone there in the first place.

Having locked away every bit of advice Glenn had offered, Josh shifted to work topics. "I have more detail on a theory around Mayor Deakins's case. I will send you an email tonight with all the details. I think there was someone in the water, waiting for the mayor to fall off his boat. I think the whole thing was planned out, and not accidental. I started the email this afternoon. I will finish it when I get home."

Hearing this, Glenn's attention snapped away from thoughts of flowers and over to the Deakins case. She motioned to her chairs. "Josh, if you're okay with it, I need you to just sit down and tell me everything about this theory right now and skip the email. To start, what evidence are we drawing on to construct this theory?"

This was right where Josh was worried the conversation would go. He hoped that explaining what made him think of this and the fact he had taken a vacation day to avoid wasting anyone else's time would get him out of the trouble he imagined was about to erupt.

"It started with a conversation with Carmen. She told me that someone could stay underwater without bubbles using a device called a rebreather. Since the theory of a waiting underwater assailant was a long shot at best, I figured I would do it myself so no one else would end up wasting their time. I did take a vacation day." While that was certainly the truth, it was not the whole truth. Josh did not believe the investigation team would take his theory seriously enough to investigate it themselves.

"The dive shop down by Little Canada, just off 35E, had sold a rebreather to a guy who paid cash for something that cost five grand, and he gave a fake name. While that isn't illegal, it is sure suspicious. I found out this morning he is going to be at Ruth's Chris Steakhouse this Friday on a date with the woman who sold him the gear. We could check for names of reservations there Friday night and see what we find."

That such a wild and paper-thin flight of imagination appeared to have actually hit pay dirt amazed Glenn. If this ended up panning out, she knew what her go-to story was going to change to whenever anyone razzed her about Ramsey County's decision to employ an 'autistic lab tech'.

In her mind, there was no "if" around staking out this kind of lead. Sure, it might not amount to beans, but if something was there, it was going to be big. Very big. And this case had nothing to it at the moment but speculation. Some cold facts would be warmly welcomed.

"I would have a hard time right now putting into words the depth of my gratitude for having someone with your imagination working here." Just thinking about finding a concrete lead in a case residing in the public eye like this one sent chills of excitement down her back. "This is the kind of thinking I don't believe anyone else could do. If this leads us to any kind of resolution, you will be receiving an immediate level raise and corresponding pay increase. I cannot tell you how excited I am right now. Don't mention the inappropriate fieldwork to anyone else, at least until this is all finished. There will be no disciplinary consequences for you taking actions you aren't authorized to do this time, but please let the investigation team do the investigating going forward, okay?"

For his part, Josh was elated over the sheriff taking his theory seriously. He was getting excited from her getting excited about it. "Thank you for your forbearance. I would not have undertaken action of my own if I thought there was a strong likelihood of actual evidence being found. I thought I would end up disproving my own theory. I will leave fieldwork to field staff from now on." Even as he said it, he thought about how much he had enjoyed the unpredictability of being out in the field. While lab tests were predictable and Josh did enjoy the simple binary options of a yes-or-no result, there had been something thrilling about uncovering the evidence, instead of just testing evidence that someone else had found.

"Thank you for sharing this with me, Josh. I do appreciate being able to talk through it, but I have paperwork that is going to bury me if I don't make some headway tonight, and I want to get home before midnight, so I am now going to ask you to leave me to it. You can email me with anything else you think of. Rest assured I will be thinking about your theory for days."

She stood up and waited for him to do the same. When he did, she put both her hands on his shoulders and, with friendly pressure, guided him out of her office. Both were smiling as they parted at the doorway and Glenn looked forward to updating the news outlets that Ramsey County

Sheriffs were making substantial progress in the Deakins case less than two weeks after it began. That would be an update that would have consequences no one could have foreseen.

Thursday — Morning

Rereading the fingerprint report detailing that the prints from Aiden's root beer bottle perfectly matched the only set of prints pulled from the black lacquer box, Talya felt she had more than enough evidence to arrest him on drug charges and even obstruction of justice for trying to frame his own father. Realizing the sneaky weasel had taken advantage of her kindness and played her like a fiddle, she now had a personal interest in resolving this case. She absolutely wanted to be there when he realized that *he* had been played by *her*, and his little game had suddenly gone topsy-turvy.

Bricks was a younger deputy who clearly spent a fair share of his off-hours in the gym. There was not one muscle on the man that didn't strain against his uniform. Despite that imposing appearance, he was the epitome of the 'gentle giant' stereotype. Talya had requested him for this job primarily because he was the most intimidating deputy on the force. In all the time he had been part of the department, she hadn't so much as heard of a civilian who had dared to test the big man's physical prowess. The two of them used to spar in the gym, but the booming sounds of bodies being slammed into the mats ended up being too much for anyone to get work accomplished in the rest of the basement and they had been told to take it to an actual gym.

The fact he didn't go easy with sparring just because she was female was only one of the reasons she felt a fondness for him. His laugh was almost identical to her youngest brother's laugh. Low chuckles built inside the chest until screams of laughter burst out, unable to be contained. She had been on one stakeout with him. They belly laughed almost the entire night, almost missing their target exiting his premises in the middle of the night. When confronted, the man made the ill-advised choice to run for it. Bricks rode him into the ground before he had gotten thirty feet away. If Aiden made the mistake of running, he wouldn't be running far.

"This should go by the numbers. He thinks he is getting a new foster family he is going to be able to bamboozle. The cuffs will be a wake-up call he won't be expecting. Remember, this is a slim sixteen-year-old boy, so no need for rough stuff. He gets cuffed, and we take him to juvenile detention. Our involvement ends there." Bricks nodded. He was happy to have a concrete duty to start his day. He was more than happy to help Talya with any request she might have. While he might have almost fifty pounds of muscle on her, she had speed and strategy. Anyone who could best him sparring, especially as regularly as she did, had his respect and admiration. He would have walked to the ends of the earth for her if she had asked.

They both drove their respective squad cars and were careful to park on the far side of the building, where they could enter unnoticed. The elevator in the back of the building was an old freight elevator. As they went up, it made a rhythmic thrumming sound that gave Bricks all he needed to start performing an extemporaneous pop and lock dance routine. He was a gifted dancer, and the sight of a 240-pound man moving like that to elevator noise had Talya in hysterics in less than a minute. Even though she was motioning for him to stop, Bricks continued shamelessly dancing his heart out.

Bent over at the waist, she tried closing her eyes, but she was betrayed by her own mind which served up the memory from behind those closed lids with perfect clarity. By the time the elevator reached its intended floor and had stopped, she was down on her hands and knees with uncontrollable laughter, perilously close to needing a new set of uniform pants. She was never ashamed of laughing hard or loud, and an appreciative audience was all the encouragement Bricks ever needed to break out the goofy shit.

When the elevator stopped its ascension, Bricks stopped his dancing, lifted the elevator gate, and enveloped the majority of her upper arm with one massive hand (Carmen referred to his hands as clam rakes, an East Coast term). He popped her up to her feet with the speed of a man tossing steaks into the shopping cart while his better half was still in the produce section. As soon as she was upright, Talya quickly nodded her thanks for the assist and beelined it down the hallway in search of a restroom. At this point, the gender of the bathroom was not pertinent; if it was unoccupied, she was using it. Her eyes were still filled with tears of laughter, which inhibited her vision but not her resolve. She found an open restroom fifty feet down the hall (a ladies' room even) and would have used the sink if someone had been in there. Fortunately, there was no need.

Stepping out a few minutes later, immediate needs taken care of, she was now all business. Giving Bricks a 'come on' hand gesture, she started around the corner and down the hall to the main common area. As she entered the room and looked around, she saw Aiden sitting in a circle with the other kids watching TV. He glanced over to see who had come in, and initially, there was no change in expression. Moments after that, he looked at who was in the door and a big smile spread across his face. "Talya! You're back!" The enthusiasm in his voice sounded sincere, and for a second, Talya belatedly wondered if the good-natured affection in his voice could be real.

Bricks came through the door just then and looked around the room at the circle of faces. As he was doing that, Aiden took in the sight of the big deputy, and the smile on his face vanished in an instant, replaced with an evaluative look. Bricks saw the boy matching the description Talya had given him and started walking around the circle to him. The boy looked at him blankly as he closed the distance between them.

A huge deputy walking towards him did not fit with any scenario Aiden could conceive of as part of going to a new foster home. Glancing at Talya, he saw her expression had changed from friendly to tense and watchful. Aiden concluded (quite correctly) that the jig was up. When the big deputy was ten feet away, he made his move.

Leaping up, he ran at a full sprint through the middle of the circle. Bricks had not expected that and yelled, "Shit! He's running," as he turned on a dime himself and dropped into a starter's stance. If Aiden had focused solely on escape, he might have made it a fair distance down the hallway before Bricks would have caught him.

Because he was still a kid, his ego now got in the way of what he was trying to do. As he sped towards the hallway, he decided he would give 'Talya the Two-Faced Cop' a hit on the way out. He changed his angle slightly, planning to run through her. Talya saw him change his path and was astounded. After all she had done, the little shit was going to check her, and not lightly.

As Aiden was about to run Talya into the ground and wipe that stupid look off her face, he closed his eyes in preparation for the impact. Consequently, he did not see her lightning-fast sidestep. He did not see her right arm come up in a clothesline, but he certainly felt it. Talya caught his neck perfectly in the crook of her elbow and powered his head to the floor. Thanks to the head of steam he had built up in combination with her strength, even as his head was rapidly descending, his feet appeared to be attempting a flip. Although she knew he had made her look like a fool, her base instincts remained gentle by nature. She drilled Aiden's head squarely on her left boot and not the unforgiving floor.

All thoughts of what a badass he was were driven from his mind as thoroughly as every bit of breath was driven from his distressed little ribcage. His mouth opened and shut like a goldfish, trying and failing to draw in some air. Talya felt a tiny bit of sympathy looking down at the gasping boy who made the mistake of underestimating her. His eyes were huge as he struggled to breathe, and the rest of his body was still not accepting nerve impulses from the traitorous brain that had led them into this predicament.

Bricks was a man of action. He rolled Aiden onto his stomach, paying no attention to the gasping. *You brought that on yourself, son,* he thought. He did not have a mean spirit, but he also was not one to engage in hand-wringing when someone experienced the consequences of their own poor decisions. He pulled both of Aiden's wrists back and cuffed them. He pulled the boy up into a sitting position against the wall, and the eyes looking back were not filled with simple fear but naked terror. With a heavy sigh, Bricks began the remedy to having your wind knocked out his brothers had always taken. Whispering to the boy, "You're going to be fine. This won't last long," he put his hands in the kid's armpits and gently bounced him up and down on his butt. Not even thirty seconds later, Aiden had enough breath to start cursing.

Taking that as a sign, Bricks stood up and switched to reading the kid his rights. Aiden looked at the deputies, smiled, and boasted he was too young for any of this to stick. Talya then told Aiden there were no prints save his own on the black lacquered box and its bags of drugs. He would not have to live with his father anymore. The attempt to frame his own father had provided sufficient grounds for Aiden to be tried as an adult. The contempt in his eyes changed to disbelief and dismay as he absorbed that last sentence and what it meant for him. He was crying like a baby as Bricks loaded him in the back of his vehicle before heading to the detention facility, as planned.

Wednesday — Late Morning

Tom Maki was going through his daily routine of morning paperwork, but his heart was not in it, and his attention was all over the place. No matter what he tried to concentrate on, his thoughts returned to the same fact: his quarry had escaped justice. Knowing that it was only due to dumb luck on his quarry's part did nothing to minimize the frustration and anger he felt as he sat at his desk. There was no location to begin a search from and there had been no activity on his credit profile or social media. The man had completely vanished off the grid. *This case is going to end up being 'the one that got away'*, he thought, and his shoulders sagged.

He had seen other officers eaten up inside by cases they just could not let go. He had never fully understood that phenomenon until now. His mind kept gnawing over the 'what-ifs'.

If Bruce hadn't had a shift change.

If Bruce hadn't been by the windows and seen them pulling into the parking lot.

If they'd gotten to the nighttime accident sooner.

If. If. If. It was nothing short of maddening how his mind kept coming back to this like a dog after a favorite chew toy.

He thought about calling local hospitals in hopes the driver Bruce must have hijacked had been admitted when Glenn knocked on his door and stepped inside. She shut the door behind her, an act that commanded his full attention. "Glenn, what can I do for you?" Shutting doors was not the sheriff's usual modus operandi, and he was curious what precipitated such an action from her.

In hushed tones, she said, "We may have a break in the Deakins case, and I want you working this. We may have a lead on the assailant. We have reason to believe he will be at Ruth's Chris Steakhouse tomorrow night. He may use the name Hans Gruber for the reservation. It is supposedly a date, so he shouldn't be alone.

"This is our first, and likely only, chance to get some real facts around this case. You and your wife should be enjoying a nice meal, on the department, before he arrives. You will be our eyes and ears on the inside. If you see someone suspicious, I want you to call for backup before doing anything. We cannot afford to squander this opportunity. Do you have any questions about what I am outlining?"

An overtime stakeout masquerading as a couple's dinner date might not have been enticing to everyone, but it sounded great to him. "Do we have any kind of physical description of the subject?" Glenn smiled and told him, "The man was described as a Jason Statham lookalike. His date will have blonde feathered hair like Farrah Fawcett and favors blue mascara. Can you tell our source for this info is in her twenties? This is a long shot, but we'll treat it like gold because we have nothing else to go on." She rolled her eyes and raised her hands palm up as if to say, *Why me, Lord?*

Pausing momentarily, she sat down in one of his chairs, leaned forward and said in a voice softer than before, "I know there's something going on with you this week because you have not left your office except to hit the can. You normally never stay in your office longer than you need. Is it the rape case falling apart that's at the heart of this?"

Not trusting his voice not to crack, Maki simply nodded in response.

Glenn's expression softened, and she said, "I kind of thought that might be it. Tom, I understand what the case meant to you. I do. Now you have to hear me tell you what *you* mean to this department. You are invaluable. You are the one keeping all the trains running on time. I need your attention *here*. I need you to control all the trains *here*. Every day you are *here*, you are making a difference in dozens of lives. Do not lose sight of that. You don't know the lives you're affecting, but your actions *here* unquestionably make a difference *out there*."

It was a perfect argument to use with Maki, and Glenn hit his emotional bullseye right out of the gate. "Shit, I need to grieve this a little more. I'll snap back over the weekend. I won't let it get in the way tomorrow night."

Glenn gave him a smile as she said, "See that it doesn't. Thanks again. Since you'll be working late, why don't you come in around noon tomorrow." She gave him a pat on the arm and an appreciative wink and left his office. He looked at the doorway, sighed, and reflected that when your boss was also a good friend, it was not a bad situation to be in (even if it meant they knew how to push your emotional buttons). He moved to his keyboard to start looking up the number for Ruth's Chris Steakhouse to discuss Friday night's reservations with them.

Wednesday — Late Afternoon

Dave White was driving back home after dropping off three packs of brats with his brother-in-law up north in Ham Lake. They were going to fuel a Lion's Club grill-out fundraiser for the children's cancer ward, a cause close to Dave's heart. The Lions' Club's past experience had shown when the fundraising grill outs used Dave's brats, they boasted around a forty percent higher profit. Armed with those facts, the district governor and regional chairwoman had sprung for lunch and essentially begged Dave for his continued assistance. He was more than happy to donate to a good cause, and being gushed over by the local chapter of Lions, of course, didn't hurt his feelings either.

As he zipped along, he saw a dead deer on the side of the road. His heart went out to the majestic animal, a veteran buck with a 14-point spread. It was a fresh kill, and the body had not yet been chewed up by multiple sets of tires. It was lying just off the road, its muzzle covered with blood. He put his lights on to alert traffic and called Public Works to arrange a cleanup for the deer.

Before the call went through, a sparkling clean pickup swung in between his car and the deer. As he watched, a nondescript man got out, dropped his tailgate, and dragged the deer by its antlers over to the waiting truck bed. Dave took advantage of the pause in his day to drain the last dregs from his water jug. He watched as the man snapped off the antlers and casually threw them into the ditch. *Not a hunter, I'm guessing,* Dave thought as he stepped out of his own vehicle.

As he approached the man, he spotted a Ramsey County Public Works sign on the passenger door, which answered the first question in his mind: "Hey there. Do you need a hand with this big fella?"

The man turned to him and smiled a goofy 'shucks, who me?' kind of smile. "Well, I sure would appreciate it. I would love a little help getting this guy up and in. Lucky deal for me I was driving by and saw your lights and the buck. I'm Peter Lewis with the county. Keeping the roads clean is my main job, so I'm driving my life away most days, looking for problems to fix. That's mighty white of you to ward off traffic with your own car; I've seen antlers pop tires on occasion.

Dave chuckled and said, "You don't know how right you are there. My last name literally *is* White."

The man's jaw dropped, and he said, "Ahhh, the hell you say! Not really?!"

"As sure as the sun's setting in the west. It's Dave White, I kid you not. Let me grab these back feet, and we can swing him onto the tailgate." He reached down, grabbed the back hooves and with the other man using the front legs, they swung the deer neatly onto the tailgate. Dave then helped the man push the deer farther into the truck and closed his tailgate.

"You're not going to dump him in a carrion pit, I hope?" It hurt Dave to think of this beauty going to waste. The thought of raccoons or possums in the pit did not concern him at all, but this trophy animal was probably coming on twenty years old. Dave felt the buck deserved better. In truth, Peter never took roadkill to the carrion pit; every dead critter was free money in his view.

"Oh, god no," came the immediate reply. I compost the animals found on the county's roads and make gardening soil out of them. It is the best boost there is for peppers, potatoes, and carrots around. Plants that use it are exceptionally flavorful. Are you a gardening man yourself? I'd be happy to spot a fellow county employee a free bag, and you could try it out yourself."

Dave considered this. "Well, I am heading home, so I'm not sure about that. What kinds of peppers do you grow? My garden has mostly green peppers in it. Jalapenos, poblanos, serranos."

"Exactly what I have in my garden. I also grow habaneros, for when I really want to punch up a recipe. May I say, it's always a pleasure to meet a fellow pepper fan. Tell you what, my place is only five miles away. Come on over, and you can taste the stuff I'm bragging about and form your own opinion. Please. I don't get to entertain guests often. I'd sure appreciate the opportunity to share what I have at home with someone who knows their peppers!"

Peter looked so hopeful; Dave couldn't bear the thought of crushing the man's hopes. Just with the brief casual conversation they'd shared, he could see why the awkward man might be starved for company. "Lay on, MacDuff!" he said with a laugh. He figured he would stay long enough to try a few home-grown veggies and then be on his merry way. He would never have guessed how his night would actually turn out.

Wednesday — Evening

Scott Johnson and Mugshot were enjoying an evening run around Lake Phalen. Mugshot's purple bandana with gold trim (not to be confused with his lavender bandana with the canary yellow trim) perfectly matched his owner's Lycra shorts and shirt. Johnson's shirt sported diagonal white lettering that spelled out Vikings, a fairly unnecessary addition for purple athletic wear inside the Twin Cities.

As they finished up lap three, the bulldog was running low on energy and willing to adopt a more sedate pace than his human, even if meant a bit of choking. Not wanting to appear uncaring, Johnson slowed his pace as well, albeit with some vocal encouragement. "C'mon pal, we can go a little longer. C'mon buddy. You can do this."

As he tried to encourage one last sprint to the parking lot, a rollerblader sitting on some rocks, wearing a Packers jersey called out, "Man, even your dog is choking in those colors!" Johnson whipped around, ready to defend his dog and his team with whatever level of aggression was warranted. As soon as he saw his heckler, he gave an inward groan. The woman was fit and quite attractive, and her smile seemed genuine, not adversarial. *Dammit, of course she's a knockout. Can't tell a knockout to fuck off. Speaking of that, maybe there's a chance for a date here. Take it easy stud, and don't throw the baby out with the bathwater just yet.*

The woman had a wide leather belt around her waist, with a shiny D-ring in the center that had a canvas leash clipped to it. Both the belt and the leash were Packer green. At the other end of the leash was a well-mannered golden lab, wearing a Packers bandana. The lab was watching Mugshot but wasn't interested enough to get up from the sunny piece of grass it had found next to the rocks.

Trying to ensure the situation stayed as light and good-natured as he could keep it, Johnson actively fought his default behavior of hostility and simply responded with, "Well, Mugshot here loves cheese so much I sometimes wonder if he just puts up with these colors because he can tell they mean something to me. He's a good ol' boy. Frankly, I think the little cheese-lover would be just as happy wearing green and gold."

He was proud of this opening salvo. It was funny, suggested openness in his thinking, and left a number of openings for a rejoinder. Looking at the sprawled lab, he noted the matching outfits between owner and dog, and mulled over the mindset required to go down roads like that. *C'mon man, play it cool for once in your life. Keep your cards close to your godamn vest this time!*

The woman skated over to him, her lab in tow. "Well, I will say it's nice to see a fellow dog owner taking the time to give their dog some matching outdoor wear, even if it is the wrong color." Johnson looked at her, and saw her smile was now spreading to her eyes, her eyebrows arching upward. That was enough to defuse his initial anger with that choice of words. If it had been a guy saying that, there would have been no defusing. *Does she even know what she's saying, and how it could be taken?*

"If your dog is a big fan of cheese, it would logically follow that you must be as well, in order for 'Mugshot' to find out he loves it. Would that be a correct conclusion?"

Although Johnson did not want to admit a love of cheese to a Packer backer, he still saw nothing mean-spirited in her face, and her tone was still friendly. Grudgingly, he admitted, "I do have a fondness for the hard cheeses. Cheddar, Swiss, Gruyere, and Edam. The cheese shop in Mall of America has a smoked Swiss that cannot be beaten. Shred it onto any frozen pizza and that pizza is elevated to restaurant quality. It's that good." Suddenly aware he was rambling, he shut the hell up.

"Well, any man that knows his cheese that well is A-OK in my book. I'm Michelle, and this is Clyde." Upon hearing his name, the lab looked up, idly hoping he was about to get a treat, or at least some thoughtful petting. When neither seemed to be forthcoming, he laid back down in the grass. "I enjoy a nice hard cheese as much as the next girl." She chuckled a bit over that. Although he certainly heard it and had a ton of rejoinders ready to go (all of them off-color), he opted to simply utter "Niiice" in a deadpan voice and tried to cock an eyebrow. It was not entirely successful, but the attempt did illicit a laugh from Michelle, so he chalked it up in the win category.

Michelle continued, "I do like Brie with something like fig preserves on French bread. It makes for a simple picnic option. Pair it with a light white wine and it's gonna be a good night."

Johnson wasn't sure if that was an offer or not. Determined not to overstep himself, he decided to continue with the cheese talk and offered, "I have a nine-year aged cheddar at home. It is pungent. It is biting. It does not care if you like it. Maybe I could bring it with me sometime and give you a taste." Once again, he was proud of himself for taking a casual stance and engaging in some fun verbal repartee. He had left the conversational doors open and he hoped she might keep things going a little bit longer.

"Well hell," she interjected. "If you two are going to be running tomorrow night, bring the aged cheddar. I'll bring the Brie and the accouterments." She pronounced the last word with an over-the-top French accent, which did make him snort with the unexpected goofiness of it. *An offer for a picnic?* he thought. That seemed too good to be true, but he was determined to ride this to the end of the line and see where it stopped.

Wanting to avoid seeming too eager, he said, "Don't tempt me. Cheese, wine, and a stunning companion after a run might be more than I can take." That should give her enough room to clarify it was just playful talk and nothing more. He set his teeth and prepared for the letdown he was sure was just moments away. Still, it had been fun to imagine possibilities and think about some what-ifs.

"I'm betting you'd be up for the challenge." Her words were the opposite of what he expected to hear. His jaw loosened, but he was able to avoid looking too surprised. "How about it? Can you be here at the same time tomorrow?" she inquired.

"We will be here," he answered. In his mind, he thought, *A team of wild horses couldn't keep away.* This was unbelievable. A hot blonde asking him to join her on a picnic? Sure, she might be a 'sconi gal,' but just talking with her was fun and effortless. No one was perfect (especially Packer backers) and expecting perfection from people was a guarantee for disappointment. As he ambled to his car, he reflected that for someone wearing green and gold, she was darn fun to shoot the breeze with. He opened his car door for Mugshot and was astounded to hear her say, "You have GOT to be shittin' me! A purple GTO Judge?!"

The fact that she recognized the make of his car left him astonished and feeling a bit sappy and daffy. He felt hopes and dreams welling up in his mind like he was a teenage boy. He slid into the driver's seat and closed the door before he was overwhelmed. "It's a good story. I'll tell it to you tomorrow night," he said through the open window. Backing out of his space, he eased his way out of the parking lot, making sure to let pedestrians cross in front of him. He would have done that anyway, but in the rear-view mirror, he could see Michelle still watching and still smiling, so he made sure to demonstrate every courtesy. He made it three blocks away before he gave in to his feelings and started pumping his fist out the window while shouting, "Yes!" with a huge grin on his face.

Thursday — Morning

On her way down to the lab, Glenn popped her head into the General Investigation office. Surprisingly, Dave White's desk was not dominated by the giant bright yellow Yeti water jug that he carried with him. It had been an anniversary gift years ago that hadn't left his side since. That jug's presence was a more reliable means of knowing if Dave was around than a canvas collar with a sleigh bell (though the jug was nowhere near as hysterical as the thought of a jingling collar on the man).

Stopping by the reception desk, she asked Callie if Dave had arrived already, possibly sans water jug. Callie admitted that most people had come through the doors, but that she had not seen Dave yet. She then added that she had talked to Gail the night before, and after an afternoon of discussion with a priest, she was feeling much better. Also, she was going to take advantage of not coming to work Friday morning to cook up a storm for the potluck. Glenn's exasperation at hearing that was tempered by the knowledge that having any kind of a goal, something to focus herself on was how Gail got through ugly situations. Selfishly, she hoped it might result in a tater-tot hotdish or a chocolate flourless torte. Gail's flourless tortes were the culinary equivalent of having a brick of chocolate smashed over your head; even the most die-hard chocolate fan couldn't devour more than one piece at a sitting.

"Did she say anything about the spa card? She better have gone down there." Glenn said with a lovingly gruff tone.

"Oh yes, it got used!" Callie said quickly. Perhaps too quickly. "There was a massage and a mani-pedi. It was so relaxing." Callie curled a set of immaculate nails under her hands as she conveyed the last part.

Not one to miss a detail, Glenn looked the young girl in the eye and asked in a low confidential tone, "Callie, did Gail give you that gift card? You wouldn't be in trouble; it was Gail's to do with as she saw fit. But I do need to know if someone who needs calming is not getting calmed."

Callie hung her head and answered, "She did give it to me. She said she needed to ease her mind, not her body. For what it's worth, she sounded good when she called last night. Calm and clear. We talked for a good hour about life and expectations."

Well, that's something, thought Glenn. In her experience, morose people in a spiral of depression or anger didn't typically reach out to talk to others. If Gail was calling Callie, it didn't sound like things were as bad as Glenn feared they could have been. While she knew that old bird was tough down to her toes, she also knew how big Gail's heart was and how strong her emotions were, deep under the surface as they might be. If Josh had been there, she might have commented to him about there being an almost Vulcan quality to the woman, but since he wasn't, she didn't.

"I'm going downstairs to look for Dave. If he comes in, let him know I'm looking for him, will you?" Callie said she would, and Glenn headed downstairs.

"Qapla!" she bellowed as she entered the lab. She felt a hint of regret as three of the four people already in the lab jumped like they'd been goosed by a longshoreman with frigid hands. That shred of regret evaporated when she saw the grin it put on Josh's face. To her surprise, the grin evolved into a series of muffled giggles. Josh's attempts to use his hands to mask the laughter were ineffective and seemed to be making him laugh even harder. With snorts of laughter of her own bursting forth at the sight of his failed attempts, she haltingly asked Josh why this ritual of theirs would have tickled him to such a degree this morning.

"I watched a video this morning of three cats laying by a heating vent, so relaxed. Their human sneezed and startled all three so badly that they jumped all over each other. Your yell startled everyone in here just like those cats...." At that point, Josh broke down into another fit of laughter that was just as unsuccessfully masked as the first one. The sight of him laughing that hard over something so ludicrous had Glenn laughing again as well.

After a minute of laughing, Glenn wiped the tears from her eyes, giving a mental middle finger to the inventor of mascara as she did. She never bothered with that kind of thing anymore except for fancy events. Years back, there had been a happy hour boasting unending laughter. Thanks to mascara, Glenn had unknowingly left that event looking like a drowned raccoon. *Never again*, she had thought to herself after seeing her reflection in the bathroom mirror as she brushed her teeth that night. True to her word, mascara had not touched her eyes before a workday ever since. It had been eleven years and counting.

"Has Dave White dropped by here this morning? I can't seem to find him, and he's not in the gym or any other rooms down here." Josh replied, "No one here but us.

When people swing by, it's unusual so we'd notice." He shrugged his shoulders, and said, "Sorry." Glenn pursed her lips and gave a little frown. She had been trying to deliver some good news this morning, but it seemed it was not to be.

"If you do see him, would you let him know I'm looking for him? On another note, Tom Maki is staking out your steakhouse Friday night. Again, if this bears fruit, I'll do more than just keep you in the loop. I wanted to let you know the progress of the case that you have made a direct impact on." With a somber wink, Glenn headed back up the stairs to her office. As she entered her office, she registered there was someone sitting in one of her comfy chairs. Their back may have to her, but the presence of a yellow water jug on the floor next to the chair left little doubt as to the sitter's identity.

"Callie told me you were looking for me. Figures it'd be on the day I'm running late." Dave said with a chuckle. "What's up Big Kahuna?" He had not referred to her as anything but 'Big Kahuna' since she had been named Sheriff. Dave's easy demeanor made it obvious his nickname for her came from a place of respect and affection. It was that demeanor that was at the heart of the news she wanted to discuss with him.

Glenn started with, "The county board has okayed the creation of a new position under the Sheriff's department. Community Liaison. I can think of no one better suited for the role than you. Carmen and Tom are in complete agreement with me on this. If you want it, the position is yours."

Dave heard what she said, but he showed no outward reaction. He was only thinking, turning things over in his mind. Exactly the kind of reaction that had led to this recommendation. "Is there a job summary page I could look at? I'd like to see exactly what the job responsibilities are before making a call on this."

"Absolutely," Glenn responded as she handed him a thin manilla folder. "Out of curiosity, why are you running late today?"

"Well, it's a funny story," he said as he sat forward in the chair. "Yesterday afternoon, I was coming back from Ham Lake and saw a dead buck on the road. I met the guy who picks up roadkill for the county. Friendly fella named Peter. As you might expect from someone who would work that job, the guy was a little off. But he wanted to show off his gardening skills, and I totally understand that. The guy was clearly starved for some human interaction. I figured what the heck - what's the worst that can happen? We get to his place, and he picks a cucumber from his garden on the way inside, slices it thin, and dusts the slices with Lawry's seasoning salt. It sounds simple, but it was crisp, refreshing, and delicious. That cucumber lasted all of five minutes."

Dave grinned, remembering how good those slices had been. Glenn murmured, "You can't go wrong with Lawry's," not wanting to derail the story but wanting to add her two cents. "You truly cannot," was Dave's reflexive acknowledgment. He purchased his Lawry's in 40-ounce containers, and they rarely lasted four months at his house. He briefly fantasized about being a spokesman for them, and then got back to his story.

"Anyway, I commented how incredible the flavor was, and he started bragging up his worm composting program, saying that was the difference. Then he broke out a black bean salsa and heated up a cookie sheet of corn chips in the oven. I told him not to go to that much trouble because I still had to get home to the wife for dinner. Well, those warm chips were the perfect vehicle to carry that salsa into the ol' yapper.

"I was also going to head out because the guy was giving off a bit of a desperation vibe to keep the interaction going and it was kind of sad. Two chips in, I called the wife and told her I wouldn't be home for dinner. Let her know the story, and she said if I didn't bring her home some of the salsa that was stealing me away from her, not to come home at all. God, I love her." His face lit up as he talked about his wife and Gail reflected how nice it was to see someone who'd been married for decades still deliriously happy in their relationship.

"I had told him not to go to the trouble of toasting the pan of chips, but we ended up polishing off three pans of those chips. And by 'we' I mean 'me'. I notice a fancy cribbage board on a side table and figure that should be an easy way to spend some time with him but avoid any uncomfortable conversation topics. I'm thinking, we play one game, I crush him, and I head out. That was how I predicted the evening would go.

"Well, shit. I'm a good cribbage player and he thumped me that first game. He was a fun shit-talker too. That always makes a game more enjoyable. He didn't skunk me, but it was close. Naturally, I couldn't leave on a losing note.

Three games later, I'm still sucking hind tit. All the games were within ten points, but he beat me every time. I have never lost four straight games since I was a teenager. I think *he* felt sorry for *me*, and let me win the fifth game, thanks to a monster of a crib I lucked into.

"I got out of there at midnight, with a bruised ego, a container of salsa, and a big bag of compost soil as consolation prizes. I would never have dreamed stopping off to chat up someone who was so desperately lonely would have ended up being so fun, but there it is." He concluded his story with a smile, a shrug, and upraised hands. Scooping up his water jug, he walked to the door, waved the folder above his head, and told Glenn, "I will mull this over tonight and let you know my decision tomorrow."

Thursday — Early Afternoon

Jan pulled into a coffee shop, planning to grab a beverage to present to Sandy from the dive shop. While this kind of thing was ideal for lowering people's suspicions (male and female alike), he did feel like doing something nice for the woman. If she lived in Amsterdam, he would be seriously courting her. He was intentionally splitting his mind, and ignoring how he knew this would have to end, and instead living in the moment and enjoying himself where he could.

Walking into the shop smiling with an amorphous sense of happiness, he noted that the few people there were mostly over fifty years of age. He was pleased to note that, as it meant less inane chatter and fewer videos being taken by children fooling themselves into thinking the world cared at all. He stepped into line behind an elderly gentleman wearing a jaunty tweed flat cap. The older man had a polished cane with him, the black wood polished to a high sheen.

"Would you, perchance, be from Ireland, the land of laughter and limericks?" he asked with a smile. The older man turned, flashed his own smile, and said, "Dubliner, born and raised. Niall O'Dell, standing before you. What's your name, son?"

Jan replied, "Noah Van den Berg, from Amsterdam, at your service." He had been using that alias for years and it rolled off his tongue. Noah was an avid birdwatcher, and prone to rambling on about the subject. That was usually an innocuous way to get people to leave him alone without raising any kind of red flags.

Niall asked him what brought him to Minnesota. Jan answered, "Well, the lakes for sure. The fall colors and family. In that order." He laughed and gave Niall a friendly shoulder bump and a knowing look, which Niall returned.

"Oh, I know boyo, I've got a lot of family here. Depending on the day, sometimes too much." The old man raised an eyebrow and shrugged. "Family is family. Am I right? We don't pick 'em, we just love 'em."

Jan reflected on how true that was, and on the unexpected delight of finding nuggets of wisdom in unexpected places. As he mulled that over, he noted that the line had not moved forward in five minutes. There was a meaty American woman with beady eyes and ample lung capacity stridently complaining at the front of the line. She was complaining that her drink didn't have the correct amount of foam, that she didn't get the flavorings she ordered, and that her name was spelled wrong on her cup.

The barista told her that they could remake her order on the house, but the woman was bleating for a manager, apparently feeling she was owed more free drinks in the future for this mistake. Niall pointed out that a name misspelling wasn't deliberate, and she was holding up the line. "Go fuck yourself, Grandpa!" was the snarled reply.

Jan stepped around Niall and stepped up to the woman, hoping to defuse the situation. Speaking in calm tones, he said, "There is no need for theatrics. Your drink is being remade. Since you want to speak to the manager, could you please step to the side so others can order?" The wording seemed logical and courteous to him, and he thought it should ease the tensions that seemed to be escalating.

His words did not have the intended effect at all. In a strident voice, the woman stated, "I'm not going anywhere until I talk to the manager. I paid my money, and I won't be shuffled to the side and forgotten! So, take Gramps' cane and fuck yourself with it, you ugly bald fuck!" If ignorance was bliss, she was in the throes of a momentous orgasm. The Dutch assassin did not react with anger. Her antagonizing words simply convinced him that words alone were not going to be the solution to the situation.

The larynx is an anatomical curiosity. Besides the protective function as part of the body's respiratory system, it is also the location of the vocal cords, used in the formation of speech. Those facts are common knowledge. Less commonly known is that strikes and chops to the larynx can cause effects running from simple incapacitation to death. The effects depend on the angle of impact and the amount of force applied. Large amounts of force to the front of the larynx will fracture or outright break the shell of cartilage, and the victim will die drowning in their own blood as the resulting blood flow drains into the lungs.

Men typically have a more prominent Adam's apple than females. Normal hormonal changes during puberty result in this difference between the sexes. The cursing woman had a small Adam's apple, and it was further camouflaged by ample amounts of subcutaneous fat. Regardless, Jan knew exactly where it was positioned in her throat. With no change in expression or any other kind of warning, he delivered a modest chop to the side of her throat with the edge of his hand. He did not use his shoulder at all, only the muscles in his bicep.

Her mouth opened and closed like a bluegill suddenly finding itself on a dock in the summertime sun. Her formerly beady eyes went wide in shock, the sudden display of the whites of her eyes seemed like a movie special effect. A small croaking sound emanated from her open mouth, and she dropped wordlessly to her knees. Jan watched her chest, ensuring she was heaving for breath. Annoying though she had been, he didn't think she deserved to die for it, and he didn't want to leave a trail of bodies for the authorities to follow.

"Well, I couldn't blame you for that! I was thinking about giving her a taste of me Shaleigh, my own self." Niall's voice was soft in Jan's ear. The girl behind the counter stood stock still, stunned and amazed at what had just unfolded in the last several seconds. The woman lying on the ground made regular soft grunting sounds, and Jan felt confident she was in no impending danger of joining the choir of angels.

Niall leaned into his new friend. "I can't believe that angry Latino woman punched her in the throat. I'll make sure the counter girl sings the same song, but now it's time you get your arse down the road." He emphasized the last part with a swat across Jan's rump, and pressed a hand into his back, pushing him towards the door.

"I would have liked to know you better, Niall. Some other time, perhaps." Jan bemoaned.

Niall replied in hushed tones, "There's a coffee shop five miles down the road. I'll be filling up there for the next week. If you're looking to find me, that's where I'll be. Now get going, before the authorities arrive." He gave Jan's arm a squeeze and Jan gripped his hand and returned the squeeze. Then without a look back, he marched straight out the door, got into his car, and drove away.

Thursday — Evening

Mugshot was showing no signs of being tired, despite finishing his fourth lap around Lake Phalen. To say the pair were taking a modest pace would have been a generous statement. Johnson was determined not to appear out of breath when he ran into Michelle and Clyde. They were wearing matching Lycra outfits tonight, a sports neutral cobalt blue and white swirls in an abstract pattern. Running shorts and shirt for him, and a loose bandana for Mugshot. Despite having done four laps, he had seen neither hide nor hair of his hoped-for picnic partner. Dejection crept in.

"Well pal, what do you say we enjoy some cheese ourselves?" He asked Mugshot. Hearing the word "cheese," Mugshot started a jumping dance to indicate he was completely in favor of anything cheese-related. Johnson admitted to himself that it really did seem like a long shot for a strange woman to suggest a picnic to someone she had just met. Worst case, it had been a fun little fantasy for a day, no matter how unrealistic.

As he started into the parking lot, he was speaking in his goofiest voice to tell Mugshot how much he appreciated the dog's unwavering commitment to him and that, of course, he was the best dog ever. He got five steps into the lot before he realized who was sitting in the grass by his parked car. He stopped walking, so surprised he was. Michelle saw them standing there and waved, trying to make certain she was seen.

Like I could have missed you, he thought as he watched her waving grow wilder, unbalancing herself. "Yes, I see you;

don't hurt yourself before the picnic!" he yelled to Michelle. Knowing she'd been seen, she bent down by the shade cast by his car and came up with a picnic basket so large that it could have been used to smuggle Tibetan refugees. "Holy shit, now *that's* a picnic basket!" he blurted out.

"This lady comes prepared for any contingency," she retorted, with no small amount of sass in her voice. "I'm dying to try your aged cheddar but let me set this up first." She fished out a large, folded blanket from the basket and with a crisp snap, unfurled it and brought it down with nary a wrinkle. She pulled out a pair of items and began screwing them together. When she was done, she set a metal camping goblet with a wine stem on the blanket before repeating the process. By the time Johnson and Mugshot brought over their cooler from the trunk, she had laid out a makeshift charcuterie board. A baguette, brie, fig jam, green grapes, and prosciutto lay out next to a bottle of open Chardonnay.

Kneeling beside his cooler, Johnson pulled out a cutting board and a small paring knife. On the cutting board, he set the wedge of aged cheddar, a block of Gruyere, and a large salami (courtesy of Dave White). It was elk, and he had been saving it for a special occasion. He also pulled out a sleeve of Ritz crackers. "Let's not forget the time-worn wisdom of Andy Griffith." He paused for dramatic emphasis, grinned, and finished with, "Everything's better when it sits on a Ritz!" Michelle responded with rolled eyes, a groan, and a laugh.

"Oh, there's a blast from the past. Hey Kool-Aid!" she shouted as she flashed a toothy smile, demonstrating she knew her commercials from the 70's as well. She was wearing a coarse white cotton shirt with gold trim. Clyde sported a matching bandana as he made himself comfortable by lying on the farthest corner of the blanket. Mugshot was not nearly so sedate, trying to sneak onto the blanket as well but with the nefarious goal of nabbing at least one of the many cheeses sitting out. His efforts so far had been thwarted, but Mugshot was anything but a quitter. His increasing girth was an ample testament to that fact.

Johnson thought a cheese pun would be just the ticket to keep things light and fun. "Well, it is certainly Gouda to see you tonight," he ventured. His line of thinking was rewarded immediately. Michelle groaned again, rolled her eyes, and laughed appreciatively. Then in a completely unexpected turn of events, she broke into a little song verse with a clear tenor voice.

"What a friend we have in cheeses... What a friend we have in Brie..."

His surprise at hearing a church song parodied that way was matched only by his appreciation of the beauty of the sound he was hearing. He wondered if she had some sort of voice training or was part of a choir. "Wow, that's amazing!" he said with awed tones, cheese puns forgotten. "Do you have any training?"

"Oh God no," was her quick answer. "I'm decent, but I just sing for fun. You get me in a karaoke bar, and I'm there 'til close. I have a ton of karaoke friends. I know their first names and favorite songs, and that's it and it's all I need to know. We laugh and sing all night long and have a great time together. Speaking of first names, I gave you mine, but I don't know yours."

She accompanied the last sentence with a pointed look. "Most folks I know just call me Johnson, so that's what I answer to," was his simple response.

"I am not going to call my date by his last name, no matter what he is used to. Is your name something bizarre like Bartholomew or Gaylord?" she asked with a smile.

He looked up at the clouds, wishing he hadn't tried to dodge the question. "No, it's just Scott, but only my mom calls me that at this point. To be honest, I would feel a little weird having someone else calling me the same thing as my mother." Hearing his own unguarded answer, he felt like he had screwed up the momentum of the conversation. He felt like had been running effortlessly through a field and then stepped into a gopher hole, falling on his face.

Michelle simply looked him in the face for a moment and then said, "If this ends up being a thing, are you okay with some third option like a nickname?" Her question seemed to indicate that maybe he hadn't sunk things before they could begin. He couldn't help the grateful tone in his voice when he replied, "I would." Michelle's straightforward demeanor was not at all what he was used to, and he appreciated the clarity of the way she talked.

"Are you always this direct or are you running a special tonight?" he asked, hoping his smile and best friendly tone would keep things light. "I am running a special tonight, but only for people on picnics," she shot back. "Honestly though, I believe straight shooting is the way to go. Say what you mean and mean what you say. That's my policy." Scott was taken aback, hearing her describe her mindset so openly. *We are not in Kansas anymore, Mugshot,* he thought with bemusement. While he considered himself a genuine article type guy, he was surprised to hear a woman not only echoing his views on how to live your life but doing it so openly and so early.

"We park our cars in the same garage," he said earnestly. The comment was one of Scott's favorites. He had swiped it from a movie he had seen long ago, and no one ever seemed to know the movie, so he felt no need to volunteer information about its origins. *C'mon man, stay cool, you overanxious dunce!* he thought as he weighed over the similarities that were already showing up. He felt his hopes rising like the regular visits of a Fiat to a hydraulic lift. Tamping them back down, he asked "Did you want to hear the story about the Judge?" He unloaded a pair of finger pistols at his car, complete with clicking sounds.

"I absolutely do, but first I want to try this aged cheddar you're bragging up." She opened the sleeve of crackers, extracted one, and topped it with a chunk of the cheese she'd broken off the wedge. "Here we go bro," she said as she popped the whole thing in her mouth, crunching contentedly. Abruptly, she stopped chewing, and her eyes widened. "Got to the good stuff, eh?" Scott chuckled at her reaction. Her face then returned to normal, and she finished chewing. She sucked her mouth's contents hard, extracting every iota of flavor.

"Mother of God! I have never had cheese like that. That is truly a 'take no prisoners' kind of cheese. I love it! Pardon me!" She grabbed a cloth and primly staunched the involuntary flood of saliva the sharp cheese had initiated. Scott noted she did not show any embarrassment about drooling like a Pavlovian dog hearing the dinner bell. While Scott felt that normally that kind of wholesale bodily shamelessness was the sole realm of the canine, Michelle seemed to have more than a little of that trait. She continued to defy expectations, and he liked it.

"Why don't you try that salami before I start the story? A co-worker of mine made that. It's elk, and it's at least as amazing as the cheese." An exceptionally naughty expression spread across Michelle's face. "Are telling me you want your salami in my mouth?" she asked. The unexpectedness of such a bawdy comment on a first date had Scott braying like a hungry donkey. His eyes tearing, he rocked back and forth with laughter. Watching the effect her words had on him, Michelle started laughing as well.

After a few minutes, Scott pulled himself together enough to announce he was starting his story. "When I was a kid, my dad's brother lived at the end of our block. His wife had died when I was six, and he was kind of a loner. Taking care of his car was what kept him going.

"When I was 12, I ran away from home one summer. I made it as far as my Uncle Al's place. I don't even remember why I ran away. He and I sat out on the porch, drank root beer, and talked about the world. Now, I know that on one of those trips inside to get more root beer, he called my folks, let 'em know I was fine, and that he'd take care of dinner. As evening came around, my little tummy started growling loud enough for him to hear. He told me to hop in his car, and we'd go to the A&W. I remember feeling like a big kid as we drove through town, and people on the sidewalk all turned to watch us drive by. I had my first bacon cheeseburger with Uncle Al. A root beer float to wash it down.

"Uncle Al told me that while parents could seem like they were all rules and telling you what you could and could not do, the only reason they bothered to do that was because they loved their kids, my dad especially. I remember feeling guilty then about running away from home and making my parents worry. Much later I found out that afternoon was like a vacation for them, and they had taken advantage of it to go to the movies. Uncle Al dropped me off at my front door that night and said I could drop by anytime. I went in, apologized to my folks, and went to bed.

"The next morning, I snuck down to Uncle Al's place, and without telling him, I Turtle Waxed his Judge to a mirror finish. When I was done, I called him out to show him what I did as a thank-you gesture. He busted his buttons seeing his car looking better than it had for a long time. He got his hankie out, blew his nose, and asked me if taking me out to the town supper club would be an acceptable payment for the fine wax job. I had never been to a super club, and it was exciting to imagine it, but I told him the wax job was a thank-you present for talking to me the day before, and you don't repay a thank-you.

"I remember him looking at me for what seemed like five minutes. Then he said, 'Since you got the old girl looking so fine, it only seems right for us to take her out and let her run.' I agreed with that. Then I told him I just had to go home and tell my folks first. He swelled up with pride like I was his own and said, 'You go do that, Scottie. Letting your folks know what's going on is always the right call. I'll pick you up at your place.'

"Ten minutes later, he pulled up in front of the house, and I cleared the house's entire front stairway in a single bound and jumped into that shiny black daydream. The first thing Uncle Al says is that he's hungry and wonders if I would be willing to join him at the super club. I told him I sure would, and we cruised all the way out there with the windows down and the music blasting. There wasn't a head we didn't turn on the way, and that includes the cows in the fields. I had the best steak of my young life that day.

"From that point forward, almost every Saturday morning, I'd wax my uncle's car, and then we'd go cruising. Both of us loved being seen in a like-new car. As the years went on, conversational topics became less about my life and more about his. Both of us looked forward to that Saturday routine. On my 20th birthday, I started doing the driving, and my uncle would relax in the passenger seat, looking cool. He passed away nine years later in his sleep. He left the Judge to me. I think about him every time I wax it, drive it, look at it. I love my dad, but I could share anything with my Uncle Al. Those two shaped me into the kind of man I am today."

He wore a contented smile as he closed his eyes, remembering Uncle Al, and let the setting sun warm his face. Michelle gave it a minute, and then said, "Wow, that's quite the story. Thank you for sharing it with me." She bowed her head respectfully as she finished. "Let's get to eating now; I'm hungry." She spread some fig jam over the bread, spread some Brie over that, and popped the whole thing into her mouth. As she chewed, she filled both glasses with Chardonnay and handed one to Scott.

"Most kind," he said as he bowed with a flourish, something he had seen many times at Renaissance Fairs.

"So fancy…" she replied, executing the best curtsy she could from a kneeling position. Thirty minutes later, there was not a scrap of cheese or any other food to be seen, and Mugshot's frequent sighs indicated how slighted he felt about this turn of events. Michelle flipped her final piece of prosciutto to Clyde. Mugshot darted towards the flying meat, but one moment Clyde was lying down, and the next second he was flying through the air, open mouth snatching the snack out of the sky.

Neither Scott nor Mugshot expected that kind of quicksilver movement from a dog that seemed to loaf around every single chance he got. While Mugshot chalked it up to just missing out on a treat and moved on, Scott's disbelief and astonishment lasted several minutes longer.

Michelle noticed Scott's stunned expression and explained, "Clyde can move fast; he just doesn't bother unless it's food-related." Sliding her jaw sideways, she considered a few options. Deciding on one, she asked, "What would you say to going out to an axe-throwing establishment on Saturday night?" While she did find axe-throwing fun, she knew it was exactly the kind of invite no straight man would ever turn down for fear of looking weak.

"I would love to!" came Scott's unhesitating reply. Being asked out on a date by a woman was not something he had experienced before, and he was a little excited by it. *I'm catnip!* he thought as thrills ran up and down his back. "Well, that sounds like a little bit of all right," Michelle said, drawing the last two words out in a sassy and brassy drawl. "I'll meet you at Bad Axe at eight o'clock then." With that, she packed the blanket and empty wine bottle into her gigantic basket and sauntered off to her car with a wave and a bounce in her step.

Thursday — Night

The door latch of the hotel suite beeped once and flashed green, allowing Jan and the man in the fancy suit entry. Laughing together, they stumbled into the room. "So the doctor says, 'That's not my duck!'" Jan could barely finish the joke, and they both laughed themselves sick over *that* one. "No more, no more!" laughed the second man. In almost every aspect of his life, the man in the fancy suit maintained a tight discipline over himself. Tonight had been a wonderful release from those constraints.

A carillon concert would have been a good evening on its own for him, but taking it in with someone well-versed in the instrument and its prominent composers elevated the experience to the sublime. The frequent interjections of the Dutchman's sardonic wit and the addition of a superb dinner had culminated in this being his most enjoyable evening out in at least two years.

"You will have to come to the Netherlands," Jan said with a happy smile. "We have many of the greatest carillons in the world. I will take you to carillons that Jacob van Eyck composed on. It may sound silly, but you can feel the energy in places like that. They are magical on their own, but going with a fellow enthusiast would be a dream come true." He looked directly into the other man's eyes and clapped him on the shoulder.

Thinking to himself, the man in the fancy suit ruminated, *Who would have thought a friendship could develop between such dissimilar men this quickly?* He was surprised at how much he enjoyed the company of an actual assassin-for-hire. Jan seemed to be the quintessential example of a book that should not be judged by its cover. When a job was at hand, he was singularly focused and all business. But off the job, he was well-read, cultured, and unexpectedly funny.

"I must retire for tonight. I had a supremely enjoyable evening." Add succinct to the list of the man's traits. Hearing that Jan had also enjoyed the time together was supremely gratifying. It made him feel even more connected to the Dutchman. "Why don't you stop by for breakfast tomorrow?" offered the man in the fancy suit. "I have a surprise that I would like to share."

Jan tipped his head forward in a gracious nod of acceptance. "That is terribly kind of you. I will be back for breakfast. Until then." With almost military precision, he turned on his heels and exited the room. Idly, the man in the fancy suit wondered if a stint in the military was in Jan's past. Although Jan had demonstrated a deductive mindset and talent for amusing analogies that evening, he had not discussed his past at all. Whether that was by design or stories of the past were simply a victim of the evening's limited time, he could not say.

Spreading out on the lush couch, he turned on the news for white noise while he checked his phone. Thumbing through his email, he deleted email after email that he cared nothing about. While he had a pricey spam-hunting app in place, it just wasn't keeping up with the rivers of shit flowing into his inbox. He promised himself thirty minutes of mindless fun playing games after he cleaned out the crap, his usual incentive. He had scarcely finished completing the mental agreement with himself when he heard a name from the television that caught his attention.

"The death of Bloomington mayor David Deakins found drowned in north metro's Turtle Lake, is now being investigated as a homicide. We will report the details as they are made available. Again, this is now a homicide investigation. Anyone with any details is being asked to contact the Ramsey County Sheriff's Department." He could only stare open-mouthed and disbelieving at the TV.

Letting his mind run through the various possibilities, from zero effect to worst case, he came to the same conclusion. His role in this HAD to remain secret. His oft-repeated saying about how to keep a secret floated up through his thoughts, inexorably growing clearer by the moment. Try though he might, he could not see another way forward.

"Fuck! Fuck! Fuck!" Each word was accompanied by both fists slamming down onto the armrest. "Goddammit! How? Fucking how?!" His voice cracked with emotion as he cried out. "C'mon, can't I have one fucking friend? Is that really too much to ask?!" It wasn't clear who he was beseeching, and after the outburst, he lapsed into a motionless silence that stretched out for quite a while.

When he finally snapped out of his quiet contemplation, he opened his phone and started scrolling through his main phone's contacts. Finding a listing labeled 'The Chef,' he initiated a call. It rang twice and went to voicemail, as expected. When the beep came, he simply said, "One unit, Marriott downtown, penthouse." Upon hanging up, he angrily threw his phone directly into a mirror decoration, destroying them both. "You deserved that, you fuck," he said to the broken phone. Its cracked face stared up, wordlessly agreeing.

Friday — Morning

Jan knocked crisply twice on the door, a smile playing across his face as he did. When the door opened, he proceeded in. On the center table was a carafe of orange juice and two circular tins with a black grainy substance in them. There were several plates of crackers and toasted croissants as well. The aroma of the croissants made him think of bakeries at home, and he felt a pang of homesickness.

"Have you ever had Beluga caviar?" asked the man in the fancy suit. Jan marveled that although it was early, he was immaculately dressed, groomed, and had breakfast ready. "I have not had any kind of caviar before."

Picking up one of the containers, the man in black used a tiny spoon to eat directly from the tin. "Feel free to have some orange juice and a warm croissant," he advised Jan. "This is Beluga caviar. It is delicious but it is a bit of an acquired taste. It's briny like an oyster but there is a savory quality to it as well. The water crackers are excellent for caviar. They don't overwhelm your taste buds. These croissants are wonderful - light, buttery, and flaky like they came directly from the Netherlands." As he said it, he winked at the Dutchman. Jan poured himself an ample glass of orange juice to wash down his second croissant. The first had not even lasted a full minute.

Unbeknownst to him, a pair of watchful eyes kept tabs on exactly what he was (or was not) eating. As Jan finished up his second croissant, he grabbed a water cracker, topped it with a heaping spoonful of caviar, and devoured it in a single bite. The man in the fancy suit relaxed imperceptibly and then asked Jan his opinion. "Hmmm. Buttery but I'm surprised how fishy it seems. And I'm well aware it's fish eggs so leave off with those comments," he said with a smile.

"Have you tied off all your loose ends by now?" asked the man in the fancy suit. Although Jan would be tying off the final knot that night, he felt asking such a question was unwarranted and invasive. Because of that, he smoothly lied, "Of course. Two nights ago." The thought that *he* might be considered a loose end to be tied off never entered his mind. Knowing how expensive caviar was, he helped himself to another heavily loaded cracker. Unimpressed with the flavor and unimpressed with the texture, he decided he'd had enough to satisfy expectations regarding the acceptance of gifts.

"I am serious. Call me when you are coming to the Netherlands, and I will show you around personally. Don't forget." Jan said as he prepared to leave. To his surprise, his words hit the other man much harder than expected. With eyes filling with water, the man in the fancy suit stood and embraced Jan in a graceless full-body hug. "You could never be forgotten," he whispered hoarsely. Jan gave him several pats on the back, extricated himself, and with a wordless thumbs-up sign, left the room.

Walking to the parking garage, he reflected on how emotionally volatile Americans tended to be. Even the most stoic ones (like his current employer) had feelings that were ready to burst forth at any given moment, simmering just under the surface. Good or bad, whatever an American felt, you could be sure they felt an awful lot of it. Normally, that kind of emotional outburst was not Jan's cup of tea, but he had really enjoyed getting to know this man. He was used to being largely treated with indifference by his employers. This job had provided not only financial rewards but also rewards of a more personal nature.

Merging onto the highway, he had a slight coughing fit. If he was coming down with whatever ailment the waiter from the night before had, he would be quite put out. He was not looking forward to 'tying off' his loose end that night. The odds were that she would never have connected a piece of equipment like a rebreather to a drowning death. Still, professionals didn't leave room for 'coulda-woulda-shouldas'. He started feeling a little lightheaded and pulled over to the side of the road, turning on his hazard lights to avoid being hit by some obese dolt paying more attention to eating their Fatty McMuffin than the road.

He realized now he was so dizzy he couldn't get out of the car. He tried getting to his phone, but his arms weren't taking orders. He was more lightheaded by the moment. He realized he wasn't drawing breath, and shortly thereafter lost consciousness. He went into the darkness happy, thinking his date that night would survive the evening. Ten minutes after that he expired. Fifteen minutes after that, a state highway patrolman stopped to check on a vehicle with its hazard lights on. His efforts to resuscitate the driver were admirable, but futile.

At about the same time, the man in the fancy suit was forcing himself to vomit into a bag. He then carefully put the lid back onto Jan's tin of caviar and tucked it into the vomit. It was crude, but it was inarguably effective at deterring the curious. He also deposited a small glass vial that had been delivered earlier that morning into the bag. The bag would be deposited in some gas station trash receptacle on the west side of town. One inexplicable death was a tragedy, two on the same day in the same part of town was a pattern. While having dots like that connected was improbable, he was always on the lookout for any way to reduce his risk exposure.

Friday — Early Afternoon

Surprising not a single person, Gail pulled into the parking lot on an official day of leave just before noon. As it was a potluck day, and everyone considered her the patron saint of potlucks, there were almost a dozen helping hands waiting for her before she even got out of her car. Popping her hatchback, she exclaimed, "Three crockpots and one container of cookies. I will be grateful to anyone who helps me carry them to the breakroom, and I will be taking names." Her grin was contagious and, coupled with the smells coming from the car, resulted in smiles aplenty, as well as several growling tummies in the parking lot.

The biggest crockpot that came out of the car looked like a children's kitchen toy in Brick's big hands. Seth Brueske took the medium-sized one, and David Anderson from the lab picked up the last one. Talya carried in the cookie container, with the spicy scent of fresh-baked gingersnaps whispering to her. Her love of gingersnaps had her seriously considering a lengthy stop in the ladies' room on the way to the breakroom that many of the cookies would not survive.

Once everything was plugged in on the breakroom tables, Gail surveyed the other offerings on the tables. Someone had brought a pair of tuxedo cakes from Costco. While she normally disdained bringing store-bought items to a potluck, she couldn't fault that selection. Not only were they the only store-bought item Gail would bring into her own home, but when she did bring them in, the cakes didn't last a week. Sure, her own cakes might be a smidge tastier, but they took at least two hours to make and then she had to clean the whole kitchen. A no-muss, no-fuss cake that was just about as yummy was a proven winner in her book.

She saw that Carmen had brought a pasta-pesto-mini-meatball entry. You could always count on Carmen to bring something solid to potlucks. It was just one of the things she respected about the woman. For an East Coaster, she wasn't half bad. There was a crockpot she didn't recognize at the far end of the table. Looking through the lid, she could only make out that the contents were bright orange and stringy. Cracking the seal of the lid, she smelled something she couldn't immediately identify, but it smelled wonderful.

"Liking that one?" asked an unfamiliar voice behind her. With a jump, she spun around. Standing there (with a slightly worried expression) was Krishnananda, the building custodian. "It's Szechuan noodles. I wanted to contribute to the potluck as well. On the subject of contributing, I hope you are doing okay. You not only acted to protect us, but you did also not take the man's life. You have the heart of a lion, and I am thankful for you." He ended his assessment with a bow and left the room.

Gail had not exchanged more than a dozen words with this man since his start that summer. Those kind words were nothing she would have ever expected to hear him utter. Like the result of a meteor hitting the sea, waves (of emotion) washed over her.

She walked quickly down the hallway, caught up to him, and said, "I didn't realize how much I needed to hear that.

Thank you." Gail wrapped her arms around him, and that act tipped her past the point of her typical Scandinavian stoicism. She started shaking from the emotions of the week's events and the impact of Krishnananda's simple, kind words.

Krishnananda simply held Gail and murmured, "It's alright. We are alright. You are alright. Everything is alright." At that moment, they were the only two people in the building, nothing and no one else existed. He was content to hold someone that needed holding, and not make them feel rushed or harried. His serene demeanor allowed Gail to focus on what her feelings were, rather than being caught up in caring for others.

After a few minutes, she no longer felt comfortable wallowing in her own feelings and her stoicism crept back. She gave Krishnananda a parting squeeze, thanked him again, and walked down to her desk to get her special potluck plate and silverware. Callie hung up the phone just as Gail walked in. "Perfect timing!" Gail exclaimed. "Let's go get us some vittles, partner!" Callie agreed happily, but privately thought, *Boy, does that southern accent need some work*.

At noon, the breakroom was nearly filled. Gail's big crockpot had housed a Minnesota Classic: tater-tot hotdish. Even at this early stage in the potluck, there was only a single scoop left. Gail helped herself to the Szechuan noodles while noting that her second crockpot (which had housed an enchilada casserole) was not only empty but someone had sponged up the saucy remnants with bread. *Won't have to do any scrubbing there*, she thought to herself. Glancing at her third crockpot, there was not even a hint of the chicken wild-rice soup that had filled it thirty minutes before. Like the previous crockpot, someone had used bread to squeegee up every vestige of the soup. She made a mental note to raise those two items on the potluck priority list.

With their plates filled, the two women headed back down to Reception. "Hey Gail!" said a voice anyone would have recognized with their eyes shut. Johnson continued, "Great job 'disarming' the suspect Monday," and let out a guffaw. The laughter he expected to hear around him did not materialize. Gail never even turned around. Shaking her head, she and Callie walked out the door and headed downstairs. In the breakroom, a dozen pairs of eyes disapprovingly regarded Johnson. "What?! That's some good wordplay!" he said, his voice both self-justifying and whiny. The unmoved expressions of disgust all around him made it crystal clear he had crossed a line he didn't know was there.

"Let's finish lunch outside," Ollig suggested to his friend, thinking that getting the motormouth outside was going to be the only way to keep this from getting worse. With a gritted teeth smile and a sharp head shake, he made it clear to Johnson this was not merely a 'suggestion'. "We are going out the back door. C'mon." Ollig said as they got to the hallway. "Fine!" was Johnson's reply, dripping with indignation.

As they got to the parking lot, Ollig turned and furiously asked, "What. The. Actual. Fuck?! Why would you say something that fucking callous to a civvy? That fucking soon after it happened? While she's still on official leave and shows up to feed your fucking ass? Good fucking job, shitwit!"

Johnson could not recall his friend ever swearing like that and had never heard him so angry. "It was just a play on words," he started.

"No!" came the answer, like a bullet. "Stop thinking of just yourself and being all proud of your semantic trick. You and I have had seminars around killing suspects and causing grievous harm in the line of duty. She has had none. Zero!" Ollig was yelling now, teeth clenched in anger, and Johnson started to think this might not be someone else's problem of being too sensitive. Maybe he really did miss something.

"Think beyond 'Oh, look at me!' Everyone likes attention, but you can't let that eclipse considering how you could make someone feel. You are a good cop and a good friend, but what you just said was selfish and thoughtless. I know you didn't mean it that way, but some things affect others in ways we might not mean. You need to make that shit right now. Not tomorrow, not next week. Now. Let her know you realized your misstep, and you weren't resting until you made it right. Now go in the front door and resolve this." Ollig thought about the situation and then added, "Please."

Ollig knew his friend very well. The addition of a 'please' would be enough for Johnson to feel he was being asked, not told what to do. Ollig understood that if his friend felt he was being told what to do, even if he agreed, his hackles went up and his heels dug in. The key was in allowing the perception of choice to exist. Even if no choice existed, simply presenting the illusion of it served the purpose, and would get him moving. *Wait 'til you're married,* Ollig thought, and not for the first time.

Walking into Reception, Johnson quietly asked Gail if he could speak to her, before looking pointedly at Callie and pointedly adding, privately. Although still miffed at the thoughtlessness of his earlier comment, Callie said she would go upstairs and see if the brass had anything that needed doing and departed.

Johnson started with, "I did not think of the possibility that my earlier comment could be taken any way but funny. It was thoughtless and I apologize for not thinking how it might make you feel." Gail reflected for a moment before responding. Knowing Johnson well enough to know apologizing was not easy for him, she said simply, "Thank you, Scott. Apology accepted."

Feeling awkward at being called by his first name by a woman who had so many similarities to his own mother, Johnson uttered a small "thank you" and walked back up to the breakroom. Looking around at all the people in the breakroom, he did not see a single smile aimed his way. Taking a deep breath, he announced, "I was made aware that my earlier comment was thoughtless. I have apologized to Gail, and she has accepted my apology. I also apologize to all of you for putting you in an uncomfortable position with my words. Thank you." Finishing his announcement, he contritely turned and sat in a far corner, away from anyone else.

He hadn't been sitting even five minutes when Bricks coolly strode past and, without stopping, said, "Class move.

Good call." Johnson murmured a quick thank you while Bricks was still in earshot and then looked at the rest of the breakroom. While there were no smiles on the faces looking at him, there were also no more stone faces aimed his way either.

Ollig appeared in the doorway, glanced around the room, and went to sit by his friend. Before he could say anything, Johnson opened with, "I don't want to admit it, but you were right in this case. I made my apologies, and it made a big difference for the better. Thanks for the advice."

Because Ollig was older (age had brought an accompanying increase in maturity), and he had children that helped him grow his maturity (and patience), he was able to refrain from saying 'told you so.' Instead, he offered, "Glad my words were helpful. I knew you'd make the right call." Ollig knew that was a bald-faced lie, but a lie he knew would help Johnson build the confidence to be humble going forward.

"Part of what helped me shift my thinking was that I met someone running around Phalen the other day." Johnson was already looking to the ceiling, remembering his date, so he missed Ollig's dramatic eye roll. Continuing on, he confided, "I'm reading up on how to be a good partner and other relationship stuff." Ollig thought of several biting comments and instead settled for asking, "Can I safely assume that you, yet again, are cautiously optimistic about this?" "Oh yes!" was the speedy reply. From there on, Johnson spun the story of Michelle and her dog, Clyde. Being the thoughtful friend he was, Ollig just listened as Johnson detailed conversations, his hopes, and his dreams.

Friday — Late Afternoon

Counting on Gail not wanting to miss out on a potluck, Ballard parked and walked in the front doors. To his dismay, he did not see Gail behind the glass, only Callie. Seeing his crestfallen face, Callie safely deduced she was not who he hoped to see. "Looking for Gail?" she asked the big detective. Ballard nodded silently. "She's upstairs, cleaning up her stuff in the breakroom." Callie received a curt nod and then she was alone again.

Ballard strode up the steps and walked into the breakroom. At this point in the potluck, almost all the crockpots were empty, and the snacks had been decimated. A rabbit would have a hard time finding enough food for a full meal. Sitting on the middle table was a partially eaten tuxedo cake. Five empty chocolate-smeared cake boards next to it served as evidence that several people bringing the same cakes was not too much of a good thing for them.

In one corner, Gail was talking with Carmen and Maki. As Ballard was walking over, Maki stood up and loudly proclaimed, "I'll tell you one thing, that cake is calling my name!" Just as loudly, Carmen responded, "Three pieces?! The only thing that cake is calling you is 'fatty'!!" Given that Maki ran 26-mile races regularly for fun, and that he had maybe ten percent body fat clinging to his bony frame, this elicited laughter from everyone who heard it, including Maki himself. "I'll get you for that one," he said, chuckling and giving a 'thumbs-up' gesture that was definitely not using the thumb. He then picked up the entire remaining cake, zipped into his office and shut the door.

Carmen took advantage of his departure to announce her own exit. With three large strides, Ballard was at Gail's side and asked if she had a few moments to talk with him. "Sure," was her friendly reply. "My last crockpot is soaking, and it could use the extra time."

"Let's use the conference room if you don't mind," he suggested. Ever chipper, Gail replied, "Fine by me. Wherever you lead, I'm with you!" Gail was curious about what could merit a private conversation with the only other person who was on leave but still in the office that day.

Once they were down the hall and in the only conference room with frosted glass, Ballard closed the door. Since Ballard clearly had something on his mind, Gail waited for him to start things out. Although she was not an investigator, she had a pretty good idea of what the subject matter was going to be. She and Ballard were the only two people in the building with crosses over their desks, and they were the only two who had severely injured others in the last week.

Ballard looked lost. He stammered, "I was able to come to peace with the physical act of killing another person by focusing on the fact that he would have killed me, and it was justifiably self-defense.

But I am really wrestling with this in a spiritual sense, and I wanted to talk with someone who is not only on the same wavelength as me but also kind of in the same boat. I haven't so much as drawn my gun in over fifteen years, never been in a fistfight, and now I'm responsible for a man's death. I'm having some trouble, and I'm hoping you might have some insight into the situation you could share.

Called that one right on the nose, Gail said to herself. "I kinda figured that would be what you wanted to talk about. I had my own demons I agonized over after Monday. Brad's selfishness at being willing to trick someone into damning themselves while he gets off scot-free, spiritually speaking. It absolutely astounds me. I have to consciously not think about it, or my blood starts boiling."

"There's a funeral home at the end of my block. Tuesday morning, I walked down there to talk with their priest. That man wasn't a priest. It was namby-pamby in a priest costume, handing out feel-good pablum and platitudes and hiding behind Scripture when asked tough questions. He actually said God forgives all sins, even broken commandments. Then what's the blessed point of having them? Of course, he started throwing out Scripture to cover his ineptitude, rather than openly discussing hard issues. I left after ten minutes, without any answers and a whole lot more ticked off than I was when I started the day."

Gail's hands had tightened to fists, white-knuckled and tight. Her jaw muscles stood out in bas relief. Ballard noted these things, dismayed he was responsible for walking her down such an aggravating path. "What did you do then?" he asked to shift her focus away from the frustrating priest.

"Well, I drove down to St. John's, just south of 694. I was determined to discuss the matter with a real priest this time. Father Kieran showed me back to his office and asked what the deal was. He's known me since I was a teen. I laid out the scenario. He had nothing but praise for not taking Brad's life. No big surprise there. Then I told him I wanted to discuss damnation and whether law enforcement nowadays is in the unenviable position of becoming hell bound through no intention of our own.

"He gave a big sigh and told me there was a big difference between the church's official stance and many of his brother's modern interpretations. He told me that strictly speaking, killing another human being is breaking the fifth commandment. The reasoning does not matter. Taking a life is breaking a commandment handed down to Moses from God himself. I don't have to tell you that really put a bee in my bonnet. Why even consider law enforcement as a career if there's a real chance of damning yourself, I asked him.

"His answer to that went way into the past. He pointed out there were no law officers with lethal weapons when the commandments were given to man, so the fifth commandment was worded using the word kill as opposed to murder because, at that time, all the killings *were* murders and only murders. At that time, there was no way to kill a person without a murderous mindset.

"Two thousand years later, that is now entirely possible. New realities require reassessment of ancient declarations. His opinion, and the opinion of many of his brothers is that the fifth commandment needs its wording updated to reflect the current world. He believes the fifth commandment should now use the word murder, to avoid the condemnation of law enforcement officers involved with incidental shootings."

With deliberate and stern eye contact, Gail finished up by saying, "That conversation focused on guns, but the idea of intention is just as central to your case. You did take a life. No denying that. It was self-defense. No denying that either. But the core element is intention. You are a genial, good man. If that guy hadn't attacked you, he'd still be alive. He forced you into an action you wouldn't have otherwise taken, to his detriment. You did not murder the man.

"As such, your soul remains untainted, and you are not guilty of breaking the spirit of the fifth commandment. Truthfully, I think that kind of updated thinking should be communicated to law enforcement across the nation. The boys in blue deserve to know their jobs aren't leading them to the devil's door. Ladies too," she added with a wink.

"I would add, it's a good thing you're a diver with some ridiculously developed legs. Your wife would not be the only one missing you something fierce if things had gone the other way." She gave Ballard's shoulder an amiable shake. "Anything else on your mind?" A little stunned by all the information she had thrown out, Ballard shook his head. "That covered the bases. I figured you wouldn't rest 'til you had some answers, and I was right. Thank you." Ballard walked out of the conference room with Gail, and with a peace of mind he had been afraid he would never recover.

Friday — Evening

Josh's hair was unusually stylish (for him) as he waited at the table for Agnes to arrive. He had washed his hair twice and had combed it three different ways before settling on the first choice. He had even taken the unusual step of asking a neighbor he passed in the building atrium if his appearance was good enough for a first date. 'You're looking aces, my boy,' the man replied. While the opinion was less clearly worded than he'd hoped, it did seem quite positive.

Kihn Do was tenth of fifteen on the list of possibilities he had sent to Agnes, and it had been the restaurant she selected. Wanting to avoid the faux pas of being late to his first date, Josh arrived forty-five minutes early (just to be sure). He had spent the time using chopsticks to pick up the various objects he'd had in his pockets. So far, only the quarter proved difficult. The USB drive and his keys had been child's play.

He was so focused on picking up the quarter he was oblivious to the waitress's approach. "Are you ready to order?" a voice asked over his shoulder. With an inadvertent yelp, he jumped in his seat while simultaneously firing the quarter into a booth twenty feet away. The couple in the booth were so focused on their indiscrete kissing, they didn't notice the flying quarter or anything else in the world. The waitress was immediately apologetic. "I am so sorry. I didn't mean to startle you! Are you okay?" Embarrassed, Josh lowered his head, letting her know he was fine, and that he was waiting for his date to arrive before ordering.

Ten minutes later, and still ten minutes early for the date, Agnes walked through the door, looking stunning. She was wearing a loose-fitting pantsuit with distinctly African coloring and patterns and a large pair of golden hoop earrings. Josh was suddenly stricken with doubts about his appearance being up to par. Before he had time to pick up speed on his downward spiral, Agnes saw him, waved, and with a wide smile, she started walking over. *Time to sink or swim,* he sighed to himself, unsure which option would play out.

Agness slipped into the other side of the booth, cheerfully noting, "I guess neither of us wanted to be late. That seems like a good sign to me." *Me too,* he thought. *Maybe both of us were looking forward to this.* Josh wondered what the incentive would be for her. The thought was not self-deprecating but merely analytical. Things seemed rather one-sided from his point of view, and he wondered if he was missing a piece of the puzzle that would make it make sense.

"Uptown is lots of fun." Josh had heard lots of people say that, so he figured it was a good starter line to get the conversation going. In truth, this was only his second visit to Uptown in as many years. "I enjoy walking around the lakes." Agnes offered. "The people-watching is unmatched. I don't believe in judging a book by its cover, and I do enjoy that when I occasionally slide into that, it can be thrown back into my face. I had that happen last week.

"For the last month, I had been seeing this white guy on the paths who had to be a bodybuilder of some kind. He was maybe 5'8" but I bet he was at least two-hundred fifty pounds of blocky muscle. He always wore a purple Lycra jumpsuit, with a massive studded black leather belt. He had an equally blocky pit bull leashed to a ring in the belt so his hands would be free as he walked. I figured he was some uber-macho hick. A real 'God, guns, and guts' kind of guy.

Last week, I saw him stopped at a bench, tying his laces. I figured I'd say hi and see how close to the mark I was in my assessment. I was expecting him to be freaked out by the talky black lady. Instead, this massive man stands up and, in a high feminine voice, starts telling me how beautiful I am and how he wished his skin was half as gorgeous as mine. His name was Curtis, and he was a dancer at the Gutherie. His dog's name was Brutus, and he was the happiest dog ever. I patted him for two minutes that evening, and now every day he sees me around the lakes, he drags Curtis over so he can get some more loving."

Agnes laughed as she remembered Brutus and his antics. Josh chuckled politely, but he thought the scenario of going up to an imposing stranger and striking up a conversation was incomprehensible. He had trouble striking up conversations with people he knew. Once again, he doubted he was in the same league as his date. *I'll enjoy it while it lasts,* he pledged to himself.

"Do you have a favorite item here?" he asked. He knew the entire menu by memory of his own favorite restaurant, including the prices. Despite having the entire menu in his head, he regularly ordered one of the same two choices every time - the Good Morning burger or a Rueben. Onion rings were the standard side item for him. His choices and his timing were so predictable that as soon as he entered the building at 6 pm on Tuesday nights, the cooks were tipped off and dropped a fresh batch of rings just for him before any waitress could ask him if it was a burger or sandwich night.

"I have several" Agnes replied. "Their egg rolls are unmatched. I always order extra fish sauce for dipping. The broccoli beef is excellent, as is the pork in garlic sauce. Honestly, those three things are always reliable, and they are filling. Money well spent, and never a regret." Josh heard her narrow list and was elated to hear some commonalities between them. "The bean noodles look like intestinal worms and the black mushrooms look like liver flukes. I don't know what it says about me that my favorites look like parasites of some kind." Josh didn't know what it meant either, if anything. He simply shrugged his shoulders and smiled.

"I like egg rolls. Let's start with an order of those." Josh felt like he was projecting confidence and feeling that he sounded that way did make him more confident. Agnes raised a hand to signal a waitress. One started heading their way. While she was still a good twenty feet away, Agnes changed her upraised hand to a fist with an extended index finger and mouthed 'egg rolls.' The waitress gave her a nod and mouthed, 'I got you' before changing course directly into the kitchen.

Josh was amazed by the entirely silent interaction. Seeing his expression, Agnes clarified, "I come here a lot. That waitress's name is Bao. Weirdly, the one up front is named Hao. The owner's name is Anh, and she is the mother of Bao. There is a single adult son who only works Saturday and Sunday nights. He is going to college for engineering, and he is nice too. Seems to be a family trait. His name is Binh." Not particularly interested in the family tree of the owner, Josh decided to use some of her own words to shift topics.

"Do you have any family traits?" he asked. Even though Agnes knew Josh had Asperger's, she was a little surprised by the abruptness of the topic change. Happily, Agnes was a 'roll with the punches' kind of gal. "Hmmm. let me think about that." After a moment, she said, "My father and siblings all have a curiosity about nature and the world we live in. My father is a published conservationist in Uganda, so all the children picked it up." Then she asked, "How about you? Any family traits on your side?"

Josh was taken aback by having the question reversed, and he was unprepared for anyone to show curiosity in him. He stammered, "I have one younger sister. We don't have much in common." He had barely finished the sentence when the eggrolls arrived, with a small container of dipping sauce for each of them. A third cup was set next to Agnes with a wink from Bao. Josh was grateful for the interruption as it gave him more time to analyze his family for possible common traits.

"I don't know that it's a trait per se, but the males in my family all enjoy good science fiction."

With a grin, Agnes asked, "By 'all the males in your family', do you mean yourself and your father? Are there grandfathers or uncles included in that group?"

While he would have preferred to keep the focus off himself, he admired her attention to detail. "I have no living male relatives anymore, so yes, just Dad and myself," he said with a noncommittal shrug.

Agnes immediately responded with, "Oh my God! I'm so sorry. Were you close to your grandfathers?"

Josh let her know he was not. "Mom's dad lived in Texas and died in a tornado before we were born. Dad's dad was an alcoholic, so we didn't see him except for Christmas. My dad has always been great. When I was young, before being diagnosed, he tried all kinds of things to find something that would calm me down. One of the things he found was watching sci-fi shows with me. Apparently, it was one of the few things that would shut me up for more than five minutes. So, I have a lot of good memories sitting on the couch with Dad watching shows."

Agnes innocently inquired, "Were any of the various Star Trek series in there?"

Hearing one of his favorite subjects being brought up, Josh's self-consciousness fell away. "They ALL were in there! Do you know Star Trek?" he asked breathlessly.

"I only know Next Generation," she replied. Any familiarity with any iteration was an awesome thing in Josh's mind.

"When I was still a girl in Uganda, it was on Sunday nights. We watched it just before going to bed. Once we moved to America, we could watch it every day after school. I loved that show." Josh heard what she was saying but could barely believe it.

"My boss is a big Trekker! We talk in Klingon all the time." The truth of it was that Glenn knew a few key Klingon phrases, but she was far from having even a conversational understanding of Klingon. On the other end of that spectrum, Josh had attended workshops on speaking Klingon, and was fluent, with a deep grammatical understanding of the language and an expansive vocabulary to match. He carried the lion's share of those Klingon conversations, so Glenn only needed to periodically grunt or belly laugh to keep him going.

He thought a demonstration might be fun. "Qapla!" he cried out in his deepest guttural tone. Appreciatively, Agnes stated, "I doubt any member of the High Council could do better. Just to be clear, I can enjoy hearing it spoken, but I cannot speak it myself. I think that you can is awesome. Given what it sounds like Star Trek meant to you, I'm not surprised you can speak it well."

While compliments usually left Josh uncomfortable and unsure how to respond, a compliment to his linguistic skills was easily received. His personal feeling was that only ignorance would explain NOT being impressed, as it *was* learning a second language (even if the language in question was man-made).

"Thank you. Most folks think it's geeky and silly and make fun of me." He was not prepared for Agnes's reply.

"Well, it *is* geeky, and that's why I like it. I'm the geekiest black woman you're likely to find, and proud of it!" She flashed a grin that showed off all of her front teeth and several farther back too.

That comment and the subsequent grin gave Josh a floaty feeling in his chest again. He wasn't sure how to respond to such a statement. It did give him hope the evening was going to be fun. It would end up being three hours of fun discussing Star Trek, altruism in the Star Trek universe versus the real universe, and selfishness versus selflessness as it pertained to societal behavior. They both thoroughly enjoyed their evening and agreed they needed to repeat it.

Friday — Night

Tom Maki and his wife were enjoying their night out. Tom had called earlier in the day to verify the reservation for Hans Gruber at eight. The host confirmed it and Maki explained that to assist law enforcement, he would like that party to be seated in a corner while he was seated in the opposite corner. He allayed the hostess's fears of a scene by telling her there was no risk of violence in the restaurant and that the evening's purpose was solely observation. He did not burden her with the knowledge that the risk of violence for Mr. Gruber would change dramatically on the way back to his car.

They were midway through the appetizer of crab-stuffed mushrooms when a blonde woman was seated at the corner table. With her blonde hair perfectly feathered, she reminded Maki of Farrah Fawcett from a red swimsuit poster that adorned his bedroom wall for the latter four years of the seventies. Had Sandy been privy to his thoughts, she would have been fiercely proud of a complimentary comparison. She was not privy to his thoughts but nonetheless sported a wide anticipatory smile, thinking about what might be in store later that night.

Maki and his wife had been together long enough that when they ordered different sides, there was an understanding that everything would be split down the middle (this was taken as a given). However, there were occasions where this strategy was abandoned by one or the other of them, and tonight would end up being one of those occasions. When the waiter mentioned that the creamed spinach was a house classic, Maki had thought to himself, *Not even if you paid me.* He was aghast when his wife indicated if it was a classic, she couldn't pass it up. He had seen garlic mashed potatoes on the menu and did not have to read further to know what his side item was going to be. Her selection guaranteed (at least to him) that this was not shaping up to be a fifty-fifty kind of evening.

Watching the far table, he waited for 'Hans Gruber' to appear. The side dishes arrived, and Tom let his wife know she was welcome to take a bite from the baking dish of his whipped taters, but he made no move to deposit half of his potatoes on her plate. He stopped her when she tried to put half of her spinach goo on his plate, thanking her for the offer as he did. Her face crinkled up a bit at that. "Are you planning on keeping all those potatoes for yourself, Mister Man?" Her voice had both a crestfallen tone and an unmistakable miffed tone. Tom had been hoping to avoid both of those reactions. He desperately hoped Hans Gruber would appear and shift the focus away from him. Alas, it was not to be.

Glancing over at the far table, he noted that Hans's companion (still alone at the table) had already ordered her first glass of wine and was already close to finishing it. She powered down the last of the first glass and signaled the waiter for a second. Clearly, no one was happy with how the night was starting out. Refocusing on the side item discussion, he pointed out to his wife that he had offered up the coveted 'first bite' of his potatoes. That should have been proof positive of his affection and love for her.

"Hon, you have to understand while to you, we are out right now and having fun, this is also a stressful work situation for me. Tonight absolutely has to go by the numbers. I have zero room for error." Then he strategically added, "I'm sorry if it affected my manners or made you feel slighted in any way." While at the same time, he thought to himself, *Christ! It's potatoes!* He knew the things to say to defuse a looming argument. It wasn't that he was lying as he said it, he just wished it wasn't a necessary thing for him to say.

His wife's face softened and embarrassed, she said, "I'm sorry too, hon. I was reading a little far into the not instantly sharing your food and thinking it might be representative of your feelings about me." Tom turned completely to his wife, held her hand, and told her, "It had nothing to do with my feelings for you." A smile spread across his face. "It had to do with my feelings about your choice of side. Good Lord!" Shaking his head, he gave her hand a loving squeeze. "After more than two decades with you, my need for you in my life is stronger than ever, and I love that."

"Well, good thing because there is no escape for you," she responded with a chuckle meant just for him. He gave her a smile, another appreciative squeeze, and looked across the room. He was just in time to see the last of the second glass of wine going down the hatch. The woman's expression was not happy at all. Looking at his watch, he saw it was thirty-five minutes past the reservation time.

Discretely, he texted the surveillance team: Dammit - looks like our man might be a no show. No sign of him yet. Companion is worth showing up for - this doesn't make sense. As he finished the text, he saw a man walk towards the woman from the bar area. Maki tensed up, and as a cop's wife who knew her husband's body language well, his wife shifted her chair back to provide plenty of room for quick action, should it be needed.

Twelve years ago, she had learned that lesson the hard way. She had been his cover on a stakeout in another restaurant. The suspect had tried to make a run for it and Maki had vaulted the table like an Olympic athlete. Unfortunately, he did not clear the head of the woman acting as his cover. One oaken thigh clipped her head, sending her speedily to the (thankfully carpeted) floor. After the suspect was cuffed, Maki checked back with her, feeling mortified he had plowed through her like that. She emphasized that she was no shrinking violet and that she was proud of her man for capturing his man.

In the intervening years, a scenario like that one had never reoccurred. Yet the lesson was now at the forefront of her mind. Her husband coiled like a cougar as he watched the man walking over. The man offered some words; the sitting woman shook her head from side to side. The man then wandered back to the bar, looking a bit deflated, His gait was nowhere near as jaunty as it was on the way over. Maki untensed, as did his wife.

By the time the Maki's were on to dessert, the woman they were watching was on her fifth glass of wine, and she looked tearful and disappointed. She was far from the only person disappointed by her date not showing up. Maki did not believe anyone could have identified him or the team's van in the parking garage as police. It stood to reason if you made the effort to make a reservation at a restaurant, you'd show up. None of this made any sense. The chance to get some hard facts on the case was sinking away like a handful of gravel thrown off a dock.

Saturday — Morning

Johnson and Mugshot had gone out for some morning fun at an open-leash dog park. With no one to meet and no place to be, they played fetch with Mugshot's favorite frisbee for three hours, and it seemed like the dog had at least another hour in him. Conversely, Johnson was at the end of his rope, as every throw in the past three hours had been a full body wind-up and hundred-foot zinger. He was drained.

Making their way back to the parking lot, Mugshot stained his leash, showing off how much energy he still had to burn. As if on cue, Johnson's phone rang. Given Mugshot's lack of composure, he figured answering a voicemail (if one was left) was the right choice. Once Mugshot hopped into the car, he pulled out his phone to check if it was someone he knew.

Surprisingly, Tom Ollig had called before nine in the morning on a Saturday. The voicemail didn't sound stressed at all, just an inquiry asking if he wanted to meet for Bloody Marys around ten over at the Ollig homestead. As he had nothing on his agenda until his date that night, he thought that would be a good way to finish out the morning. He enjoyed Ollig's kids, and they enjoyed Mugshot. Maybe the kids would tucker out Mugshot.

Getting in, he tousled Mugshot's ears and asked, "Who's the good boy? Who's the best boy? It's you, isn't it? Oh yes it is! Oh yes it *is!*" With the windows up and no one around to hear, he let his inner goofiness out with exaggerated inflections. Mugshot enjoyed the vocal gymnastics and jumped into the front seat, play-bowing and barking in excitement.

Smelling himself as he sat in the driver's seat, he was glad the invite was for ten so he could go home and shower off his pungent post-frisbee stench. Mugshot didn't seem to mind, but Johnson did mind. He was reminded of one of his father's classic lines: 'Damn boy, you'd knock a fly off a gut wagon!'

Half an hour later and now fresh as a daisy, he headed over to the casa de Ollig with Mugshot. As he pulled up in front of the house, he noticed a man standing in the yard he didn't recognize. As soon as the engine was off, the man hustled over. "Hi there! I'm Tom's brother Harry! I'm a bit of a gearhead and muscle car fan.

"Tom said he had a friend with a Judge, but I never dreamed it'd be this good-looking. That purple flake paint has got to be custom. Listening to you pull up, am I right in thinking there are 370 horses under the hood? Oh! This is like stepping back in time! Your car is absolutely gorgeous!" The man almost vibrated with excitement.

Tom shouted from the front the front door, "Harry! Let the man get a drink first. Calm your ass down!" Chastised, Harry hung his head and stepped back from the car in silence. Conspiratorially, Johnson whispered to Harry, "I will not leave today until we have the time for a proper geek-out. I have loads of stories to share about the old girl."

As he stepped away from his door, Mugshot took the opportunity to leap out, determined to meet this new friend and give the man the chance to meet such a good boy as himself. Harry did not disappoint. "Well, hello!" he exclaimed, "Who is this?!" he asked as he gave Mugshot an energetic backscratching.

"That is Mugshot. He might lick you senseless, but he doesn't bite," Johnson offered as he walked away. He had only gotten halfway across the yard when cries of 'Mugshot!', 'Mugsy!', and 'the Mug-sti-nator!' erupted from the house as both boys burst forth, beelining to the middle of the yard.

As exciting as it was for Mugshot to meet a new friend, it was nothing compared to the fun he always had with the little humans. Their yells were scarcely out of their mouths when the bulldog turned and hurtled to the middle of the yard in a muscle-stretching sprint. All three bodies got to the middle of the yard at the same time and collapsed into a writhing, rolling pile of arms, legs, and paws. Giggles and barks came from the pile.

Content to leave the dogpile as-is, Johnson continued to the house, clapped Ollig on the shoulder, and went up to the front door. Entering the living room, Johnson saw the coffee table loaded up with Bloody Mary fixings, in addition to a half-devoured plate of bacon-sprinkled deviled eggs. "Thanks for the eggs, Gwen!" he shouted, recognizing the artistry in the spiral yolk patterns as her handiwork. He grabbed a glass, admired the tangerine-sized ice cubes, and began making his drink.

"There's a freshly opened jar of pickles in the middle of the table if you want to add a little magic," Ollig suggested playfully. Johnson closed his eyes and counted to ten.

Opening his eyes, he put an entire deviled egg in his mouth to shut himself up. It helped that he knew they were always delicious. Shoveling them in was always the right thing to do.

Harry came in, red-faced. "Chasing around that dog of yours is a young man's game. He's way too quick for me and these knees and hips. The good news is I knew drinks were a-waiting!" He smiled and started making himself a drink. Johnson let out an audible sigh as Harry poured a healthy shot of pickle juice into his glass. Turning to the source of the sigh, Harry commented, "There are none so blind as those who will not see. My brother mentioned you were a purist in most things. The Olligs are tradition breakers from way back." He laughed and solemnly finished, "And that has made all the difference."

Gwen came in from the kitchen and admonished both Ollig brothers, "Leave him be, you outlaws. Try this on the eggs and let me know what you think." She put a spice shaker on the table with a Flatiron Pepper label. Without hesitation, both brothers theatrically moaned, grabbed an egg, and liberally applied the flakes before throwing back the entire shebang. The moans increased in volume, and Harry began to chortle as well. "Hot *and* flavorful. You cannot go wrong with Flatiron. Thank you, Gwen!" Harry hadn't finished completely swallowing and thus sprayed a few bits of egg as he yelled his thank-you, but his appreciation of those pepper flakes trumped his manners.

Johnson tried a light sprinkling on his egg. Hot was certainly one word to describe it, although he felt that blistering might be more apt. He drained his drink and chewed up several of the cheese curds that had been intended for garnish and hoped they'd help with the burn. They did take the worst of the heat away, although the slow burn in the back of his throat remained untouched.

Astoundingly, the brothers were eating more eggs, and applying more and more of the flakes. While his competitive urge wanted to show that he could hang with the big dogs, his throat reminded him that would be pure foolishness. Even just five years ago, his self-preservation would have lost immediately to his ego in a contest like that. He felt a little pride in his maturity journey that he could put down one last egg without the need to punish or prove himself by adding even one more pepper flake.

The three men laughed and traded stories from days gone by. As is typical when brothers get together with any kind of audience, embarrassing stories came up, alternating subjects from one brother to the other. Johnson trotted out a few colorful stories from his own youth as a matter of decorum; certainly, they were not needed to keep the conversation rolling.

When things were winding down, Johnson asked Harry if he'd like to take a ride and do a little cruising. They ended up driving around for forty minutes as Harry asked question after question about the car. When they got back, Mugshot was playing fetch with the boys. His pace was noticeably slower than when he arrived. *Those kids never fail,* Johnson thought to himself. It would be an early bedtime for someone while he was out on his date that night.

Saturday — Night

Crossing the street with more than a little steam in his stride, Johnson's smile was apparent from a block away. Stepping through the double doors of Bad Axe, the first thing he noticed was that the place was huge. The second thing noticed was the sound of many grunts of exertion. Looking around he counted at least fifteen lanes, almost all of them taken by large groups. From the desk, a man loudly greeted him. "Welcome to Bad Axe! How can I help you tonight?"

Johnson replied he was waiting for a date. The man behind the desk winced as he heard those words. "It might be a goodly while before we get an opening. Saturdays are our biggest night. Would you have made a reservation?"

Uncertainly, Johnson volunteered, "Well, *she* might have. Maybe under the name Michelle?" The man behind the front desk looked up. "Michelle? Fit blonde gal?" Somewhat taken aback, Johnson simply nodded. "She's the best gal we've got on our league team." Looking at his monitor, the man then confirmed his suspicions. "You two have the league lane. Number eleven. If you want to warm up now, you can grab a basket of axes. Order a drink here, and we'll bring it down to you."

Taking all that in, Johnson realized he would be well served to lower his expectations for the number of games he would be winning that night. Walking down to their lane, he picked up a basket of the newest-looking axes. Once at their lane, he took several practice throws. Not one of them stuck. One did bounce back far enough that he had to jump out of the way. He was happy to see no one was paying any attention to anything but their own games, thus no one had seen him jumping around like an epileptic frog.

He was gathering up the thrown axes when he heard Michelle say from behind him, "Getting in a few practice rounds, eh? I will let you know now, I don't play for money. So no hustling." He turned around with a grin. Michelle was wearing all black. Black boots, black slacks, and a black short-sleeved shirt that read, "I don't bury hatchets; I throw them." The shirt did make him chuckle, but he couldn't look away from her hair. Her entire head was encircled by braids of various sizes. Noting his gaze, she explained, "I have a niece who needed to practice braiding for her cosmetology final. I think she did a good job." Johnson agreed, a little surprised by how much it changed her appearance.

"I understand I'm on a date with a ringer. Are you really in a league?" Johnson inquired.

"I am on a league team with five guys. They all throw axes and knives. I just throw axes, and occasionally very cute temper tantrums." She laughed long and loud at that. Johnson laughed as well, although he wondered how much truth was in that statement. 'When someone tells you who they are, believe them.' His mother was an ardent fan of that saying.

"I think we may need to come up with a way to even the odds." He racked his brain and then said with a smile of his own "For instance, we could say that you must sing and dance when you throw. That way, even when you crush me like a flabby grape, I'll still be entertained."

Michelle looked at him, clearly baffled. "Seriously?" was all that she could muster.

"As a heart attack. This is already looking to be an ego-decimating evening for me. I would request you give me a little something for agreeing to walk into this lion's den with you." Michelle weighed this over. It was a ridiculous idea, but this was a first date and fun should be the goal. "Deal. Maybe for fun, we can say every fourth throw, you do something goofy too." Johnson agreed that sounded fair and, even better, fun.

With the ground rules laid, they flipped a coin to see who would start. Michelle called 'heads' while the coin was on the way up. Johnson caught it in one hand and slapped it onto his other hand with a flourish. "Oh, what showmanship!" Michelle remarked. Removing the covering hand, they saw Gentleman George looking up, reminding both of them that in George's day, it had always been 'Ladies First'. Michelle grabbed an axe and stepped to the line.

Without warning, she started bobbing up and down, knees splaying outwards. While holding her arms straight down, she started to sing with a Cockney accent so thick you could slice it. "Ahh-ve got a lurverly bunch a coconuts, there they are, standin' in a row…" Johnson couldn't help guffawing at the unexpected sight and sound of this spectacle. Michelle whipped her axe from a crouched position, sticking it a few inches to the left on the bullseye. That dried up Johnson's laughter.

Michelle gave him a deep curtsy and a smirk, then stepped off the line. Johnson grabbed the newest-looking axe, hefted it a few times to look like he knew what he was doing, and threw the axe with all the force he could muster. It hit the target sideways, vibrating it hard enough to shake Michelle's axe free. He looked back hopefully. "Does that count for anything?" "Nothing at all, although that kind of force is impressive on its own," was the mirthful reply.

"May I offer a suggestion?" she asked warily. This would often get prickly. Lots of guys got their dander up getting advice from a woman in anything perceived as a manly subject, no matter what the woman's credentials were. Happily, her date indicated he was open to anything she might share. "Make the same throw every time, and only change your distance from the target. Once get your magic distance figured, you'll be unstoppable." She stepped up the line, tangoed her way to the side and back, and then threw her axe right in the middle of the bullseye. Johnson gave her a low whistle of approval, which she accepted graciously.

Stepping up to the line, Johnson noted he was about fifteen feet from the target. Cocking his arm, he did his best to copy the easy throw of Michelle. The axe spun through the air and embedded itself in the bottom middle of the target board. While he was surprised and pleased with himself, he was a little surprised when, from behind, he heard Michelle give a victory shout and then yell, "You big stud! Nice throw!"

It reminded him that the evening was not supposed to be adversarial, but recreational. He turned to face her. "Thank you, thank you. I would like to thank my mother for making me possible," he said with a bow and a grin. Michelle started playing music on her phone. "If I'm going to be doing a song and dance as part of every throw, I want some backup," she explained. She sidled up to the line and started swinging her hips as she sang "Black Velvet." While the hip-swinging was provocative and something he would normally focus on, it was her singing that left him transfixed again.

"Good God," he stammered. "That is amazing. Why aren't you in a band?" he asked earnestly. Michelle answered, "Aren't you sweet? No, the closest I come to singing gigs is a karaoke night with a bunch of gals. Some of them are super good. Regardless of who's singing, we can always count on a good time." She smiled, thinking of her last time out with them. One of the gals had brought a friend along who not only had wonderful tips on hair care but also received a standing ovation from the entire bar when he perfectly belted out the theme song from the show *True Blood*. One of the gals followed that up with *Dancing Queen* and had a little choreographed routine to go along with her singing. It was the kind of night where you went home with sore ribs from all the laughing.

Switching topics, Michelle asked, "Since things are going well between us tonight, can I run a few possible nicknames past you?" That sentence made Johnson's heart soar. He had also been thinking the evening was progressing well, and to find out that she thought so too, without having to fumble around to acquire that info, was exhilarating. "Fire when ready, Gridley!"

"How does Scottie Mac grab you? I know you aren't Scottish, but it would be fun to say." The one-sided grimace that slid across his face was answer enough. "Okay, how about schmoopsie-poo?" That got an involuntary chuckle. Johnson replied "Absolutely not. Let's try another."

"Fair enough," Michelle said. "Since we both know what a johnson is slang for, what do you think of Heavy D?" While Johnson did know of and even liked that artist, he was a little wary about outsized expectations that could accompany that nickname. He answered, "I'd prefer something original, but I like that line of thinking!"

Michelle responded with, "Since we know where johnsons like to end up, how about confounding expectations, and I call *you* Muffin? Maybe Mr. Muffins if I'm feeling extra lovey?" Johnson tried to scowl, quite unsuccessfully. That suggestion was so ludicrous he couldn't help but laugh. Michelle chuckled as well. "Let's call that the temporary winner, and if we come up with something better down the road, we can always modify as warranted." Johnson nodded in agreement, still laughing at the abject silliness of it.

"I believe it's your throw, Muffin," Michelle said with a sugary tone. Trying not to show just how much he liked having a secret pet name, Johnson stepped to the line, measured his distance from the target, and threw. The axe sailed to the target and again stuck in the bottom middle. "Right on!" Michelle shouted. Her enthusiasm made him feel a lot better about losing. Michelle stepped up and threw a perfect bullseye.

Knowing he would be seeing many more of those from a league player, Johnson consciously decided to be a good sport and loudly cheered the bullseye. It did not go unnoticed. Michelle was feeling some excitement of her own. Finding a man who could put his ego aside and could also laugh at himself was like finding buried treasure. Finding one that could celebrate others' victories even when he knew it was at the cost of his own victory was even rarer. The night played out even better than either of them had hoped.

Sunday — Morning

Gail and Steve Ballard strode through the doors of the Robbinsdale shooting range displaying a confidence Gail wished she felt. The fact that she had to bring someone to accompany her underscored how helpless things seemed. Her favorite pastime, which had been a source of joy for decades, was now badly tainted, and she could only hope to find some kind of mental reset. Ballard had offered to help Gail the way she had helped him and had volunteered to spend his Sunday morning with her.

Passing through the mantrap, they walked to the far lane and began unpacking their gear. Gail selected the far lane because she wanted as much privacy as she could get. If she was going to lock up again, she did not want anyone else to see it. Opening her gun case, Gail took her Glock-24 to the range tray and then came back to load her clip. So far, so good. She felt nothing that could get in the way of a good time yet. Carrying the clip to the range tray, she slapped the clip firmly into the gun and racked a bullet into the chamber. Again, so far, so good.

"Here you go," said Ballard as he attached a paper zombie target to the target bar and sent it downrange, stopping around the thirty-foot mark. They were intentionally avoiding targets with any kind of humanity. Ballard stepped backward out of the shooter's box. Gail picked up her gun. No issues were creeping in, she observed. *Maybe I just needed to have someone by my side*, she speculated.

She pulled up into her shooting stance and drew down on the target. That was when things fell apart. She felt a flutter in her chest and was suddenly hot everywhere. *Just like menopause,* she groused. As she tried to aim, a bead of sweat trickled into her eye. "Dammit!" she cursed, putting the gun down and wiping her forehead and temples angrily.

"Gail, what's happening with you right now? What are you feeling?" Ballard asked with a concerned tone. "Everything seemed to be fine right up to your aiming." Frustrated, Gail lamented, "Everything *was* fine! As soon as I brought the gun up, I got a hot flash and a feeling of dread." Looking at Ballard, she plaintively asked, "What's wrong with me? I don't like this."

Ballard looked directly at her and said, "Gail, there is nothing wrong in the slightest with you. You experienced a massively traumatic event. You are, at heart, a kind and good woman. An extenuating circumstance forced you to protect people you love with potentially lethal force. Even then, your nature wouldn't allow the taking of human life. You might be horrified by what you did, but you did it because you wanted to avoid any loss of life. While you are clearly upset by what you had to do, you also need to remember that you couldn't have known that his gun was empty. You took the actions you did to arrive at the best possible outcome. I will tell you straight out, you are a fucking hero. A. Hero. Always remember that."

Gail took this in. Her Scandinavian heritage did not want to accept such self-aggrandizing sentiments, but then she weighed it over in her mind and decided there was a fair bit of validity to what Steve was saying. His words actually did make her feel better about herself, and she thanked him for it. "That means an awful lot to hear that from someone in our line of work. Thank you for putting that in a way I needed to hear it. I'm not a bad person for shooting someone who looked like they were going to shoot my friends. You're an awesome friend for helping me see that." Ballard told her he was just painting the lay of the land in a way that she could see it for what it was, and he was helping a friend who had helped him.

"Now let's dust some zombie fuckwads!" he said as he put his arm around her shoulders, giving her a friendly squeeze. Gail slung an arm around his waist and returned the squeeze. "Let's do. And thanks again." Between the two of them, they went through twenty-five zombie targets in the next hour. Feeling more herself than she had since the actual shooting, every shot of hers was a headshot. That was not a claim Ballard came close to making, but helping Gail find some peace was what he considered an ample reward.

Monday — Lunch

One more reason to love autumn in the office was that there were ten birthdays in three months, which translated to a potluck-o-ganza. Bricks was in the breakroom, eyeing the offerings spread out on the tables when a young woman he didn't recognize walked in with crockpot. While late additions to potlucks were not unusual, the woman herself was quite unusual. Jet black with no hair, Bricks had never seen anyone like her.

"There's normally not much color at these potlucks. I think you might have enough color for five or six people." He grinned as he said it to make sure she would know how he meant it. Agnes grinned back.

"This coming from a brother who barely passes the brown paper bag test?!" Bricks laughed out loud. "OK, you got me. Who are you here to see?" The level of her confidence had his money on Carmen, who didn't seem to have friends who weren't brassy and wildly confident.

"Josh Dubrik. Do you know him?" Luckily Bricks was not drinking anything yet, or he might have made quite a mess. As it was, his eyes widened, and his jaw dropped comically. For sure, Josh would have been his dead-last choice. Agnes was not terribly surprised by the reaction, but she did find Brick's facial reaction laugh-out-loud funny.

"What in the world has the darkest ebony sister I have ever seen coming to see the weirdest little white guy we've got?" Bricks wasn't being mean; it was genuinely incomprehensible to him. Agnes let him know she was looking for someone with intelligence over anything else.

"He does have that in spades," Bricks admitted. Pausing for a moment to replay what he'd asked out loud, he added "no offense" with an over-the-top grin. Agnes dramatically rolled her eyes, then chuckled as well.

"My name is Agnes. What is yours?" With a shrug, Bricks said, "Everyone just calls me Bricks. Nice to meet you, Agnes." Agnes offered a head nod and then asked, "Is that moniker related to you being built like a brick shithouse?"

"It is not," answered Bricks.

"Well, do tell," Agnes prompted.

"Many years ago, when I was a trainee, we got a call where a guy had two bricks thrown through his windows. We show up and the guy is going berserk. He's demanding we fingerprint the bricks. I'm trying in vain to explain why you can't get fingerprints off a porous brick and this guy is having none of it. My trainer breaks in and tells me to put the bricks in the car, then he tells the guy if we get usable prints, we'll call him. He gives the guy a report for insurance, and we head out.

"He stops at a construction site a few miles away and says to me, 'Let me show you how we process bricks,' and chucks them next to a dumpster. Then he tells me that 'No one wants to hear we can't do anything for them, even if it's the truth. So instead, you tell them the evidence is being worked. A few days later you call and tell them no prints matched the federal database, which technically is true. Everyone ends up happy that way.'

"I was so impressed with the genius of this that I retold that story to everyone and at every happy hour for weeks. Eventually, someone commented that since I loved to tell that story so much, maybe folks should just call me Bricks. It's been Bricks ever since."

He finished his story and opened his arms wide. Agnes gave him a little burst of applause. "That's a story worth telling," she said with admiration in her voice. "If I kept it to myself, would you be willing to share your real name with me?" Bricks looked at her and then dramatically looked around the room. Leaning in, he raised a hand to shield his mouth from view and stage whispered, "It's Cedric. But you didn't hear that from me." He gave her a grave stare and then his poker face cracked, and he laughed at himself. Agnes laughed as well and let him know she would keep that information to herself.

Josh walked up to the doorway, saw Agnes standing there, and let her know he had to talk to the sheriff and then he would be right back. Agnes gave him an exaggerated thumbs up and, in her best authoritarian voice, said, "Make it so, Ensign Dubrik." Josh grinned ear to ear at that. Bricks rolled his eyes and said, "It's becoming clearer why you are here for him."

Walking down the hallway, Josh knocked on the door frame. Glenn looked up from her phone call, saw it was Josh, and motioned him in. Finishing her call, she mentioned that Josh was becoming quite the social butterfly. "You don't know the half of it! I invited Agnes to come to our potluck and she accepted! She's talking to Bricks right now. However, I have something completely different to talk about. I have a new theory on the Deakins case," Josh declared.

Hearing those words, Glenn stood and moved in front of her desk. "Tell me you found some hard facts somewhere," she said with anticipation evident in her voice. Josh was excited as well, moving to sit on the front edge of a chair. "Well, after Friday night fizzled, I took the liberty of putting out a BOLO for rebreathers with the TSA and the state patrol, in case our guy was trying to leave. I didn't figure he'd leave dive equipment worth thousands of dollars behind. This morning, state patrol called to say on Friday they found a dead driver on 35W with a suitcase and a rebreather in his trunk. The picture of the body looked like someone who looked like Jason Statham. I would like to take the picture to the dive shop for confirmation, but I think they will confirm he was our bad guy."

Glenn's hope for a speedy resolution to the case seemed to be coming to fruition. She let out a long sigh and dropped her head. While she was dismayed their only possible suspect was dead and unable to confess, she tempered that frustration with the knowledge that he wouldn't be killing anyone else. "Again, that was brilliant insight and superb initiative on your part. This would be followed up as an accidental drowning case if not for you. Consider your pay raised as of today." She felt a warm rush of gratitude for Josh and the unusual way his brain worked. With a savage voice, she shouted, "Qapla!" and jumped up, raising her fists above her head, pumping them in victory.

"Oh, there's a lot more" Josh trembled with excitement. "When they ran the prints on the driver, it turns out his name was Jan de Boer, and he was on Interpol's wanted list. He was a hitman for hire. Top shelf, by all accounts. That fits with the circumstances around Mayor Deakins' demise. But why would a hitman from Holland care about a Minnesota mayor? The answer is because he was paid to care by someone.

"The sale of the rebreather also included a small air tank with an integrated mouthpiece. That was *not* in the car. Why? I believe it was used up when whoever got Deakins out there on his boat jumped into the water after Deakins was killed and the assassin then towed him underwater to the shore. No one would notice two divers come out on the shore in the evening. The hitman died the morning after we announced Deakin's death was a homicide, not a drowning. I don't believe that's a coincidence. The ME had asphyxiation as the cause of death for this Jan guy. Who asphyxiates in a car on the open road? I believe whoever hired him was tying off loose ends."

Glenn listened to Josh spin his theory. She went from exultant, to incredulous, to angry. "So are you saying if we get a positive ID from the sales staff to confirm this Jan guy bought the rebreather, he is likely the murderer? But we would have nothing on the person who hired him or the reason why?!" The emotion in her voice made Josh afraid to answer. He offered a timid yes, and Glenn exploded, yelling "Goddammit!" Josh reacted by trying to make himself as small as possible in the chair. Seeing that, Glenn clarified, "I'm not mad at you, Josh. I'm mad at the situation. Wild as your theory is, it feels right to me. Without you, we would not have connected these dots. It just doesn't look like there are more dots to connect going forward."

Josh made a face of sorrowful agreement. "That is where I see the investigation drying up as well. Without some clue from the hitman, we have no way forward from here. I requested his phone be sent here for analysis in hopes we get something from that." Josh didn't like the idea of an unsolvable puzzle and was ready to put every ounce of his attention on the phone when it arrived. Out loud, he said "Nothing to do but wait around until we get his phone. I'm going to the potluck now. Would you like to meet Agnes?"

Glenn responded, "Would I like to meet the woman who is bringing my top resource out of his shell?! Hell yes I would! Let's go!" Josh was happy to have someone to show off and to eat with. Walking into the breakroom he started out with introductions. "Agnes, let me introduce Glenn Campbell, Ramsey County Sheriff. Glenn, this is Agnes Okelo of the BCA." Josh had commented on Agnes's appearance, but Glenn was a little taken aback by how striking the woman was. On the surface at least, it appeared as though Josh had outpunted his coverage.

"I brought a stew as our entry," Agnes volunteered. "Chicken with potatoes and carrots." "Well, that sounds grand," said Glenn. "Why don't you two start in? I have some things to tend to before I eat." That was an understatement. Josh's information bomb was still going off in her mind and she needed to do some thinking without any interruptions.

Josh grabbed a plate, handed one to Agnes, and surveyed the offerings. The first crockpot in line was Gail's and it had been scoured clean. Only the scent of something south of the border remained. Happily, Josh saw there was still enough tater-tot hotdish left in the second crockpot that he could have a full scoop while leaving enough for Agnes.

Little of what was left looked good to him. He took a ladle's worth of Agnes's stew and grabbed some cheese and prosciutto from the picked-over remains of a decimated charcuterie board. Sitting down, he tried Agnes's stew first and was surprised by the light flavor. "Agnes, this is wonderful! What is the flavor here? I cannot identify it."

Agnes felt a wave of pride at his enjoyment of her cooking, and relayed to him that nuts, fruits, and vegetables were a huge part of Uganda cuisine and that in this stew, the flavor he was trying to identify was crushed cashews. Playfully she softly said, "I know my way around handling nuts." Her attempt at flirting never even made it onto Josh's radar.

Slurping up the last of the stew, he said, "I guess you do! I really liked that." He looked up at Agnes and gave her a wide smile to underscore how much he meant what he was saying. Agnes gave him a smile back and realized her keen flirting game wouldn't amount to much in this relationship. But when you could have a cute, intellectual man who was monogamous (if even that), retiring said game seemed like small potatoes.

Monday — Evening

Given that the weather was cooling down and this might be one of the last evening parking lot potlucks for the year, it was no surprise most people showed up and were enjoying themselves. Dave had used his new extension cord to bring his roller grill out, and even with his wife bringing the large cooler filled with brats, they had not been able to get out ahead of demand. As soon as one batch was finished, they were gone within minutes. The steel holding pan intended to hold the surplus brats was emptier than a Ponzi schemer's heart.

Talya was sitting beside Dave with a small cooler of her brats by her side. She had gone home to get her brats and had also brought three one-pound bags of sauerkraut with her. Half of one bag was all that was left at this point. To Dave, Talya's brats were like a time machine, consistently taking him back to trips from his youth. Closing his eyes as he finished his third 'Turkish brat,' he could see the stands of various spice vendors and felt the excitement he had lived with constantly at that time in his life. It would be easy to suspect there might be some 'extra ingredients' in those brats, given Dave's relaxed stance as he lounged in his chair with a complacent, dreamy smile, but it was only his joy of reliving those days.

Bryce Miller was regaling Bricks and Tom Ollig with a story of a co-worker who had been in the bathroom for thirty minutes towards the end of the day. When Bryce went in to check on him, he heard strained and extended grunting from the stall. That groan ended with a cute <bloop> as something tiny hit the water. Given the amount of exertion for such a meager result, Bryce had barely made it back out into the hallway before collapsing in gales of laughter. Bricks and Ollig were both in tears of laughter, just hearing the story secondhand. Bryce completed the tale with, "The kicker was, I ended up pissing my own pants right there in the hallway. Had to go home early. That was a soggy drive." Bricks heard that last line and started screaming with laughter. That finishing line had the opposite effect on Ollig, who was almost paralyzed with laughter. Ollig was wheezing and was staying upright only by slinging an arm over Brick's massive shoulders. That someone else was laughing so hard they had to support themselves by clinging to him only extended Brick's screaming fits of laughter.

The noise had everyone looking for the source. When they saw that Bryce was in the middle of it, most immediately knew who was to blame and went back to their conversations.

"Now that is the very definition of an odd couple," opined Callie to Gail and Glenn as she looked at Josh and Agnes. Glenn replied, "You never know where you might find a good partner. Remember, just because something doesn't make sense to you doesn't mean it doesn't make sense. While it might not surprise you to hear Josh is a Trekker…"

"It does not," Callie interjected in a low voice.

Carrying on, Glenn added, "It might surprise you to know I'm a Trekker from way back, and Agnes is a Trekker, too." Callie immediately regretted her comment, bowed her head, and focused on the clenched hands in her lap. "In this case," Glenn continued, "Star Trek is the common element that brought together young and old, black and white. I think that's pretty cool."

"It sure is!" Callie quickly agreed, hoping to minimize the snarky impact of her earlier comment. Thinking of other things she knew Glenn liked, she offered "Who knows, maybe ABBA could cross those lines too, you just don't know it yet." The evening would indeed be taking an unexpected turn into ABBA territory shortly, but no one would have imagined it.

Johnson's car pulled into the lot, its headlights sweeping the area. Surprising everyone that looked over that way, someone got out of the passenger side. Even more surprising to onlookers, it was a woman. The two of them were heading over to the brats when a voice called out disbelievingly, "Michelle?" Looking around, Michelle excitedly shouted, "Dancing Queen!" She hopped over to Glenn and hugged the sheriff. Not one person knew how to react to such unbridled affection being showered on their boss. Seeing the sheriff laughing and hugging the woman back only increased everyone's feelings of disbelief.

"I would not have guessed you were police," Michelle declared.

"She is the Sheriff of Ramsey County" Callie clarified.

'Apple polisher', Johnson thought to himself.

Glenn said nothing, merely shrugging. A huge smile suddenly spread over Michelle's face, and she started to fiddle with her phone. Glenn had a good idea of what her friend was up to. "Don't do it," she advised Michelle.

ABBA's hit *Dancing Queen* surged from Michelle's phone. Glenn was well aware that every eye was checking out the commotion. "I am not singing this at my work," Glenn protested. The entire parking lot started cheering, "Glenn! Glenn! Glenn!"

Glenn was able to hold out through one verse and one chorus, shaking her head in protest. She sang softly with the second vers, resulting in boisterous cheers and whistles. With that encouragement (and to the surprise of everyone except Michelle), she really belted out the next chorus and finished out the rest of the song, accompanying the singing with some vintage disco moves. The parking lot dissolved into chaos, with war whoops, cheers, and general clapping. "Big Kahuna!" came a shout from the brats area. With the spell of the song now gone, Glenn stood there with an 'I-can't-believe-I-did-that' look on her face. Michelle led the crowd in a chant of "Glenn! Glenn! Glenn!" with a huge grin on her face.

A woman entered the parking lot on a bike, firing into the turns like a race car, and skidding to a halt in front of Bryce. She was wearing a tightly buckled trench coat. To him, she said, "You should come home now. Naughty Gretchen is waiting." She opened the bottom of the jacket so that only Bryce could see. The message delivered, she got on her bike and pedaled back the way she'd come from. Even though he had been in the middle of telling another story, he stopped, locked his folding chair shut, and slung it over his shoulder. Ollig chuckled, "She's got you on a short leash tonight, Bryce?" To which Bryce replied, "You don't understand, and I wouldn't expect you to. Naughty Gretchen is a version of my wife who is very open sexually, and very adventurous. She shows up four or five times a year. You could superglue me to this chair, and I'd still make it home now!" Flashing a risqué grin, he hit the bricks at a crisp pace, a man on a mission.

Tuesday — Late Afternoon

Josh knocked on Glenn's door. Given the serious expression on his face, Glenn asked him to close the door on his way in. Josh sat in one of the comfy chairs and began with, "I have a lot of information for you." Glenn felt a thrill in her stomach anticipating more information about the Deakins case. She marveled at how comfortable Josh was getting at meeting women face-to-face, and wondered how much of that could be attributed to having Agnes in his life.

"I received Jan de Boer's phone this morning. There was a single number in Recents, and the same number was also in Texts. That other number was a burner phone that we ended up locating in a Minnetonka gas station trash can. There were no prints, but we confirmed that those phones were communicating with each other. There were several texts calling for a meeting in various hotels. Every one of those rooms had been booked under a false name. The person signing for those rooms was clearly aware of the camera systems and was disguised. So that line of attack gave us nothing but dead ends."

Glenn cursed the luck they were running up against now. While it was a good thing the murderous puppet was out of the picture, she really wanted to nab the puppeteer. Things were not shaping up well for that to happen. Josh didn't seem like he was finished detailing his findings, so she still held out some measure of hope there was good news yet to come.

"I took the photo of the dead man to the dive shop to get a confirmation he was the purchaser of the rebreather. I did get that confirmed." Josh didn't believe the saleswoman's crying jag over seeing her dead 'husband-to-be' in the photo was anything the sheriff wanted to hear about. "So, we can reasonably conclude that Jan de Boer did the actual killing of Mayor Deakins. We have no clues as to who would have hired him. His round-trip ticket to Amsterdam was paid for in cash. I have exhausted every possibility I can think of. As far as this case is concerned, there is nothing else that will provide further information about who did the hiring."

Glenn's hopes came crashing down, knocking the wind from her sails. "So the guy that set this whole thing in motion gets away Scot free?! Shit!" She couldn't believe the case had hit a brick wall like this. It took a minute, and then she realized there was no sound in the room. Looking at Josh, she saw he was sitting motionless, staring straight ahead. He looked like a taxidermized pet. Apologetically, she confided in Josh, "I'm just upset the architect of this is not going to face the justice he deserves. I'm pissed at the situation. However, without you, we never would have tied Jan de Boer to this crime. You have performed magic with this case and that is no exaggeration. It is remembered by everyone involved with this case. Please let me know if you need anything, because you deserve a reward for your work on this."

While Glenn wasn't expecting any requests from Josh, his next comment threw her for a loop. In a quiet voice, Josh began, "I really enjoyed hunting the information down for this case. I would like to apply for the next Investigator position that comes along." Glenn tried to reason through this. She started by asking Josh, "Do you realize that will put you in a position where your job will be talking to strangers all day, every day? You have been exceptional with this case. No doubt. I am proud of the job you've done here. I'm just a little shocked to hear you have any interest in taking on a public facing position. This is completely unlike the man I've known for eight years, who only started talking to me face-to-face in the last two weeks."

Josh analyzed the situation more as well. "That does seem to be a disqualifying aspect I hadn't considered. Is there any position on the investigation side that doesn't require that kind of daily interaction?" Glenn racked her brain, then conceded she couldn't think of one off the top of her head. Slumping in his chair, Josh looked every bit the epitome of dejection. Not wanting to run the risk of Josh looking for greener pastures, Glenn offered, "That doesn't mean we couldn't create a position that formally would let you stretch those creative muscles. Let me work something up and run it past a few folks."

Josh was not a political animal, but he knew the creation of a new position was always a political process. He was grateful to hear Glenn was willing to make that effort. He looked forward to telling Agnes about how his talk went with the sheriff. Glenn was dead on suspecting that having Agnes in his life was expanding his horizons.

The sheriff was an excellent judge of character, and she liked Agnes out of the gate. The woman didn't seem to have any ulterior motives regarding Josh. That relieved Glenn's maternal feelings regarding Josh. Despite his towering intellect, he was still quite naive and an easy mark for liars and manipulators. Seeing the two of them together was not something anyone would have predicted, but they both clearly delighted in being with each other. Looking at this from Josh's side of things, it looked like puppy love. Glenn truly hoped this would not end with someone's heart being broken.

ONE YEAR LATER

Tuesday — Lunch

Bill Larson looked around the breakroom and spotted his old trainer, Lance. He sauntered over and sat down, a toothy and joyless smile on his face. "Remember the drunk driver case last year in North Oaks? The driver killed a little girl?" Lance gave a wordless nod. Bill continued, "I took today off because it finally went to trial. The defendant was dressed to the nines, trying not to look like the soulless piece of shit she is. The prosecution showed pictures from the little girl's autopsy, including a picture of her face with a Mercedes logo imprinted in it. The jury took all of twenty minutes to deliberate before coming back with a guilty on all counts verdict.

Bill sat back, stretched his shoulders, and exclaimed "HA!" in what Lance thought was a sterling example of schadenfreude. Lance decided to offer one last piece of wisdom to his former trainee. "I'm glad to hear there was justice but let me offer some advice: This job *is* dealing with awful shit. If you let it, it will eat you up from the inside and burn you out to the point where you won't be able to do the job. Caring about others is never a bad thing, but not everyone can do this job. We can't afford to lose the people who *can* do it to burn out. Just a thought for you."

Bill heard the advice and struggled with it. Lance's wisdom was usually to be heeded, but today he didn't want to temper his angry joy at seeing this selfish poser getting what she deserved. Ironically, he knew it was exactly what Lance had just described, he simply wasn't in a place to implement it. *Going forward, I'll calm the hell down*, he thought to himself. Out loud, he said, "That's good advice. Thank you." He got up, and walked out, feeling a bit deflated. He had really wanted to gloat with someone over justice being served, and that second helpings were going to be mandatory.

He passed Johnson on the stairs, and they exchanged mumbled hellos. Johnson came in and sat down next to Ollig. "I need to talk to you and get some relationship insight," he threw out.

"I'll do my best, but I promise nothing!" Ollig smiled as he repeated one of his favorite pet phrases.

"This is going to be pretty personal. Are you okay with moving to the conference room?" Without a single word, Ollig stood up from his lunch and walked down to the conference room.

Johnson entered behind his friend and closed the door. Ollig wondered what subject would require this kind of privacy with his friend. Johnson began, "Michelle and I have been together almost a year now. We have pet names for each other, we have a couple name, we enjoy a lot of the same activities, we laugh a lot. But I'm struggling with one thing.

"In my entire sexual history, I am used to being the sexual aggressor. Up until now, my pattern for the majority of my sexual activity follows this tried-and-true pattern: 'You don't want to, I talk you into it, you like it.' Michelle is WAY outside my experience. She is constantly the sexual aggressor. Naturally, I had no complaints for the first couple of months, but then I realized I was operating outside my usual comfort zone.

"That's the thing. Remember the first part of my established sexuality is, 'You don't want to?' That is not a part of being with Michelle. A year in and there is nothing I have brought up that she isn't game for, nothing I have to wheedle and negotiate to get. If anything, she is way more adventurous in the sack than I am."

Ollig threw out, "Poor you. How awful that must be. If I get missionary twice in a month, it's a good month!" He was confident that would lighten the mood. To his surprise, it didn't even raise a smile. "Sorry, please continue," he muttered, feeling regret about interrupting.

"My dilemma is this: Other than sex, things are great. But the sex is not in my comfort zone. At all. I feel like a pansy admitting these feelings. This is eating at me. Can you offer any insight? You're my only friend with a working long-term relationship under his belt."

Ollig gathered his thoughts for a minute then offered, "Sex is a wonderful thing. For a non-telepathic species, it's as connected as we get with another person. You are literally physically connected. It can also be a mental connection. Best case, it is additionally a spiritual connection. It can be magical.

"But as amazing as it is, you have to recognize sex is just one piece of the puzzle. It's an important piece, a glorious piece, but the key is to remember that it is still only a piece. If everything else is working, you owe it to the puzzle to try everything you can to resolve the things that aren't working.

"That said, the only practical advice I have is to talk with Michelle about what's bothering you. If she is willing to do anything sexual, then maybe she'd be willing to role-play to give you what you need. Communication is going to be the way you can solve this. Even if you feel ashamed to admit some things, admit those things to your partner. Honesty and trust are what relationships are built with, and those two things are necessary to create a future with your partner. Just my two cents."

Johnson processed the advice and then nodded and said "Yeah, you're right. I have thought that, but my pride doesn't want to admit any feelings or fears." He paused, thinking hard about what his friend had said. "I'll have to lay it all out tonight. Thanks for listening to all this. You're the only person I could open up to about this."

Ollig gripped Johnson's shoulder and gave him a friendly jostle. "I'm always happy to listen. Whatever happens, Gwen and I are always in your corner. That's a given." Johnson felt a little overwhelmed by that admission. "Thanks, man," he said with a voice hoarse with emotion and with a now hopeful outlook. Together they then walked back to the breakroom and the remainder of Ollig's sandwich.

Tuesday — Evening

It had been a grand day for the man in the fancy suit. Ground had been broken on his hotel, and they were already ahead of schedule getting the foundation poured. He had made several sports bets and all but one made him even wealthier today. Lastly, a business rival had been found guilty in a rape trial and would no longer be a fly in his ointment. The day had been nothing but an unending stream of good news.

He stopped at his favorite club for a drink on the way home. The wind was picking up, so he skipped the putting green and headed directly to the bar. The bartender gave him a friendly smile and opened a special locker. Pulling out a bottle of 50-year-old Macallan, he poured a generous three fingers worth into a chilled glass. He didn't dwell on the fact that the scotch he was pouring was worth more than his car. He offered a modest bow and a "Sir" as he presented the glass. He knew that particular customer preferred solitude and was an impressively heavy tipper when he got it. He turned and busied himself arranging the evening's glassware.

Everything was coming up roses for the man in the fancy suit. He sipped his peaty treasure and thought of the Scottish Highlands. His one visit had etched Scotland forever in his mind. The mountains, the history, the people. Amazing, one and all. He had been revolted by the idea of haggis, prior to that trip. Once he arrived, he steeled himself and ordered some at a local pub, just to check it off the bucket list. He had been shocked by how much he enjoyed it. He was equally shocked when he was in a grocery store there and saw TV dinners for 'Haggis, Nips, and Taties'. God knows the Scots love their haggis. He ended up having haggis eight days out of the fourteen he had been there, and it had been consistently delicious.

Sadly, it was one of those things that didn't translate well at home. The difference between Scottish and American haggis was that America didn't allow lungs in the ingredients. He would not have thought lungs had much flavor, but American haggis had never measured up to its Scottish brethren. He had stopped trying to replicate the satisfaction he remembered from that trip, resigning himself to a haggis-free lifestyle at this point.

Finishing his glass off, he lifted his index finger, indicating he would enjoy one more. Appreciating the bartender's reserve, he put a crisp hundred-dollar bill on the bar and moved in front of the five-foot wide wood-burning fireplace. He lost himself in the crackle and warmth. After ten minutes, he snapped back, looking around for anything out of the ordinary. Seeing nothing untoward, he renewed his sipping. He felt a pervasive happiness as he sat there with a good fire and good scotch.

Once he finished his second glass, he felt it was time to get home. The bartender returned his friendly, exciting salute, and he walked out the doors. As he stepped out, he was blown sideways a step or two. The scotch was not enhancing his equilibrium. He regained his center of gravity and headed to the parking lot. While still a good fifty feet away from his car, he watched as an SUV pulled in next to his car. He felt more than a little apprehension as the driver moved to exit.

That apprehension was well founded. As the driver opened their door, the wind ripped it out of their hand and slammed it into his car hard enough to tilt it almost fifteen degrees to one side. He had spent $200,000 on it and waited two months to get it. Even from this distance, he could now see a dent big enough to bathe a cat in.

"Jesus Christ! What were you thinking, you brain-dead moron?" he screamed. Only then did the driver make it all the way out of the car and, with quite an effort, closed her car door. She was wearing a waitress's uniform and stammered "Oh my god! The wind is so strong! I'm so sorry!"

Seeing red over his prize vehicle brutalized, he advanced on the girl. "Look at my door, you stupid girl!" His words dripped with venom and contempt. "You'll pay for this repair! Every goddamn cent!" He couldn't believe his formerly great day could end like this. He stepped up to the girl, his face inches away from hers. "Speak! What do you have to say!"

She could only sputter. The man's fury was terrifying. Trying to step back, her feet tangled, and she fell backward. Rather than offer her a hand up, the man stepped closer, towering over her. "This car is practically brand new, you simple little cunt! And now look at it!" Feeling frightened for her wellbeing now, the waitress couldn't help but start crying. Unfortunately, her tears only further enraged the screaming man.

"Oh, here come the waterworks! That isn't getting you out of this, you pathetic nothing!! You are making this right!" He, in his fury, and she, in her terror, failed to notice a white pick-up truck that had stopped on the side of the road, just outside the parking lot. The driver watched the scene in the parking lot play out.

Dropping down so he could yell directly in her face, the man promised, "You are going to regret being so careless, you worthless nitwit!" The waitress put her hands up, shaking as they were, to fend the screaming man off.

That was enough for the pick-up driver. He firmly adjusted his ballcap, got out of his truck, and headed into the parking lot to help.

A chance to make an author happy today!

If you enjoyed the book, please consider leaving a review.

While it wouldn't take much from you, the benefit to me would be significant, and I would be appropriately grateful.

If you are willing to recommend the book to others, I would be most thankful.

Word of mouth is the best advertising an author can hope for.

You can find details about my upcoming writing projects on my author page.

www.RyhntopiaWritings.com

Thank you

Steve

Gail's Classic Minnesota Tater-tot Hotdish

1.) Slice half an onion (the kind doesn't really matter—I like purple) into small pieces. Throw them into an oiled skillet on medium-high. Stir regularly.

2.) Once the onions start to sweat, pour in enough water to cover them. Let them soften, and let the water boil off. You should be left with nicely browned onions.

3.) When the onions are mostly dry, throw in a pound of ground beef. Remember: fat equals flavor.

4.) While the hamburger is browning, season with pepper, salt (smoked or Lawry's), and five or six squirts of Worcestershire sauce.

5.) When the burger is mostly dry, throw in a spoonful of minced garlic and stir.

6.) Layer the burger mix in the bottom of an ungreased 9x13 baking dish.

7.) Layer 2 cans of drained green beans evenly over the burger.

8.) Mix 2 cans of Cream of Mushroom soup goo with 1 can of milk. Once whisked smooth, pour evenly over the entire pan.

9.) Top with an entire bag of frozen tater-tots (Ore-Ida brand for company, store brand otherwise). Bake at 350 degrees for 30 minutes.

For Cinco de Mayo, season meat with taco seasoning. Replace green beans with a layer of refried beans and jalapenos. Use onion tater-tots.

Cast of Characters

Central Victim

David Deakins – Mayor of Bloomington, found drowned in Turtle Lake.

The Brass

Glenn Campbell – Sheriff of Ramsey County

Carmen Shapiro – Undersheriff, and Head of the Aquatics Division

Tom Maki – Deputy Sheriff

Regular Officers

Steve Ballard – General Investigations, Aquatics Division

Tom Ollig – General Investigations

Scott Johnson - General Investigations

Talya Cetin - General Investigations

Cedric 'Bricks' Williams - General Investigations

Dave White – Special Investigations

Lance Miller - Trainer

Bill Larson – recent transfer

Reception

Gail – Reception

Callie – Reception Intern

Ramsey County Lab

Josh Dubrik – Head of Ramsey County's lab. Diagnosed with Aspergers.

David Anderson – Lab tech

(Mitch) – Unseen lab tech

(Becky) – Unseen lab tech

BCA Evidence Intake

Agnes – Ugandan BCA EI staff, romantic interest in Josh Dubrik

(Carla) - Unseen BCA EI staff

(Julia) – Unseen BCA EI staff

Civilians

Michele – romantic interest in Scott Johnson

Gwen – Wife of Tom Ollig

Bryce Miller – Funny guy, lives very close to the department

Gretchen Miller – Bryce's wife

Kelsey – Dive shop staff

Sandy – Dive shop staff

Antagonists

The Man in the Armani/Fancy Suit – Puppeteer of Jan

Jan De Boer – Dutch hitman

Pete Lewis – Murderous cannibal of 'shitsacks'

Bruce Swanson – Serial rapist

Martin Marquez – Violent drug dealer

April Davis – Drunk driver

Aiden Jesup – Teenage delinquent

Made in the USA
Monee, IL
31 May 2024

59169272R00184